Of Ruins and Romance

I0519937

Rosie Chapel

First printing 2017
ISBN: 978-0-9954303-5-8

Ulfire Pty. Ltd.
P.O. Box 1481
South Perth
WA 6951
Australia

www.rosiechapel.com

Cover artwork by H.E Rodgers

Other Books by Rosie Chapel

The Hannah's Heirloom Sequence

The Pomegranate Tree ~ Hannah's Heirloom ~ Book One
Echoes of Stone and Fire ~ Hannah's Heirloom ~ Book Two
Embers of Destiny ~ Hannah's Heirloom ~ Book Three

Etched in Starlight ~ Hannah's Heirloom Prequel

Regency Romances

Once Upon an Earl
To Unlock Her Heart

For Jess
Sometimes, great friends are those you've never actually met!

Acknowledgements

Thank you very much Janet and Jess for your generous help in the editing process, your diligence is greatly appreciated.

Thank you also to Graham from A Fading Street Publishing Services.

Of Ruins and Romance

Prologue

Finally! This was it, no more long hours studying, no more assignments, no more exams, no more referencing — oh the relief! She had one more day and that was only because she had already paid the rent on her lodgings, then she was free. Kassandra Winters — Kassie to her friends — whooped in a most unladylike manner as she walked briskly across the quadrangle to the Arts Department where her course coordinator had his office. She was a little early for her appointment with him; a final interview of sorts she believed, after which she expected that he would return her last assignment. Official results would follow in a couple of weeks.

She slowed her steps as she reached the entrance and paused for a moment, turning to look back over the old, rambling buildings that made up her university college. She had spent three years of her life here and, although she had loved the exercise of taking a degree, soaking up the knowledge her lecturers shared, they had not been easy years. Innately shy and coming to university as a mature student, Kassie had tended to remain in the background, unwilling to push herself forward into the groups of enthusiastic youngsters straight out of high school. This same reticence meant that she struggled with presentations and group work; and as she had needed a part-time job to help with her expenses, she had missed out on much of the socialising. Still, she had a tight knit, albeit small, circle of friends and knew that they would keep in touch long after their academic life ended.

Pushing open the heavy wooden door, she slipped into the cool of the hallway and took her time climbing the stairs, not wanting to arrive dishevelled and out of breath. As she meandered along the corridor, she heard the rumble of voices coming from Professor Hardwick's office. Unwilling to interrupt, she stood and casually read the notice board while she waited for whoever was visiting to leave. Checking her watch, she saw that there were still several minutes before her appointment.

Idly scanning the flyers, Kassie spotted several that were advertising trips: to Italy or Greece to study ancient ruins; archaeological digs in either Jordan or Turkey or, closer to home, Hadrian's Wall or Chedworth, even the Isles of Scilly. She sighed; they all looked so fascinating and, except for Hadrian's Wall which was a stone's throw from where her family lived, and possibly Chedworth, completely out of reach.

Suddenly, she heard her own name and, mindful of what is said about those who eavesdrop, Kassie stepped away to avoid hearing their conversation. She frowned, curious as to why they needed to be discussing her anyway, the temptation to move back so that she listen in, almost irresistible. The second voice, not one she recognised seemed to be asking a question and her professor replied in his usual booming voice.

"Oh, she's very clever, unquestionably; mature enough for the job but totally unsuitable for that type of venture. Too shy, too plain, a bit ungainly if you must know and rather on the plump side, not at all what's needed for such things; you need someone with a bit of glamour and panache. I don't think she has the charisma required to hold the attention of a group and they'd grow bored. No, definitely not a good fit for your scheme..." there was a pause and it seemed as though the second person made a comment because then the professor continued, "...no, no, I mean it's up to you, of course, but I wouldn't consider her. Kassandra would be far more suited to a job in an archive office or a university library. I know she's been working in the archives here, far more appropriate for such an introvert."

There was a muffled reply, followed by further conversation and then quiet laughter. Kassie was mortified and more than a little irked. Were they laughing at her? She knew her cheeks were bright red and that she needed to cool down before she knocked on the professor's door or she might just blow her top. Fleeing into the nearest cloakroom, Kassie ran her hands under the cold tap and, pressing chilled fingers to her burning face, studied herself in the mirror, dispassionately — plain and ungainly indeed. How rude! Kassie was under no illusions about her looks; she was far too tall and knew that she wasn't conventionally pretty, but she thought that her long wavy hair was okay and her eyes were an interesting colour. As for being plump — well okay, so she wasn't skinny, she never had been, but neither did she think she was overweight. Maybe a little curvy but she considered herself to be nicely proportioned. Even if she was, what business was it of theirs? Humph — she glared at her reflection — plump my foot.

Tilting her head to one side, she decided that she really wasn't all that bad and, after making sure she looked tidy, straightened her back and swung out into the corridor. She was almost at Professor Hardwick's office when a giant of a man strode through the door, knocking her flying. As her legs went from under her, an arm shot out steadying her against a hard body. A large hand snaked around her elbow drawing her upright, sending a frisson of something she could not discern along her arm.

"I do apologise, I wasn't looking where I was going. Are you all right?" The deep voice resonated from a concerned face. Blue eyes twinkled down at her as she pulled away, rolling her shoulders to right her backpack. Unable to help herself she glowered at him. So, this was the gentleman with whom her lecturer had been talking, she thought to herself, morosely. Who the heck was he? Why did he have to be so darned handsome and why was he still holding her?

"Yes, thank you I'm fine," she answered primly. The man continued to twinkle at her until she began to think she had a smudge on her face or twigs sticking out of her hair. "What?" she demanded pinning him with her gaze.

"Are you by any chance, Kassandra Winters?" Kassie's brow furrowed at his question. Why did he want to know?

"Yes. What of it?" she rapped out, in less than civil tones, still smarting from her professor's remarks.

"You are not at all what I expected," he replied cryptically and releasing her arm, disappeared down the corridor. Kassie stared after him in bewilderment, wondering what he meant, then dismissed it as nonsense and knocked on the professor's door.

"Kassandra! Come in, come in. So, how does it feel to be finished?" Resolved to read nothing into his earlier comments, Kassie plastered a smile on her face and chattered away gaily about her plans.

The next day, once she was satisfied that everything was packed ready to go home, Kassie joined her friends outside the Ref — their preferred eatery on campus. It was a beautiful day in early June, the warm air held the promise of summer but it wasn't so hot that you needed to seek the shade. Their gossip was full of excitement about the future and Kassie experienced a twinge of sadness that this was the last time they'd meet like this. The coterie that she was a part of came from all over the world and, after today, everyone would go their separate ways. Determined not to remind anyone and put a dampener on the proceedings, Kassie pushed all that aside and threw herself into the fun of the day.

Much later and after many promises had been made to keep in touch, to arrange visits and — if nothing else — text, Kassie was strolling back to her rooms to collect the last of her luggage, when she was suddenly confronted by the same man who had barged into her the previous day. She tried to sidestep him, but he planted himself right in her path giving her no alternative but to make eye contact.

"So we meet again," he smiled gently, his rather austere countenance lightning up. He appeared genuinely pleased to see her, which she found peculiar. She regarded him steadily, trying to weigh him up, thinking that he seemed vaguely familiar, but how or from where wouldn't come to her.

"So it seems," was her less than encouraging response. He raised an eyebrow.

"Why so grumpy? Aren't you looking forward to the holidays?" She frowned at him, unsure why he was asking her questions.

"Not particularly, I rather liked being here. Now I have to go and find something suitable to do." She couldn't quite bring herself to repeat the words she had heard yesterday, but a mischievous imp inside her really wished she had.

"What was your major?"

"Classics and ancient history, with some medieval thrown in." For the life of her she couldn't infuse any life into her voice. All she could think about was that blasted conversation. Serves you right Kassie, she thought, you know nothing good comes from overhearing stuff. He was watching her, quizzically and she'd had enough.

"I'm sorry, I have no idea who you are or why you care about my major or my plans. I've had a long day and still have to get home, so if you would please excuse me, I have to leave." She flushed, as irritation overrode her usual politeness. Taking a breath, she apologised, "I'm sorry. That was uncalled for, but we've never met and I am at a loss as to why on earth you are interested in a plain, ungainly student who has a tendency to plumpness." To her horror, she could feel tears forming. Get a grip she instructed herself, you are twenty-six years old, not a baby. She made to go around him, but he stopped her by grasping her slim hand in his huge paw.

"So, you heard?"

"It wasn't as though Professor Hardwick tried to keep his voice down, I was at the other end of the corridor. I'm more surprised the whole faculty didn't hear him. Anyway, it is of no matter. Apparently, I am only suited to libraries and archives so it is a good job that's what I will be doing," her tones bleak. She shook off his hand and, lifting her chin, rushed down the path, without so much as a goodbye. The man stood motionless, watching her go, that genial smile still playing around his lips.

Had anybody had been listening, they might have heard him say very quietly,

"Oh, Kassandra, you are suited to so much more."

One

Rome ~ two years later,

Kassie sat in the shade while her group explored the ruins. Sipping from a bottle of still cool water, she watched as they clicked away with their cameras or pored over their guidebooks. It was Wednesday and so, as indicated on this week's schedule, they were at Ostia, the old port of Rome and she had given them an hour to themselves before they needed to catch the train back into the city.

Kassie loved it here, well if she was honest, she hadn't come across a site she didn't love, but Ostia was always so peaceful. Even in the height of summer, the sheer size of this place meant that it was nowhere near as crowded as the Forum or the Colosseum. Most tourists didn't even know it existed. She leaned against the wall, admiring the dappled light through the trees and listening to the umbrella pines whispering in the breeze.

It was late August and Kassie had been living in Rome for just over two years. Initially resigned to staying on in the university archives for a little longer, she had been astonished, almost as soon as she had finished her degree, to receive an invitation to work in the administration department of one of the international schools. She had applied for the job with absolutely no expectation of even getting an acknowledgement and had been stunned when not only did she get said acknowledgment, but also that she was asked to attend an interview.

The interview was held at the University of York, which gave Kassie the chance to spend some time in that most ancient of English cities, and she could easily have spent all day wandering the old walls. The interview itself was more like a chat over coffee and by the end of a very interesting hour Kassie had the job. They wanted her to start immediately; so, she went home, packed her bags, waited for the tickets they duly sent, and left.

Kassie loved her family, but she had lived away from them since she was eighteen, first because of her job and latterly her studies. It had been too far to travel to and from university every day and she preferred the peace of her own room on campus to the chaos that seemed to always envelop her parents' home. They were sorry to see her go, but they too were not used to her being around and she felt rather in the way.

One day, about six months after she'd arrived in Rome, while traipsing around enjoying the sights, she had come across a group of visitors who were utterly lost, having no idea what to do, where to go or how to get there. Taking pity on them, Kassie had asked what they wanted to see. Once she had managed to get a word in edgeways, she had talked them through the best way to find everything, showing them how to get there on the maps they carried and linking up those sights that were close together, giving them the most expeditious way of viewing everything in the time they had available. She had also suggested they might like to talk with one or two of the agencies who offered great tours without the hassle.

They had been very pleased and one of them had taken her contact details, in case they got lost again; although how anyone managed to go astray in Rome was beyond Kassie, she found it one of the easiest cities to traverse. A few weeks later and with no idea how they found her number — although it seemed likely that her little group of lost sightseers may well have had some involvement — she had received a call from one of the tourist agencies, asking whether she might be interested in doing some temporary work for them, while one of their staff was on maternity leave. They needed someone who spoke English fluently and who knew the city. Another interview and she had another job. Kassie had taken pains to make it clear that her priority was her position at the international school, but they came up with a roster that suited everybody and still gave her a little free time.

She worked four days a week at the school and the remaining three as a tour guide. Her days were full and she loved it.

Bringing her attention back to the present, she glanced at her watch and noticed that it was coming up on the hour. Strolling over to where the group had begun to gather, she shoved her large straw hat over her sun-streaked hair and corralled them along the path towards the exit of the site and on to the station. Just as they reached the Porta Romana necropolis, she heard a familiar voice. Unable to place it, Kassie spun on her heel, squinting in its general direction and, for some inexplicable reason, was not surprised in the slightest to see him. The man from her professor's office, the man she had also run into the day after, the man whose rather random conversation still perplexed her.

As she stared at him, a most peculiar sensation ran through her, but was gone before she had a chance to think about it. He must have felt her gaze boring into him, for he too turned and their eyes locked. For a split-second Kassie was certain that the world shuddered and aware that earthquakes were not unknown here, wondered whether it was a tremor. The man smiled, that same gentle smile, said something to his two companions and sauntered towards her group.

"Well, if I'm not mistaken it's Miss Kassandra Winters. How lovely to see you again." He ran his eyes over her willowy form, appreciation glinting in their sapphire blueness.

"I doubt that," she murmured, for his ears only, which elicited a low laugh. "You have me at a disadvantage, Sir, I am afraid I do not know your name."

"An utter travesty and a state of affairs that cannot be allowed to continue." He grinned engagingly. "Gabriel St Germain at your service." He bowed slightly, which had anyone else done so would have seemed foppish, with this man, entirely uncontrived. She smiled then and to the tall man watching her it was as though the sun had just come out from behind a dark cloud.

"I apologise, I did not mean to interrupt your afternoon. I just never expected to hear someone I recognised. I must get my group back to the city. It was nice to see you again." She started to walk away when his voice halted her.

"Are you staying in Rome, Miss Winters?" She did a slow about-face and nodded, unable to see his expression for the sun was right behind him. "Maybe we could meet for a drink one evening?" Kassie stood for long moments debating with herself.

"You can find me at the Discover Antiquity agency," was her only reply and she hurried away, a soft chuckle following her down the ancient road. Ignoring both the warning in her head and the warmth in her stomach, Kassie spent the next little while answering any amount of questions from her small group and, by the time they had boarded the train for the short journey back to Rome, she had herself in hand.

Depositing her flock at the tourist office, Kassie trudged home, looking forward to an evening with her feet up, a glass of red wine and some pasta. Walking into her apartment building, she called a 'buonasera' to Emilia, the elderly lady who lived in the ground floor apartment and who always looked out for her young neighbour, before slowly climbing the two flights of stairs to her haven.

Once inside, she switched on a lamp or two and threw open the large French doors onto her balcony, taking a few moments to lean on the railing and breathe in the balmy evening air. Kassie loved the view out over the city; the light over the soft hues of the coloured roofs was magical at any time of the year. The grumbling in her stomach, however, made her turn her back on the sunset and after changing into more comfortable garb, set a pan of linguine simmering. While the pasta cooked, she heated some pesto sauce, stirring through chunks of cooked chicken and sliced mushroom before adding the linguine and tossing it all together. Pouring herself a large glass of red wine, she applied herself to her meal with gusto.

As she relaxed with a second glass of wine, Gabriel St Germain's face swam across her vision. His name rang a very distant bell, but in what regard eluded her. She ruminated on it for a little while, to no avail, eventually giving up. If it proved important enough it would come to her sooner or later.

For the remainder of the evening, Kassie sat at her desk by the open windows, typing away on her trusty laptop and was very satisfied that she had managed well over a thousand words before slumber called.

The following days were no more or less exciting than every other day. Kassie loved her work at the school but it was quiet now. It was the height of summer and many of the staff were involved in projects away from the city, leaving little to keep her occupied. Even though this was the most expensive time of the year to travel, Kassie had begun to mull over the possibility of taking a holiday. She hadn't had one in the two years she had been in Rome, and she spent a relatively fruitful hour or so browsing the Internet to see what was available within her price range. Tuscany was somewhere she really wanted to explore, as was the Amalfi coast, oh, and the Italian Alps — her list went on.

Rather more than two weeks since their last meeting, this was how he found her; lost in imagination, an open travel brochure on the desk and likely seeing rolling hills and vineyards rather than her tidy office. Unwilling to disturb her reverie, Gabriel St Germain, simply leaned against on the doorjamb and enjoyed being able to study Kassie unawares; his observant gaze perceiving more than his subject would have been comfortable with. Her long hair pulled back into a loose plait, no make-up spoiling the clear skin of her heart-shaped face and clothes that suggested a frugal lifestyle, not unfashionable as such, more that they had been chosen for durability over style. He noticed too, that she looked tired and speculated as to the reason.

She had taken some tracking down. The tourist agency was not prepared to divulge any personal information, which was fair enough, but after several phone calls and numerous visits, they had finally relented, suggesting he try contacting the international schools, as English speaking staff could often be found within their hallowed halls. To his frustration, this proved just as challenging for, as Kassie's job was administration, she wasn't listed on any of the websites. It was pure fluke that, while searching through the gallery of images for this particular school, Gabriel had come across a photo of some celebration or other and there she was, in the background, grinning cheekily and raising a glass of champagne towards whoever was holding the camera.

Her face, the face that came to him in dreams, leapt off the screen and he had found her.

Two

He knocked quietly and watched as Kassie came back to earth, her vision refocusing, the rather drab office taking the place of endless Italian vistas dotted with pencil pines. A slight shake of her head, a hand automatically patting her hair to ensure it was still in place and she assumed her professional persona, standing to welcome him. Recognition flooded her eyes and she smiled in surprise.

"Oh, I do beg your pardon, Mr St Germain, I didn't hear you. Have you been waiting long?"

"Just long enough," came the enigmatic reply. She frowned, suddenly uncertain, but decided to ignore it and invite him in.

"Please, take a seat, Sir. How may I help you?" Good one Kassie, she thought, just the right tone of polite interest.

"I was hoping you might be able to help me out of a sticky situation." Kassie raised her eyebrows enquiringly. "I am about to take a group of people to several of the ancient sites, most are in and around Rome itself, but also Pompeii, Herculaneum and Oplontis. I did not expect there to be any more than ten, but it's grown to, at the last count, fifteen, and one guide is simply not enough. It's too hard trying to keep so many together and makes exploring some of the sites a bit problematic." He paused, watching for a reaction. Kassie just looked at him, her face expressionless.

He continued. "Anyway, I know that you also work as a tour guide and wondered whether you would consider coming along as my assistant." Kassie began to speak, but he interrupted, "It will be in an official capacity and you would, of course, be paid for your time. Accommodation and certain meals are also included." He smiled encouragingly.

"Why me?" she asked, puzzled. "There are hundreds of tour operators in Rome, you could have your pick. Why me?"

"Because I know you, well I know of you and I think you are exactly who I need. My group are quite elderly and do not need to be rushed through at a gallop. They appreciate the finer points of ancient history and archaeology and I prefer someone with a common sense attitude. Someone who will gladly take the time to accompany them through the sites and who has the patience to answer their questions, not a young go-getter who prefers to sit in the bus texting her latest boyfriend and whose sole purpose is to hustle the group through as quickly as possible so she can meet said boyfriend in the bar."

Several things ran through Kassie's head at once. The most important being that he thought she was old, or at least not young — that stung a little. His explanation as to why he wanted her to assist, while quite laudable, made her sound like a stuffy spinster. Was that how others saw her? Professor Hardwick's words from two years ago came back to haunt her and, unexpectedly, she wanted to cry. Good grief, Kassie, she admonished herself; every time you meet this man he has the same effect. Grow up!

Gabriel watched her eloquent face with interest, her sudden wistfulness tugging at something deep within him. Guessing that something was niggling at her, Gabriel didn't press the issue, hoping he might get the chance to coax it out of her sooner or later. Handing her a leaflet, which detailed the tour, he added that he would drop in the next day to answer any questions she might have and find out whether she was interested in taking the job. Then he was gone.

Kassie just sat, completely still, for what felt like an age, although it was probably less than ten minutes. She turned the flyer in her hand, but the words didn't make any sense, all she could see was his face. A buzzing on her desk jolted her attention back and she saw it was her mobile. A text, 'I hope you will decide to join us. Gabriel.' It was from him. How did he have her number? She stared at it, her finger stroking the screen, still mystified. Recalling that tomorrow was Wednesday and she wouldn't be in the office she texted him back, a brief 'Just remembered, I won't be here. Taking a tour around the Forum from 10 until 2.' And left it at that. It was up to him to find her.

Putting the leaflet aside for now and shoving the travel brochure into the bottom drawer of her desk, Kassie turned her attention to the few remaining items cluttering up her in-tray.

The rest of the day ticked by slowly, lack of anything interesting to do making it seem interminable. Her mind kept going back to the meeting. Despite being far too shrewd to read anything more than polite courtesy into his request, Kassie could not stifle a growing sense of anticipation that she might see Gabriel the next day. She knew he was way out of her league; everything about him implied that he moved in far more exalted circles than her. Even his clothes, casual though they were, screamed expensive designer wear, but she still wanted to see him. She was also moved to wonder what had prompted him to conduct a tour with elderly visitors; it seemed an odd pastime for one such as he.

While she was enjoying a late afternoon coffee, she picked up the leaflet again, glancing through it quickly, before reading it thoroughly cover to cover. It was the perfect tour. In between the ancient sites, he had included options such as a tour of the Vatican, or the Borghese Gallery; afternoon tea at Babingtons or an evening at the Opera. If she had planned a tour just for herself, these are the things she would have included. The mere thought being part of it making her heart skip with happiness. She had visited all the ancient sites he had listed but, where possible, Gabriel had managed to gain access to restricted areas. She was very impressed.

Before she was half way through the pamphlet, she knew she could not possibly turn down this opportunity. If she could book the time off she would do it. Her decision, of course, had nothing whatsoever to do with the devastatingly handsome man who was organising it.

As she read the last page, she felt her cheeks grow hot. Gabriel wasn't just anyone; he was *Professor* Gabriel St Germain, specialist in the Flavian and Trajanic periods, renowned archaeologist, author of several volumes of work and currently guest lecturer at the American University of Rome. She was absolutely mortified. As a student of ancient history, how could she not have known who he was?

Out of the blue, she recalled why he had seemed familiar the second time they had met. During her third semester at university, she had been in the middle of a presentation on the Pantheon, when someone had asked her an idiotic question.

Kassie hated being in the spotlight and at the time had not possessed the assurance to talk off the cuff, to chitchat with her audience. She had stuttered a response, and even though she had been quite correct, those trying to trip her up had made fun of her diffidence, causing the whole auditorium to laugh at her expense. It had been utterly humiliating, more so because a visiting lecturer had been invited to watch, an expert in the period of history they were studying — Professor Gabriel St Germain.

Kassie couldn't believe she had forgotten. Mind you it was not a day for which she had fond memories. She had struggled through to the end of her talk, presuming that all her hard work, preparing her slides and coming up with a less than typical angle to address, had been ruined by a bunch of witless wonders. She had been very surprised to discover that she had managed to scrape a high distinction, her very first; but even this accolade had not been enough to cancel out her discomfiture and, where possible, Kassie had avoided — like the plague — any units that included such presentations. Ironic really, as half of her working life now involved doing exactly that, often to people far more judgemental than a group of heedless students.

Hopefully, he had forgotten too. He showed no sign of recognition during any of the times they had met. She studied his photograph at the bottom of the brochure. Just looking at his career stats suggested that he must be at least thirty-five — oh my, Kassie, such a grand old age — he didn't look that old, closer to thirty she would have guessed. Not that it mattered; he had absolutely no interest in her anyway.

Dismissing it for now, Kassie finished her day and, after requesting some long overdue leave and tidying up her already neat office, walked back to her apartment in the warmth of the late afternoon. She decided to take the long way, past the Pantheon. Once there, she sat for while on the steps of the fountain in the piazza opposite the entrance to the monument, and breathed it all in. Whenever she felt out of sorts, Kassie would come here and just admire the magnificence. She loved this building, she felt that it spoke to her and it never failed to lift her heart. To stand on the same marble floor where emperors once stood, and to gaze up at the same oculus, through which Hadrian would have looked out of nearly two thousand years ago, was a privilege she never took for granted.

Lost in thought, Kassie sat there until the light began to change, the harsh brightness of the day waned into subdued mellowness — the Pantheon fell into shadow and it was time to go home.

The next afternoon, up on the Palatine Hill — the vast palace complex adjoining the Forum — Kassie was answering a question about Domitian's stadium and how could it possibly be here if there was already one under the Piazza Navona, when she noticed that, surreptitiously, Gabriel had joined her group. She cleared up the confusion for the young woman, explaining that it was presumed this stadium was probably for private sporting events, such as foot races, at the invitation of the emperor, rather than for public spectacles. Then, as no more questions were forthcoming, Kassie informed her charges that they had the rest of the afternoon to themselves.

Thanking them for their attention and complimenting them for being the best group she had shown around for a long time, she turned them loose to amble through the ruins to their hearts' content. Collapsing onto one of the long wooden benches that overlook the stadium, Kassie took a gulp of water from her ever-present bottle, and rested her poor aching feet.

Gabriel strolled over and sat next to her. They didn't speak. For Kassie, it was lovely just to sit with no need to talk, she had been talking for hours: the twittering of the birds, the whisper of the breeze through the pines and the muted conversations of the other tourists wafting over her, was far more preferable. Shutting her eyes, she lifted her face to the sun and as she did so, her large, floppy, straw hat slipped off her head. Without thinking, Gabriel caught it, placing it on Kassie's knee while she reached out blindly to grab the dratted article and, as their fingers touched, the oddest tingle vibrated up her arm. Abruptly she sat up dragging her hand away, a delicate pink colouring her too pale face, plonking the hat back on her head more to hide her flushed cheeks than needing the shade it provided.

"Static," was Gabriel's considered opinion, grinning at her reaction. Suddenly, Kassie relaxed and grinned back; she couldn't help it, for all his academic prowess and his stature in the world of antiquities, he seemed so affable, an old-fashioned gentleman; easy going and probably quite imperturbable. She studied him from under the brim of her hat. Even sitting down, he was huge, she guessed he was well over six feet, but not heavy, his body looked trim and muscular, in fact, surely he'd be better off playing basketball rather than lecturing.

He was wearing a pale grey, linen shirt, its cuffs rolled up, revealing tanned forearms — the result of years working on digs, no doubt. Faded jeans over well-worn, scuffed leather, lightweight walking boots completed his outfit. He looked like everyone's ideal image of an archaeologist, yet it suited him and appeared totally unpretentious. His dark hair, intriguingly something between black and brown, was covered with a wide brimmed Akubra style leather hat as battered as his boots, and his eyes, those incredible, deep blue eyes, were watching her.

"Seen enough?" Caught out, Kassie flushed, shifting in her seat so she was facing Domitian's palace, unable to think of a clever reply. She twiddled with the strap of her bag and muttered something about going home, but felt strangely unwilling to leave. He reached over and pressed her fingers. "Don't go, I'm sorry, I didn't mean to embarrass you." She turned her head and stared into his eyes, searching for mockery and finding none.

"You didn't." He raised a sceptical eyebrow. "Well, maybe a little, but I just wanted to, rather it was nice to be able to, I never get the chance, oh dear…" Her words tripped over one another and she faltered, coming to an awkward halt. It wasn't the done thing to tell a stranger and a man to boot that she wanted to study him in much the same way that she might study a Bernini sculpture; to admire his chiselled features and the taut planes of his muscles covering his powerful physique. No, that was not generally something she should say to a man she'd had less than ten minutes worth of conversation with over two years.

Kassie, in turn, intrigued Gabriel. During the day, he had been able to follow her group for some time, without her seeing him. He knew everything there was to know about the Forum and usually the tours were two a penny; they all had the same banter and none came off script. With Kassie, it was as though she hadn't been given a script. She talked about the ruin as though she had lived there, as though she had mixed with the emperor's household, or was a member of his administration. When she was explaining the different sections of the complex to her group, Kassie was a confident, vivacious, enthusiastic young woman, breathing life into the timeworn stones, conjuring up the colourful, exciting and dangerous world of ancient Rome with a passion that left him breathless. He could have listened to her all day.

Now she was quiet and withdrawn, her lack of self-assurance at odds with what he had just seen. If he hadn't witnessed this same duality previously, he might think she was feigning; but he had, several years ago, and he was beginning to think that Miss Kassandra Winters needed someone to persuade her to believe in herself.

Hoping to divert her from her obviously uncomfortable train of thought, Gabriel asked Kassie whether she'd had a chance to look at the leaflet. Her whole countenance changed and she became that animated young woman again.

"Oh, it looks marvellous. If I was able to customise a tour just for me, this is exactly what I would want to see and do. If you think me capable, I'd love to help." She chattered on for a little while, clearly enthused by the idea of assisting him with the tour. Gabriel heaved sigh of relief. The most important part of his plan was in place, moreover, he could not imagine anyone else more thoroughly suited. Now he would have three weeks in her company, a most delightful prospect and he hoped it would be enough.

"How about we go and find somewhere to have a coffee, or a glass of wine and discuss it further?" he asked.

Kassie hesitated, but couldn't refuse him, even knowing that this was a bad idea, that her traitorous heart was already halfway lost. The, admittedly almost imperceptible, practical side of her brain insisted that he was simply showing friendly interest in the person who would be helping him, while her hopelessly romantic side whispered that for one evening it couldn't hurt. She nodded, smiling guilelessly, gathering her bag and stood on her tired feet, ready to follow wherever he might lead.

Three

Familiar with the area, Gabriel asked Kassie whether there was a café to which she was partial. Shrugging she named a few, but commented that she was happy with anywhere that served decent coffee or, more preferably, a cool beer. After talking all day her throat was tired and a chilled drink would ease the ache. Taking her hand as though it was the most natural thing in the world, Gabriel spoke of this and that, ideas he had for the tour, the length of time they would stay in Rome, whether it was better to stay in Pompeii or Naples on the days that they would visit those ruins, this and that.

Kassie listened, interjecting here and there with the odd suggestion, carefully worded so as not to seem pushy. By the time they arrived at a trattoria that Gabriel assured her was the ideal spot for all their wining and dining needs, they were totally engrossed in their discussions. A beer led to dinner with wine and it was well after eight before Kassie glanced at her watch.

"Goodness me, I had no idea just how long we'd been talking. Please, I hope I haven't kept you from something." Kassie said, feeling guilty for dominating so much of his time. Gabriel smiled his lazy smile and leaned back in the comfortable chair, sipping the last of his wine.

"Nothing spoiling," he assured her. Not really the most encouraging response, but at least he hadn't dashed off.

"Well, I'm sure you have better things to do than waste the whole of your evening with me and I should be getting home anyway. I have a couple of things to do before tomorrow." She gathered her things together, pulling some cash out of her wallet to pay for her half of the meal. Gabriel shook his head.

"No way," he said in a tone that brooked no argument. "I was the one who suggested this. My treat."

"Thank you." She accepted his gesture, graciously. "I've really enjoyed it. Will you need to meet again to finalise details, or do you think we've sorted out everything to your satisfaction?" Gabriel was quite certain that everything was organised within an inch of its life, but he wasn't about to tell Kassie that. He would enjoy spending more time with her; she was funny, clever, insightful and, despite her reticence, nobody's fool.

"I'll let you know. We may need a couple more get togethers, I'll just have to check my timetable," was however, all he said. "Now come on, let's get you home." Kassie shook her head.

"I'm fine, really. I often walk the city at night, it's quite safe." Gabriel shuddered at the thought but forbore to comment.

"Humour me." He smiled, grabbing his jacket and going over to pay the bill. Giving up, Kassie nodded.

"Okay then, but just this once." He grinned at her and she felt her heart flutter. Stop it, Kassie she instructed herself, he's just being kind. Their account paid, the two made their way to Kassie's apartment. She steered them past the Pantheon, slowing as the huge structure came into view. She couldn't help it; there was something so evocative about its grey majesty. Unwilling to say anything for fear Gabriel would think her daft in the head, Kassie just gazed and as they turned along the narrow street leading towards her neighbourhood, had to glance over her shoulder before it was lost to sight.

"It's really quite something, isn't it?" Gabriel ventured. Kassie glanced up at him, nodding mutely, words didn't seem appropriate; after a few minutes, he added, "I love it too."

"I can't explain it. I don't think there are enough adjectives to do it justice, and I feel that it calls to me." She blushed. "Sorry I know that sounds totally crackers."

"Never apologise for loving something, it shows that you have empathy." She bent her head for, regardless of his words, she felt ridiculous. She remained silent for the rest of their short walk and suddenly they were at the apartment.

"I'm up there." She pointed in the general direction of her flat. She turned to say good night and found herself facing his chest. He lifted her chin with one finger and smoothed his thumb over her bottom lip. She couldn't move and simply stared at him through wide eyes

"Sleep well, Kassandra," murmured Gabriel and vanished into the darkness. Kassie stood there, motionless, her jaw somewhere near the floor, trying and failing to work out what the heck had just happened. She was sure people who were just being friendly didn't brush someone's bottom lip with their thumb. Or did they? She hadn't had a serious relationship; she'd barely even dated. She knew she wasn't the type of girl that men fell over themselves to go out with, in fact, it dawned on her that she hadn't been kissed properly either. One or two of the guys she had been on the odd date with had pecked at her mouth, but that was all. It hadn't really bothered her until today. Now she felt rather gauche.

Oh well, she thought, as it's unlikely that Gabriel will ever want to kiss you, he'll not know how green you are. With that less than comforting thought she skipped upstairs and let herself into her flat. The evening was not yet over for Kassie; she made a hot drink and resumed her usual position by the open balcony doors, immersing herself in another world until she heard the soft chime of midnight from one of the local church clocks and thought it prudent to go to bed.

Kassie didn't hear from Gabriel for a few days, but as she had been asked to do some archiving at work, was busy enough that she didn't have time to notice. Once her supervisor approved her request for leave, Kassie spent a couple of hours listing everything she would need to have in order before her holiday. Well, it wasn't really a holiday; but as her mum often pointed out, sometimes a change was a good as a rest. It would have been far more relaxing to spend a couple of weeks lying on a beach, soaking up the sun and reading her way through the huge pile of books she had sitting next to her bed, but this would be far more interesting. She didn't like being in the sun much anyway.

She had texted Gabriel to advise him that she had been granted time off and to check whether there was anything else she needed to prepare for the tour. He had replied that it was in hand and he'd let her know. A brief message and totally unsatisfactory, but what else could she expect? She was only his assistant after all. Continuing to ignore the warning bells clanging in her head, Kassie applied herself to both of her jobs with her usual enthusiasm and the days flew by.

The Sunday before they were due to set off and while Kassie was guiding a group around the Vatican, she became aware that Gabriel seemed to be shadowing her footsteps. Her soon-to-be employer had wanted to hear her in a setting other than ancient ruins, to see how well she handled what he assumed would be a less familiar environment. After another long round of calls to her agency, he had managed to find out that she was scheduled to conduct a tour around the Vatican and St Peter's Basilica that day.

Arriving sometime after the tour had begun, Gabriel caught up with the group as they strolled through the Gallery of Maps and quietly latched onto them. Hoping that his presence wouldn't distract her, or cause her to clam up, Gabriel kept his distance, but stayed close enough to hear her commentary. Funnily enough, Kassie didn't seem unduly bothered, she was totally focussed on the group, sharing as much information as possible without overwhelming them.

There was no doubt she had done her research thoroughly, her narrative was lively and engaging, but it was clear when they came to Raphael's Rooms, that this was her favourite space. She obviously knew the frescoes in detail and her love for the artist and his work shone from her face, which, as far as Gabriel was concerned, lit the suite of rooms. Her delight was infectious and by the time they had moved along, heading towards the Sistine Chapel, her followers were as enamoured with Raphael as her.

As they left the Vatican and walked around to St Peter's Basilica, she chatted with the members of the group, taking questions, some of which were ludicrous in the extreme, but she treated each one as though it was the most important question she'd heard that day. She made eye contact with whomever she was answering and Gabriel knew that she could have told them the Basilica was made of cheese and they would have believed her. The longer he listened to her, the more convinced he was that he had made the right choice, that Kassie was the best person to accompany his group. That he could not wait to spend three weeks with her was another matter entirely.

Ninety minutes later, Kassie finished up by mentioning that, if they would like to see further manifestations of Papal extravagance, San Giovanni in Laterano, was also worth a visit and then thanked them for choosing Discover Antiquity for their tour. They, in turn, thanked her profusely for her time, which she graciously accepted and tried to tip her, which she refused but so tactfully that her group felt as though she was the one tipping them.

"That was really well done, Kassie," a deep voice said, as a tall figure detached itself from the marble pillar against which he had been leaning.

"Thank you," she replied, grinning. "To be honest, I find St Peter's totally overwhelming, which is why I mentioned San Giovanni. It has an understated magnificence which I find easier to cope with; plus, it has the doors from the Curia, for me a win, win!" Gabriel chuckled at her expression, which reminded him of a mischievous child. "Oh boy, do I need a coffee," she said, hesitating a moment before adding, "would you like to join me?"

"I would like that very much," he replied. Then, in much the same way as he had done the last time they met, he took her hand and the two meandered slowly along the Via Della Conciliazione, across the Pont Sant'Angelo before wending their way to the Piazza Navona, chattering as though they had known each other for a lifetime, not the very few hours they had spent together. Gabriel filled Kassie in on the last-minute details of the trip and confirmed that the coach would pick her up from her apartment at 8am this coming Friday. Kassie felt excitement begin to stir; she was really looking forward to this tour, which had nothing at all to do with the tall professor walking beside her.

Kassie pointed out one of her favourite cafés and the two found a table outside, watching the world go by, over an espresso or two and a cannoli each. Kassie knew she had to be careful, too much coffee and she wouldn't sleep, but she didn't want the afternoon to end. She enjoyed his company, he was such an interesting companion; witty, intelligent and, even though she knew it was mere politeness on his part, made her feel as though she had the whole of his attention.

Of the few times that she'd been taken out, Kassie had noticed, to her chagrin, that more often than not, the guy's concentration wavered, generally as a far more attractive prospect entered his line of vision. It was one of the reasons she had given up on the whole thing, it wasn't a great boost to your morale when your date asked whether you knew the hot brunette that had just entered the club.

Gabriel watched Kassie as she talked, noticing, again, that she looked tired and too pale and wondered, absently, whether she ever got enough rest as, unbidden, an image of her in his arms while she slept popped into his head. An image that made him smile. Kassie caught the smile teasing at his lips and wondered at its cause. Gabriel said nothing, however and she didn't know him well enough to ask.

The afternoon faded into evening and Kassie decided that she should make a move; it was too easy to think this was more than it was. Excusing herself for a moment, she disappeared into the café to pay their account, coming out to see Gabriel waiting for her.

"That was sneaky," he chuckled, "I was about to go and settle that bill.

"Yeah, I thought you might, but it was my turn," she replied, with an impish grin. He grinned back and catching her hand, entwining her fingers in his, turned in the direction of her flat.

"Past the Pantheon, right?" She glanced up at him sharply, thinking he was being facetious, but his expression was bland, no hint of derision.

"Thank you," was all she said, but felt a slight increase in pressure on her fingers as he gently squeezed her hand. Too soon, they were in front of her building. Accepting that she couldn't stretch this out any longer, Kassie said, very politely, that she was looking forward to Friday and she hoped he had a good week.

Gabriel's fingers were still interlaced with hers and he was gazing into her eyes as she spoke, huge fathomless green eyes into which he could quite happily have fallen. He didn't want to let go of her hand, her slender fingers felt so right in his large ones; he tried to think of a way to extend the evening but his brain wouldn't come up with anything, so he did the next best thing. He kissed her.

Four

Kassie was floored, she didn't know what to do, this wasn't some half-hearted peck on the mouth, it was a caress, a promise, an endearment. Gabriel's lips were firm and warm and, never having been kissed like this before, Kassie just emptied her mind and let instinct take over. Tentatively she moved her own lips under his and as their kiss deepened, all sorts of interesting sensations stole up her body. Gabriel still held her hand, but his other arm went around her, drawing her close, until she was moulded to him. She could feel the erratic beat of his heart, which echoed hers and her body began to melt.

Gabriel's head told him that he shouldn't be doing this, that it was too soon, that Kassie didn't know how he much he cared, but dear Lord she felt so good in his arms. Her perfume tantalised his senses and the innocence of her response was enchanting. He had wanted to kiss her since first they met in the corridor outside her professor's office, but nothing could have prepared him for the barrage of emotions from which he was suddenly reeling. His breathing went haywire and he felt Kassie sag against him, inordinately pleased that she was as affected as he.

The longer they kissed, the less Kassie was aware of her surroundings. It seemed as though the world had receded; it didn't matter that they were standing in front of her building, that it was still daylight, that anybody walking past could see them. She was unaware of everything except his embrace, which sent ribbons of heat singing along her veins and she had never felt more alive. Oddly, it seemed that her body was now boneless and she couldn't stop her legs from buckling, but Gabriel didn't let her fall, simply pulled her more tightly against him. Unable to help herself, she brushed cool fingers up his jaw, stroking over his cheek and up into his hair, feeling him shudder at her touch.

He lifted his head, his eyes dark with hunger; he had to stop this before it got out of hand.

"Kassie," he muttered gruffly, transfixed by her eyes. "This…I never intended…I didn't mean." He couldn't form a sentence as his gaze was drawn back to her very kissable lips and, with a groan, he recaptured them, feeling Kassie sigh with pleasure, as his tongue tasted the sweet softness of her mouth.

Time seemed to pause and then Gabriel broke their kiss, but did not relinquish his hold. He needed Kassie to believe that this wasn't a whim, that he wanted more than just a kiss, but he didn't know how to frame the words.

"Oh, must you stop?" she whispered ingenuously. He looked down at her and tall as she was, he towered over her. Her hair was awry, her cheeks flushed and her eyes, oh those eyes.

"I must sweetheart. We're standing in the middle of the street and even though I could happily kiss you for the rest of the night, I don't think this is the best place to do so." She watched him as he spoke and he thought he caught a flicker of something deep in her gaze, but it was gone before he could define it.

"You could come up," she suggested, shyly. "There's a pizzeria along the street, I could order takeout and we could…" she paused, unsure of whether she should say what she wanted to say, going instead with "…continue our discussion." The thought of spending the rest of the evening with Kassie was far too tempting and Gabriel vacillated for several seconds until he capitulated, knowing that if he left her standing in the street now, he would kick himself later.

"Sounds great," he said, and she smiled, her face lighting up, causing his breath to catch in his throat. He knew this was a mistake, he should be taking this slowly, he didn't want to rush her, but neither did he want to be apart from her. How was this even possible? Gabriel couldn't explain it to himself, didn't even want to try. For now, it was enough that it was so and, he could only hope that one day Kassie would feel the same way.

Half an hour or so later, a glass of red wine poured, they were wolfing down the steaming hot pizza as though they were starving. Gabriel had to admit it was excellent, one of the best he'd tasted, from the tiniest of pizzerias — more a kiosk than a shop — but it was delicious. Kassie giggled at his groans of enjoyment.

"Sorry, but this is so good." He grinned at her and, as they ate, they resumed their comfortable conversation. Gabriel tried to draw Kassie out of herself, to tell him about her family, her life. For so introverted a person, she had chosen to live and work in one of the world's most vibrant cities, yet she was alone. He thought her family lived somewhere in England, but from the little he had seen of her, she didn't seem to have any friends — apart from her co-workers — and for some reason that saddened him. She needed someone to go shopping with, to wander through art galleries with, to have dinner with, to laugh with, to cry with, to share her secrets with, and — as he watched her trying not to drop her slice of pizza — he knew without a shadow of a doubt that he wanted to be that person.

Kassie had no idea what was going on in Gabriel's head, which probably, was no bad thing. She wasn't confident enough in herself to suppose that he could possibly want to be with her as anything other than a friend. Gabriel was drop-dead gorgeous, successful, incredibly sexy — although she had an inkling that he wasn't aware of either the former or the latter — he could have the pick of any woman he wanted and she imagined that she wasn't his type at all.

Finishing their meal, Kassie asked whether Gabriel wanted his wine topping up, he nodded and went to stand at the balcony, gazing out over the city, watching the evening fade into night. Kassie brought his glass over and they stood shoulder to shoulder, admiring city lights, the Capitoline Museum gleaming white against the encroaching darkness.

"What a view! I could stand here all night," Gabriel commented.

"I often do," Kassie replied. "In the summer especially, I leave the doors open, turn off the lights, drag my chair over to the window and just lose myself in the night. It's the best way to unwind after a hectic day." Gabriel turned to study Kassie, who coloured a little under his scrutiny, moving to sit back down on the chair, curling up her legs underneath her and resting her glass on the arm.

Gabriel was about to do the same when he spotted the little table, on which lay a pile of notebooks, one open to a page covered in jottings. He attention was caught as he noticed the odd name, names he recognised, names from antiquity. Puzzled, he set down his glass and picked up the top one. He scanned the writing and, although realising that this could be private, was unable to stop; he scanned the pages, there was scarcely a line without some note or other scribbled on it. He was confused for a few moments, not understanding what he was reading, but the more pages he checked the clearer it became. Kassie was writing a book!

He glanced up to see her watching him, dubiously. She was withdrawing; her body language told him she was expecting ridicule.

"How long have you been writing?" He breathed the question, stunned at the details contained within the notebook. While he waited for her answer, he picked up two more and leafed through them; her research covered some unusual aspects of life in the Roman world, aspects that were more along the lines of academic research than lightweight novels. She still hadn't answered and he paused in his examination of her jottings to look across at her.

The minute Gabriel spotted her notebooks, Kassie stilled, unsure what to do. Dammit, why hadn't she moved them? Well 'cos you weren't expecting company, you wally, she admonished herself. Awesome! Now he would see her mindless rubbish and realise that not only was she lacking in beauty and poise, neither was she much in the high achiever department.

Gabriel was silent; the apprehension in her face causing a pang in his heart. He went over to where she was sitting and knelt next to her. Under normal circumstances, she would have found this very funny, he was still way taller than her, even on his knees, but this was so far beyond normal that she wasn't sure of the rules. He took the glass — the stem of which she had been twiddling — out of her hand, placing it on the low coffee table and then clasped her hand in his, feeling her trembling.

"Kassie, how long have you been writing?" She regarded him in the soft light of the lamps; he didn't look as though he was going to mock her.

Taking her failing courage in both hands she replied. "About four years."

His mouth fell open in shock. Four years!

"How did you…when did you…what did you…?" he couldn't get his head around it. "Have you published anything?" She stared at him for such a long time that Gabriel, who could almost hear the debate going on in her head, thought she wasn't going to tell him. Finally, she nodded, ever so slightly. "How many?"

"Six." Now he was gobsmacked, there was no other word to describe his astonishment.

"SIX?" His deep voice bellowed the word. "Six! You're kidding me? I didn't think I was easily surprised, but this, this is incredible. What are they about? Where can I find them?" Gabriel carried on asking questions about the books until he realised she hadn't responded. She pulled her hand away and tried to put some distance between them, not easy when he had her trapped in the chair. "Kassie?" His tone eased and he sat back on his heels, tilting his head to study her expression.

Kassie had never wanted anyone to know; this was her secret, she had loved that no one else had a clue about her other self. The person who disappeared into another life, another world and wrote silly romance novels set in ancient Rome.

"If you don't mind I'd rather not say any more," she said, defensively. "It's not like you'll have ever read, or even seen one. I cannot imagine that they're your type of book and you won't find them in any bookshops."

"How do you know what my type of book is?"

"Well I can almost guarantee that it won't be what I wrote."

"Might you let me be the judge of that?" She stared at him, trying to figure out whether he was serious. He looked serious. His deep blue eyes crinkled and he was smiling, but not in jest, in encouragement. Still, she wasn't ready to share that part of herself.

"They're just light fluff," she whispered. "Please, just leave it." He studied her for several seconds, reading the panic in her eyes and realising that she was scared; scared that he would think less of her, that those words Professor Hardwick had uttered two years ago were true, that she was only really suited to libraries — shelving the books not writing them. Gabriel cursed his old mentor then, wishing that Kassie had never heard his declaration. He wasn't sure whether he'd ever persuade her that he had already known she was capable of so much more.

"Okay, I'll let it go for now, but I won't forget. I would love to see your work. Honestly." Pondering, as he said this, whether he might be able to work out which books she had written, if he searched the online bookstores with specific refinements. Kassie relaxed, and suggested a hot drink. Needing to divert her attention Gabriel accepted and she went through into the little kitchen to boil the kettle. While she was gone and, even though he experienced a twinge of guilt for prying, Gabriel took the opportunity to have a final flick through one of the notebooks, hoping for a hint of a book title or a name. A few things stood out, which he stored away for later use and by the time Kassie came back with the drinks, he was standing on the balcony looking out at the night.

The rest of the evening passed without any more discussion on the books. Gabriel concentrated on their upcoming tour and, after a little while, Kassie's normal enthusiasm for all things ancient re-surfaced. It was late when Gabriel left. He didn't want to go, but they both had a busy week ahead, at the end of which he would be able to enjoy three weeks of her almost undivided attention; three whole weeks — the mere idea sent his pulse rate into overdrive.

With a marked lack of enthusiasm, he shrugged into his jacket and walked to the door, Kassie ahead of him, her hand on the latch. Before she could open it, however, Gabriel pulled her close, cupping the back of her head and kissing her gently. Kassie's hand fell away from the door, coming to rest on his lower back. It was barely a touch, but it felt like a brand and he sensed, rather than heard, her sharp intake of breath as she leaned into his embrace, their passion flaring once again.

Minutes ticked by then, "Kassie," he said in undertones, "you are going to make me lose all restraint."

She smiled against his mouth.

"Would that be such a bad thing?" she said, shyly, blushing at his words and her own response. Such intimacy was uncharted territory for Kassie and she was caught between wanting him to take it further and panicking because she had no clue what to do should that ever happen.

"No," he said, quietly. "I think it would be the most incredible thing, but I do not want to rush you. You deserve to be courted properly, not thrown over my shoulder and carried off into the woods." Kassie spluttered with laughter at the image he conjured up, all the while her heart fluttering. He wanted to court her? Did that mean what she thought it meant? As far as she could tell, old-fashioned romance never happened anymore; still, it sounded intriguing and she was happy to let this unfold slowly. She met his eyes; his deep blue, unreadable, eyes and felt the world tilt a little.

"Well, if you feel so inclined, it would be most unfair of me to stop you." She winked at him, softening the formality of her reply, yet her words were in keeping with their mood. Gabriel smiled down at her, dropping one last kiss on her forehead. He unlatched the door and, after saying he was looking forward to Friday, disappeared down the stairs.

Five

For Kassie, the week seemed never-ending. Every day dragged, even the Wednesday when she had two groups to guide around the Colosseum. Each evening, when she got home and before sitting down for a meal, she would pack a few more things until, by Thursday, she was done. She had explained to Emilia that she would be away for three weeks and why; that astute lady reading more into her somewhat convoluted explanation than Kassie realised.

Suddenly it was Friday and, unexpectedly, Kassie was nervous. She didn't know whether this was because she would be acting as tour guide all day, every day, or whether it was because she would be in Gabriel's company for nearly a month. She hadn't seen him since Sunday evening, but he had texted and emailed her every day. Some were business-like missives relating to the tour, others were akin to mini love letters and Kassie treasured them, re-reading them every night before she went to sleep.

She knew she was acting like a schoolgirl on her first crush, but she couldn't help it and now she would be seeing him in less than an hour; the realisation that she would be in such proximity for an extended period, daunting. She didn't want him to think she was throwing herself at him, but he was the one who'd said he wanted to court her. Problem was, she simply could not understand why. What was it about her, Kassie Winters; too shy, too plain, a bit ungainly and maybe a little more curvy than was fashionable, that made him kiss her as though she was the only woman in the world never mind Rome?

She had tried to figure him out, but so far all she'd come up with was that, to Gabriel, she was probably a pleasant diversion and a useful asset and, if she was honest, she worried that his interest in her was more to do with her going along as his tour guide, than any real curiosity about her as a person. She didn't think that he was that shallow, but the thought refused to be banished, nibbling away at her newly found confidence.

Determined not to let it spoil her holiday, Kassie shoved it aside. She would deal with all matters of the heart when the tour was over, hoping that by then everything would seem much clearer.

Although Gabriel had said they would pick her up outside her apartment, Kassie had persuaded him that it would be easier if she made her own way to the group's meeting point. It was far too difficult to get a large coach up to where she lived and the walk from her home to the Piazza del Popolo was always pleasant. It was a beautiful morning, the sun was shining and the sky was blue, just a few fluffy clouds to soften the glare; the air was cool but promised a warm day ahead. Kassie strolled along the narrow street that skirted the Borghese Gardens before navigating down the steepish zigzag hill to the piazza, dodging reckless drivers and mad cyclists. She was a few minutes early, so went to sit on the steps under the obelisk, watching those tourists already there, snapping away with their cameras and children dashing about, making the most of their freedom as the long summer holiday drew to a close. It was all noise and movement, a typical day anywhere in Rome.

Lost in reverie Kassie didn't hear footsteps nor did she have any awareness that she was no longer alone until a large hand grasped hers, the unanticipated contact making her jump. She spun around sharply, ready to yell at whoever presumed to get hold of her hand, and looked straight into a pair of twinkling blue eyes.

"Oh, it's you," she said momentarily flustered. "You want to be careful doing that, I was all set to flatten you."

"My apologies, I didn't intend to startle you and by the time I realised that you were in your own little world there, it was too late." He didn't look particularly repentant, his engaging smile tugging a responding grin from her lips.

"Just be warned, next time you might not come off unscathed," she said reprovingly, then changing the subject, "are they here?"

"Yeah, just over there." Gabriel pointed towards the arch, where Kassie spotted a group of elderly people, surrounded by a huge pile of luggage.

"Goodness, I hope you've chartered a reasonably sized coach or we'll never get all that luggage in." Kassie giggled. Gabriel chuckled, agreeing with her sentiment, adding that he'd travelled with this group before and, thus forewarned, had booked accordingly. Kassie stood; brushing the dust off her three-quarter pants and running her hands over her hair to make sure it was still in its ponytail.

"You look great." Gabriel assured her and she smiled gratefully.

"I don't know why I'm so nervous; it's not like this is in any way new to me. I do it every week, but I've got butterflies."

"Maybe this will help," said Gabriel and pulled her close for a quick, hard kiss. Kassie forgot to breathe and her heart rate doubled. Well, that wasn't going to calm her nerves, but it did distract her, most effectively, for a few seconds. As Gabriel released her, she stumbled backwards and his hand shot out to steady her, sending that now familiar jolt of electricity pulsing up her arm.

"Careful, love. You don't want to go bashing yourself up before we've set off." Gabriel smiled gently, as Kassie took a deep breath and tried to concentrate, too many conflicting emotions running through her head. She should never have let him get this close, how was she supposed to conduct herself in a professional manner if he insisted on kissing her without warning. Straightening up to her full height, Kassie made a decent attempt to get a grip on herself and deliberately schooled her features into a bland expression.

"Thank you," she said, recovering her composure, "do you think you should introduce me to the group?" Gabriel studied her for a moment, his brow furrowing at her impassive face. Where was that vivacity he was so used to? Then he noticed her clenched jaw and realised what she was doing. Somewhat concerned that she was putting up a wall between them for the sake of propriety, he let it go for now and, collecting her suitcase, led her over to the group.

Gabriel was thorough with his introductions; there were five couples, Jenny and Bill, Harry and Claire, Penny and Tom, John and Ella, George and Lillian, as well as five singles, Dot, Tony, Hugh, Walter and Anna. Once names were swapped — Kassie hoping she'd eventually remember them all — the group expressed their pleasure at her presence, discussing the tour with unfeigned excitement. They pressed questions on their tour guide, until laughingly, she put up her hands in mock surrender saying that they could ask her anything they wanted, but preferably one at a time and maybe once they were settled on the coach.

Gabriel watched this amusing interlude; again struck by Kassie's innate ability to make each person feel important and that nothing they asked her would be viewed as beneath her consideration. While they had been gossiping, a large coach had pulled up at the other side of the archway and Gabriel began to usher the vociferous group towards it. Their driver Dominic, whom Gabriel greeted with a friendliness that suggested this wasn't their first meeting, quickly stacked all the suitcases in the luggage hold and soon they were motoring out of the city. Today they were driving to Naples, where they would spend a few hours at the National Archaeological Museum before travelling onto Pompeii where they would be staying for three nights.

It took a little while for Dominic to extricate the coach from the snarl of city traffic, but before long they were flying along the autostrada, the genial driver telling them that all being well, they should be in Naples around 11am. Trying to ignore her qualms regarding the ungodly speed of the bus, Kassie turned her attention to the group. She guessed that everyone, except for Gabriel and her, was in their seventies, but looked sprightly and in good health. She answered all their queries, explaining their plans for that day and those of the following three.

The next day they would tour the ruins of Ancient Pompeii, the day after they would visit both Herculaneum and Oplontis, leaving the third day free, in case they would like to return to Pompeii, or spend the time discovering the modern town. The ruins were so extensive that it would take more than one day, in fact probably more than two days, to explore them properly.

This pleased Kassie, as she was more than happy to potter around the ancient site as often as possible. Their hotel served breakfast and — should they choose to eat there — dinner, meaning they need only to organise their lunches, but as there were cafés within both Pompeii and Herculaneum, Gabriel didn't foresee any problems food-wise.

Eventually, the chatter amongst the group quieted and they began to admire the scenery, one or two dozed, the sun soporific through the windows. Gabriel moved to sit next to Kassie, ostensibly to go over their itinerary, in reality because he needed to be near her. Not seeing her for five days had been torture and it was only by sheer force of will that he had not joined her afternoon tour of the Colosseum two days previously. Kassie tried to remain detached, a wasted effort for the minute his leg touched hers, all her good intentions evaporated.

"Told you so," was his opening comment. Kassie raised a questioning eyebrow. "They already love you, you'll have them in the palm of your hand before we reach Naples."

"Don't be daft." Kassie was amused by his assertion. "They're just being friendly. They seem like a lovely group though, really interested in everything we'll be doing. It will be a joy to take them around; way more fun than trying to instil some passion for the ancient world into people who are only doing the tour because they think they're supposed to, in order that they can claim to have seen this that or the other, but couldn't care less either way. It's soul destroying sometimes."

Gabriel watched as she spoke, knowing that she was completely unaware of how she charmed him. It was only the fifteen other people around them — who might be rather agog at their tour organiser suddenly dragging their tour guide into his arms and kissing her until she lost her senses — that prevented him from doing precisely that. He was hoping that during this trip, he might be able to orchestrate some time together, just the two of them, so that Kassie would see how serious he was about her.

Kassie glanced out of the window and realised that they were already on the outskirts of Naples.

"How much longer do you think? Before we arrive, I mean?" she asked Gabriel, who reckoned a little over half an hour, traffic permitting,

"It can be rather tricky in the centre and it'll be easier for the coach to drop us and park elsewhere. I think we'll have about three hours around the museum."

"Oh, will that be long enough?" Kassie ran her mind over the exhibits and artefacts on display in the museum, knowing she could spend all day studying them. Guessing her thoughts, Gabriel grinned.

"Remember our group are not young. It's more than likely that they'll have had enough after an hour or so and will find a quiet corner to sit and soak up the atmosphere. Three hours is a long time, but we can always have a coffee or some lunch to fill in time while we wait for the bus to come and pick us up." Kassie nodded in understanding and began to move through the coach explaining that they were not far from their destination and to make sure they had everything that they would need with them.

Shortly thereafter they pulled up in front of the museum, gathering at the entrance with varying degrees of agility and Gabriel, who had pre-booked the tickets, led them into the cool of the interior. Almost two hours later, having seen the Roman and Greek statues, admired the stunning mosaics — including the breathtaking depiction of the battle of Alexander against Darius — along with the huge collection of artefacts and frescoes from Pompeii, Herculaneum, Boscoreale, Stabiae and Cuma, the group was tiring.

Except for the odd interjection from Gabriel, Kassie had done most of the talking and she was desperate for a drink, coffee preferably. Gabriel had been impressed with her breadth of knowledge; the museum contained a vast assortment of treasures, yet she seemed comfortable discussing anything displayed within. He was coming to realise that ancient history was Kassie's passion; that she drank in everything she could regarding it, like a man dying of thirst would drink suddenly offered water.

Not far from the museum were several cafés and the group trudged along, found seats outside one and relaxed with a coffee and a late lunch. They took the opportunity to find out more about their guide and, once again, Kassie was showered with a host of questions. Most centred on her personal life and went along the lines of; how was it that such lovely young lady wasn't married yet? Did she have a current boyfriend? Did she know that young Gabe here was single? What made her move to Rome? Tell me all about yourself dear and so on. She fended them off good-humouredly and Gabriel noticed that she managed to answer their questions without disclosing anything much at all.

Kassie was interested to hear them calling Gabriel, 'Gabe.' It suggested that they knew him well, and had for a long time. She studied him, while he was engaged in a lively debate with Harry over the conservation of artefacts. He suited Gabe, but she felt more comfortable calling him Gabriel, or while on this tour, Professor St Germain; it wouldn't do to seem too familiar. His face, usually rather grave in repose, was animated and cheerful; his relationship with this bunch, obviously congenial. Kassie felt her heart do that strange flutter and purposefully dampened it down, going into the café, ostensibly to get another coffee, but in reality to try to calm her chaotic emotions.

The coach arrived and they were soon heading for Pompeii. During the shortish drive, Kassie explained that the modern town surrounded the ruins and that for the most part was a typical Italian town; one that, had there not been an archaeological site of international significance bang slap in the middle of it, would barely be noticed. This intrigued the group and they said how much they were looking forward to exploring both ancient and modern Pompeii.

Their hotel was situated, conveniently, across the road from one of the entrances to the ruins and once Gabriel had checked them all in, he handed out their respective keys, dispatching them to their rooms saying that they were free for what little remained of the afternoon. Dinner was booked for 7:30 at a local trattoria, but until then, they could do as they pleased. Most chose to have a rest in their rooms and a few relaxed in the little garden at the rear of the hotel.

Kassie, however, excited to be back at Pompeii, decided that since the site was still open and there were a few hours of daylight left, she would treat herself to a brief visit. Slipping her camera into her backpack and checking to make sure she had her purse with her, she dropped her room key at the desk and walked out into the sunny afternoon.

Six

The entrance near their hotel was the one near the amphitheatre and was nearly always quiet, as most of the large tour groups came in at the far side of the ruins. Kassie bought her ticket and declined a map — she had been several times and knew her way around. It was around 4pm; the sun was still quite high and the afternoon warm. Tall umbrella pines whispered in the light breeze and the only sounds were the chirping of birds and the drone of bees.

There was no one around, which was exactly how Kassie liked it. Sauntering over to the amphitheatre, she walked through the cool tunnel into the arena, imagining the roar of the crowds as they cheered on their favourite gladiator; it was so evocative. Leaning against the aged stone, she let the history wash over her. The tranquillity of the day, at odds with the violent spectacles that took place there millennia ago.

Brushing aside her whimsical thoughts, Kassie left the amphitheatre and stood for a few moments at the palaestra, where young men trained in all manner of sports, and then dawdled aimlessly along the cobbled streets past the ruined houses — some of which she ventured into — and on towards the Forum.

Once there, Kassie found a relatively secluded corner and just absorbed it all. She enjoyed watching the world go by and it was pleasant to do so without worrying about losing a member of a tour group. This most fascinating of sites never ceased to enthral her. Even though there were major issues regarding the preservation of Pompeii, Kassie knew there was an enormous effort underway to halt the decay and conserve what remained. The cost was astronomical, but it would be worth every penny. Pompeii was a snapshot in time, a moment from antiquity, frozen forever and its protection was vital.

She had been sitting for at least half an hour when she heard a familiar footfall. Tilting her head, she saw Gabriel striding towards her. Her eyes hidden behind dark sunglasses,

Kassie drank him in. He mesmerised her, with his athletic physique, his unruly hair and his piercing gaze. She could not let herself fall, knowing, even as the thought crossed her mind, that it was too late; Gabriel had ensnared her heart that day in Ostia and every time she saw him, he stole a little more. Forcing herself to remain calm and despite a pulse rate that would put the beat of a hummingbird's wing to shame; she managed a creditable job of appearing composed.

"Kassie, I guessed you would not be able to resist." Gabriel grinned as he reached her makeshift seat.

"I love coming in towards the end of the day when most of the big tour groups have left; there's only the sad acts like me, obsessed with antiquity. On the plus side, you can take your time and roam at leisure." She smiled back, although Gabriel thought he detected a reticence in her response. Unsure what had prompted it, he chose to ignore it and simply sat next to her, the two relaxing in the shade of their ruined section of wall.

As they sat, the afternoon began to fade, the harsh blue of the sky taking on a gentler hue, bathing the ruins in an almost magical light. Gabriel wanted to put his arm around Kassie and pull her close, nestling her against his shoulder, entwining her hand in his. Kassie wanted much the same thing, but even though they were almost touching, suddenly and inexplicably the gulf between them seemed vast.

"How many times have you visited Pompeii?" enquired Kassie quietly, trying to find a way to breach the gap.

"Several," was Gabriel's less than satisfactory response. He was leaning against the wall, his eyes closed.

"Errr…so, this group, how long have you known them?" Floundering, yet needing to keep their conversation going

"Oh, quite a few years." Gabriel's tone suggested disinterest and Kassie gave up. This was too hard. It was clear he didn't want to chat and she couldn't keep sitting so close to him, when he so obviously found her company boring. Irked that he had spoilt her afternoon — he had sought her out, not the other way around and now he was behaving as though she'd interrupted him — Kassie picked up her backpack and, snapping a stilted goodbye over her shoulder, stalked away, disappearing down the street that led to the amphitheatre.

Gabriel watched her go, knowing that he'd upset her, yet unable to find the words to put it right. He knew it was because he was battling with a welter of unfamiliar feelings, but it was unfair to take it out on her. She had no idea what was going on in his head and much as he wanted to talk to her about it, he feared it would scare her off. At thirty-three, Gabriel had indulged in very few casual relationships and as his work often took him away for long periods of time, they rarely lasted. He had never expected to find someone with whom he wanted to share his life, someone who would challenge him on every level, someone whose face haunted him and whose body bewitched him.

Then, quite by chance, he had met Kassie and in the most unfortunate circumstances. Following that little incident, he had contrived to bump into her the following day but it was evident that she had overheard Hardwick's comments and, presuming him to be complicit, had reproached him. Despite her annoyance with him, as he watched her glorious eyes fill with tears, Gabriel had lost his heart. She had walked out of his life once and he didn't think he could bear it if she did so again. He had to tell her, even if she didn't feel the same — although if her response to his kisses was anything to go by she wasn't unmoved by him. Sighing in frustration, Gabriel stood, stretched his long limbs and trudged back to the hotel.

The evening passed pleasantly enough. Kassie took pains to sit as far from Gabriel as she could and although she seemed happy to chat, excused herself before the meal was over, claiming she had a headache and returned to their hotel.

The next morning, after a very sumptuous breakfast, they all gathered in the hotel lobby and Kassie led the way across the road to the ruins. She had gone over earlier to collect their pre-booked tickets and so all they had to do was show them to the attendant.

She walked the legs off the group, showing them as much as she could in the time available. Once again, Gabriel was astonished at her knowledge. She made the place live, talking about Pompeii in the same way she had done when at the

Forum in Rome, as though she had lived there. It made the plight of those killed following the eruption of Vesuvius much more poignant, for everyone in the group felt as though they had known the victims personally.

Making sure, however, that they took proper breaks, coffee, lunch and then another coffee mid-afternoon, Kassie didn't rush the tour and as they wended their way back to the Forum in the late afternoon, suggested that they finish here. They could stay longer should they choose, or were free to leave and everyone would meet at 7:30 for dinner.

Most decided to return to the hotel for a short rest; Hugh and Tony wanted to visit the Villa of the Mysteries at the far side of the site, a proposal that John and Ella jumped on and the four strolled off along the street towards the Via Consolare, out to the Porta Ercolano and said villa. Kassie confirmed that she would hang around a little longer in case they had any more questions, waving her hand in the general direction of the café.

Treating herself to yet another espresso — she'd be bouncing off the walls soon — Kassie sat on one of the benches just outside the café, resting her tired back; which was where Gabriel, whom she'd avoided with a modicum of success for much of the day, found her; eyes closed, head against the wall and that ridiculously large hat on her knee.

"Kassie." His rich baritone voice broke through her daydreams and she opened sleepy eyes, straight into a pair of deep blue ones, gazing at her with an inscrutable expression.

"What?" she demanded, churlishly.

"Please may we talk?"

"I'm not sure we have anything to say to each other," she said, her voice cool.

"Just give me a moment." Kassie stared at him, searching his face and finding apprehension there, his eyes shadowed. Gabriel uncertain — that couldn't be right; he was always so confident. Kassie fidgeted, not wanting to hear what she imagined he was going to say yet knowing she really had no choice. Well, maybe she should face it now; it would be like pulling off a sticking plaster, painful but over with quickly.

Gabriel watched all this flickering across her expressive face and felt his heart contract. She looked as though she was steeling herself for bad news and, although the last thing he could countenance was hurting her, it gave him a glimmer of hope. Maybe she did care. Finally, she nodded and he sat down on the bench next to her. She shuffled away, needing to keep some distance.

"Why did you walk away from me yesterday?" he asked in a low voice. Kassie sat, unmoving, for so long that he didn't think she was going to answer.

"Because it was patently obvious that you didn't want me there," she said, so quietly that he wasn't sure she had spoken at all. Gabriel ran his hands through his already unruly hair, making it stick out at crazy angles, the gesture distracting Kassie and she wished he wasn't so darned cute.

"I'm sorry Kassie, I didn't mean to upset you. I was trying my best not to drag you into my arms and hold you close and kiss you. I didn't know…I wasn't sure how you felt, so I forced myself to detach and then you left, so I wondered…" He trailed off. Kassie gawked at him. Wasn't she the one who was supposed to be all awkward and insecure? He looked utterly endearing in his discomfort, but she wasn't going to let him off that lightly.

"I left because you seemed totally disinterested in being with me, which really bugged me, as you came to find me not the other way around. One minute you were all chatty and friendly, the next you answered my questions as though I was disturbing some Zen moment and you became closed and cold. If this is some kind of game, I do not wish to play; I don't know the rules. I fail to see why you want to kiss me anyway, I know you said you wanted to court me properly, but that must have been the wine or something or you were just being polite or you thought it was the easiest way to persuade me to join this tour. Well it worked; I'm here, so you can stop pretending. I know I'm not a catch. I'm under no illusion about my looks or my figure or my nature." Her cool tones became glacial.

Gabriel heard the pain in her voice and wished Professor Hardwick could see the damage his words had caused. He had long ago worked out that Kassie had never been particularly self-confident but to harbour the belief that he'd been stringing her along and that she was a nonentity, bruised his heart. He took her slender hand in his.

"Kassie, firstly, I do want to court you, more than anything in this world, the wine had nothing to do with it and this is no pretence, nor is it a game. Secondly, I think you are beautiful; your hair shines like burnished gold, your eyes beguile me and there are things I crave to do with your body that should not be discussed in such ancient surroundings, for the ghosts of this place would rise in consternation. One thing you are not and, in my eyes have never been, is ungainly or plain."

Kassie's jaw had dropped during this little speech.

"You don't think I'm old, or stuffy?"

"Huh?" He was flummoxed. "Where on earth did you get that idea?" She reminded him about the day he came to her office, when he told her he was looking for someone with a common-sense attitude, who was not a young go-getter. Gabriel groaned, seeing why she would think that.

"No, you goose. I wanted you…well I wanted you because it was the only way I could think of to get you on your own for three weeks," he said, smiling at her dumbfounded expression. "But also, because I'd seen you with tours. You love what you do and it radiates out of you, connecting you with whatever group you happen to be taking around, in a way that makes them feel as though you really care about their experience and, in this day and age, that is a rare gift."

Kassie was silent; she had lost the ability to speak, her mind whirling. He thought she was beautiful? He thought she was beautiful! She couldn't get her head around that.

"I think you probably need your eyes testing," she said, eventually, when her mouth finally listened to her brain. "Beautiful my arse."

"Yes, I'm sure that part of your delectable anatomy is beautiful too." Gabriel grinned, watching hot colour flare up Kassie's cheeks. Then he became serious again, "Kassie, I believe we share something very special here, something that should be cherished and appreciated. I'm not looking for a quick fling, I want it all." He paused there, unsure whether he'd stated his case clearly enough, realising that she hadn't said anything about her feelings. He studied her face, watching her process his words, her green eyes holding him spellbound.

Kassie started to speak and then thought better of it. She was baffled and as she regarded him steadily, trying to figure out what he meant precisely, her eyes touched his soul and Gabriel's control shattered.

Seven

"Oh God, Kassie." Unable to wait any longer he cupped his hand around the back of her head, twisting his fingers into her long, luscious hair and kissed her with all the pent-up desire that he'd been trying so hard to quash. Kassie shuddered and, without conscious thought, moved closer, her body just brushing his. Gabriel heard her breathing quicken and smiled against her mouth, she felt something; did she care for him too? Releasing her hand, he pulled her against him, feeling her heartbeat rise, imitating the unsteady rhythm of his own.

Kassie couldn't think straight when he kissed her, so there was no point trying. Even had she wanted to maintain some kind of distance, her body betrayed her. Her arms went around his waist and her hands stroked up his back, fingers splaying out across his shoulders, anchoring him to her. He was like a drug and she was hooked. Distractedly, she mused that as addictions go, this had to be one of the more preferable ones and she couldn't see herself coming down from the high anytime soon.

After what seemed like an age during which hundreds of delicious shockwaves ran rampant through Kassie's svelte frame, Gabriel lifted his head and stared down at her, taking in her dazed eyes and delightfully tousled hair. He didn't speak however, simply tucked her head into the crook of his neck and held her close, his large hand trailing up and down her spine. They stayed like that for long moments and then Gabriel turned her in his arms and ran one finger along her jawline, tilting her head so she had to look at him.

"Tell me what you're thinking," he asked quietly, hesitantly. Kassie stared into his blue eyes, warm now reflecting the desire she was sure must be in hers also. She dithered for a moment then plumped for honesty. She had nothing left to lose.

"That it's too late."

Gabriel blanched at the baldness of her words. His heart sank and his head pounded.

"You mean I've ruined everything?" His voice was hoarse and she could hear panic in his tones.

Chuckling softly, she hastened to clarify. "No, you nitwit. I was lost the moment we met in Ostia and, by too late, I mean that despite everything I've done to fight my feelings; trying to persuade myself that you aren't interested me, that you just want a tour guide and you were merely being friendly, my heart had other ideas."

She stopped abruptly.

Oh, bugger, should she have said heart? That seemed a bit forward. He hadn't told her he loved her, what was she thinking? Such declarations, however indirect, sent men running for the hills. Oh, Kassie you dope, now you've gone and blown it and he was doing that so well all by himself.

"Are you saying you love me?" Gabriel's voice now held a note of wonder.

"N-no, n-no, I never s-said that, you m-misunderstood me." Kassie stuttered, cursing herself for being so rash.

"Yes, you did, you said your heart has other ideas. You do, you love me."

Kassie lost her temper then, she was flustered and he had caught her off guard; what did he think he was doing, sending her nicely ordered thoughts into complete disarray. She all but stamped her foot in her agitation.

"Well, so what if I do? It's all your fault! I was fine, absolutely fine until you came over here, invading my safe little world, appearing out of nowhere, treating me to coffee and kissing me and holding my hand and being tall and handsome and...and...tall." Coherence, never her strong point, abandoned her and she could feel treacherous tears building, dashing her hand across her face to scrub them away. Mortified, she tried to disentangle herself, her need to run, far outweighing her need to behave like the adult she was. Gabriel simply pulled her closer, refusing to let her flee and whispered in her ear

"I love you too." Kassie froze and then squirmed so that she could see his face. He held her gaze, no cheeky smile and no sign that he was winding her up. Her breathing hitched and she tried to respond, but all she could manage was a rather feeble little squeak. Gabriel didn't care about that, leaning in to kiss her tenderly, his lips moving over hers like an embrace, sending quivers right through her and making her toes curl.

"Oh my," was all she said when he finally lifted his head. "Gabriel, that's so kind but you didn't have to say that. Anyway, you can't possibly love me, I'm not your type at all and it's only been two weeks and I'm sure I'll get over it…" her words tumbled out too quickly, as she tried to backpedal. He put his finger on her lips, stopping the avalanche of denials —

"Kassie, there's nothing kind about it and I don't want you to get over it. I think I've been in love with you since I knocked you flying outside old Hardwick's office. In fact, no, since we're being honest, it probably happened the day I saw you present on your favourite building. Your reaction when those students tried to derail you made my heart ache. You had been going so well, I had no idea that you weren't comfortable with public speaking, you made it look effortless. Then when they made fun of you, all the light left your face and you sort of closed down and I realised how hard you found it. All I wanted to do was rush up into the stage, wrap you in my arms and tell you it was going to be okay. It just took my head a little longer to catch up with my heart."

"You really, truly love me?" Her murmured question was nearly lost on the breeze.

"I really, truly love you, my beautiful Kassandra." Kassie smiled then, and to Gabriel it was as though they were surrounded by the glow of a thousand stars.

"Well…errr…well…how do we? Should we? What about the group?"

"What about the group?"

"Well, it's probably not particularly appropriate, us being…well…err…I mean…" Not sure what they were, Kassie clammed up.

"A couple you mean?" he said, smiling as she fumbled. "I don't think they'll care one way or the other, Kassie; if they get their daily dose of antiquity I doubt they'll even notice. Anyway, I'd rather like to hold your hand while we walk through the past." Gabriel grinned as he watched her brow crease in thought. "No use frowning about it, love, just get used to it."

"I s'pose it should be okay," she muttered rather dubiously. "I'm just wary of how it might appear. I'm supposed to be a professional, I don't want them to think I'm some kind of…well, I don't know what you'd call me. A groupie?" Gabriel spluttered with laughter

"That implies you threw yourself at me and I couldn't throw you back. How about saying you're my girl."

"Oh, that sounds rather lovely…your girl…" Kassie ran that one through her head, but before she could say any more, Gabriel kissed her again. There in the middle of one of the most fascinating ancient sites in the world, on a warm summer's afternoon, just as the sun began its slow descent towards the horizon and in full view of several tourists, not to mention a few inquisitive birds, Gabriel stole the last remaining piece of Kassie's heart.

Minutes ticked by and still they kissed. Kassie luxuriated in the feel of Gabriel's arms encircling her; it was as though she'd been waiting for this moment her whole life. She never imagined that a kiss could be so earth shattering, heat flickered through her and she forgot everything except the spell that Gabriel was weaving around them.

His heart rate going through the roof and his own passion flaring, Gabriel knew he had to stop this now, or who knew what would happen. Reluctantly he broke their kiss, whispering that maybe they should go back to the hotel. Kassie shivered, the implication clear. She wasn't sure she was ready for the next step, but she was equally sure that she had no willpower when it came to Gabriel. Nodding shyly, she turned to find her hat, which had slid onto the dusty flagstones at their feet. As Kassie glanced up, a small crowd of tourists, who had obviously witnessed their embrace, clapped. Hot colour flooded her cheeks and she rammed her hat on her now totally messy hair, trying to cover her embarrassment.

Their applause didn't faze Gabriel at all; as standing, he bowed with a flourish, saying. "She just agreed to be my girl."

Huge grins appeared on the faces of their audience

"Gabriel!" Kassie muttered, mortification clear in her voice, "Must you? You're making me sound like a giddy teenager."

"Yes, my darling, I absolutely must." He took her hand and turning it upwards, kissed her palm. As one, the group tilted their heads, sighing in delight at the sheer romance of such a gesture. Gabriel went over to them and murmured something in low tones. The group looked at Kassie, who didn't know where to put herself and back to Gabriel. Lots of nods and handshakes ensued, leaving Kassie totally bewildered. The group walked slowly away, chattering and occasionally glancing back, their faces still wreathed in beatific smiles.

"What? What did you just say to them?"

"Nope, I'll keep that to myself a little longer. No," he said, as she protested. "You'll find out soon enough."

"Not fair," she grumbled.

"Oh, I think it's quite fair, you have your secrets, so I think I'm entitled to mine." He grinned at her affronted expression and, taking her hand drew her along the path towards the amphitheatre. They discussed the next day's plans as they walked and suddenly they were at the hotel. Kassie's stomach was tied up in knots; half of her wanted this, while the other half was quietly freaking out. It was all very well when taking this, whatever it was, to the next level was an improbable dream — okay it was a most alluring and irresistibly sensual dream — but a dream nonetheless, now it was reality. To admit to the man, whom you were convinced was 'the one,' that you'd barely been kissed never mind the rest of it was something Kassie wasn't quite ready for.

Retrieving their keys from the receptionist they climbed the few stairs to the first floor. Coincidentally their rooms were next to each other and by the time they reached her door, Kassie was a bundle of nerves. Swiping the card, she pushed open the door and stepped into her room. Gabriel followed and as the door swung shut, he drew her close for a quick hard kiss.

"Gabriel," she muttered, trying to concentrate, he ignored her and their kiss deepened. "Gabriel, please just a minute." He pulled back and studied her face, she was quite pale and her eyes had a trapped look, like a deer caught in headlights.

"Hey, what's wrong, love?" Stroking her cheek.

"I think, no I know, I want this as much as you do, but please can we slow down. It's just…I'm…I can't go from kisses…heady though they were…in a Roman ruin, to wild sex." Gabriel chuckled.

"I'm gratified that you think it will be wild." He grinned, leering at her in a most unattractive fashion. Kassie gurgled with laughter and nudged him.

"You are silly. No, it's just, look, yes okay I want this…" she waved her hand about randomly, suddenly unable to verbalise what they had been about to do, "errr…this next bit, but I'd like us to take our time. You said you wanted to court me, well court me. Take me to dinner, take me for a walk, talk to me, tell me about yourself. What are your dreams? What are you hopes? Hell, what is your job, for I have no idea? Yes, we have something special happening here but I don't want to spoil it all by missing out on the journey." She paused and looked at him, "Do you see…?" she whispered uncertainly.

"Yes, love, I do see and, while I would like to register my interest in the whole wild sex part, I would be glad simply to court you. Would you do me the honour of joining me for dinner this evening? There will, of course, be fifteen other people in our entourage, but maybe we could chance a moonlight walk later."

Kassie smiled shyly.

"That sounds absolutely marvellous. Oh, and one other thing," he raised a quizzical eyebrow, "do you prefer Gabriel or Gabe?" He gaped at her not expecting so mundane a question right at that moment. "I only ask because the group all refer to you as Gabe, so they must know you very well; a question I posed yesterday and one which you sidestepped very neatly, by the way."

"I don't mind, whichever you prefer is fine with me." Still avoiding the issue Kassie realised, but she let it go for now.

"Hmmm, I can't decide, they both suit you. Regardless, I'll still refer to you as Professor St Germain during the day. I think calling you by your given name is a bit too overfamiliar for a tour assistant." Gabriel smothered a laugh, commenting that if that's the way she wanted it, who was he to argue, but her use of the honorific would be quite ridiculous when he held her hand.

"Oh, I hadn't thought of that. Maybe you shouldn't hold my hand then."

"Stop panicking Kassie, just let things unfold naturally. Now, since an afternoon of debauchery is off the table, I think I'll go next door and take a very long, cold shower." That made Kassie laugh again, a golden sound so full of uninhibited joy that Gabriel knew right then, he could never let her go.

Eight

The next day was engrossing, fascinating and utterly exhausting. Herculaneum and Oplontis were new to the entire group except Gabriel and Kassie, and all were riveted by the state of preservation of both sites. Although both Pompeii and Herculaneum were buried, it was the way they were buried which now provides archaeologists and tourists with unique perspectives on each town.

When Vesuvius erupted in AD 79, vast amounts of ash drifted southeast towards Pompeii, followed shortly thereafter by a deluge of pumice and hardening larva, quickly filling the streets as it was scattered across the town; the weight of which eventually caused the roofs to collapse. Next, a series of pyroclastic surges spewed down the mountain swallowing Herculaneum first and then Pompeii burying everything in its path. It was the intensity of the superheated gases that caused instantaneous death to anyone and anything and, was so hot that in Herculaneum, it carbonised the wood, preserving it. Once the surges reached Pompeii, however they were just cool enough to ignite, rather than carbonise, anything flammable thus destroying any wooden structures. This explains why Herculaneum still has many buildings with intact upper floors, wooden support beams surviving the devastation. Both towns are archaeological miracles in their own right and the group spent quite some time discussing the similarities and differences, plying Kassie with a multitude of questions.

Once satisfied that they had managed to absorb everything they could, Gabriel suggested they move on to Oplontis. Often referred to as Poppea's Villa either because it was reputed to have been built by Nero for his second wife Poppea or owing to its possible association with her family, it is presumed to have been built as a seaside holiday retreat — although now, the coastline is much further away. While its state of preservation is remarkable, it is the frescoes that are the most astonishing part of this villa. Many of the stunningly beautiful and delicate wall paintings have survived almost intact and offer a valuable insight into how lavishly the wealthy decorated their homes in the mid to late first century AD.

Oplontis is not a large site, neither is it usually overwhelmed with visitors and Kassie felt more than comfortable, after a quick guided tour to let them simply wander at will. After telling them to come find her should they have any questions, she retired to a bench at the edge of the colonnaded walkway and let the peace of the villa envelop her. Gabriel found her there about fifteen minutes later and they talked quietly until the group decided they were ready to move on. Dominic drove them back to Pompeii via the scenic route, avoiding the busy motorways where possible, making the journey much more pleasant.

The following day was free and Kassie, unable to help herself, went back into the ruins at Pompeii. She slipped out of the hotel very early and was lost in history before most of the others had even had their breakfast. Gabriel guessed her plans, but left her alone for the morning. By the afternoon, however he wanted to see her, so sent her a quick text asking whether she would meet him in the café behind the Forum. She pinged back a brief 'yes' and he strolled along the Via dell'Abbondanza whistling softly to himself.

She was waiting for him on the same bench where he had told her he loved her two days previously. Once again, she was resting her head against the wall, her eyes closed and her hat on her knee. He stopped several feet away and just studied her. The sun picked up the highlights in her hair and even from this distance he could see the smattering of freckles across her nose. She had a very cute nose he decided and he might quite like to kiss it.

As though sensing his scrutiny, she opened her eyes and turned her head in his direction, a bright smile making her face glow as she saw him, and his heart missed a beat. In four strides he was at her side and, asking whether she wanted a coffee — which she did — he went into the café, ordering two espressos as well as two slices of pizza and, once served, carried them outside.

"Oh, thank you, I didn't think I was hungry 'til you brought these out." She grinned. A distinct rumble belied her words, making them both chuckle. They ate in companionable silence and sipped the rich coffees.

"So, have you enjoyed your day, love?" Gabriel asked once they were finished and Kassie had dumped their plates and cups in the bin. She nodded.

"It's been great, I was on my own until about half ten and it was so peaceful. I managed to get right over to the other side before the hordes landed, and explored all those villas I missed the other day. Then I came back this way and checked out the gladiator school and the theatre. Now my feet ache and I don't think I can get back to the hotel." Pulling an agonised face and making Gabriel chuckle.

"Well, I expect we can sit here for a while and just people watch," he mused. "I'll get us an ice-cream in a little while, that'll keep the café people happy."

"Oh, ice cream, scrummy," was Kassie's childlike response. Gabriel took her hand in his and resting both on his thigh began to talk about the upcoming part of the tour. They would be leaving Pompeii the next day and travelling back to Rome.

"Wouldn't it be easier for me to stay at my apartment?" Kassie asked, as Gabriel paused for breath.

"Not for me." He winked. She blushed becomingly and he kissed her hot cheek.

"I was just thinking that it would be more cost effective if you had one less hotel room to pay for."

"Yes, it might be, but the rooms are sorted and don't you want to feel as though you're on holiday? I know it's more of a working holiday, but at least in a hotel you don't have to wash the dishes or do the cleaning. Surely you must enjoy being spoilt occasionally?" Kassie had to admit it was rather nice not to think about all her usual mundane chores and was easily persuaded that the hotel was by far the more pleasant option.

Without thinking Kassie leaned against his shoulder and, still holding her hand, Gabriel tucked his arm through hers, holding her to him. He carried on talking about the tour until, suddenly, he realised she wasn't answering him anymore. Glancing down, he saw that she'd dozed off. Smiling at her serene expression, he shifted slightly so that he could slip his arm around her, nestling her against his large frame. She fitted perfectly, she half woke and then snuggled in and Gabriel couldn't recall the last time he had been this content.

She felt so lovely and her scent drew him in, whatever perfume she was wearing was doing the most peculiar things to his senses. While they sat, he stroked his fingers up and down her arm, trailing them lightly over her skin, pondering his continued seduction of Miss Kassandra Winters.

They remained like that for well over half an hour. The afternoon began to wane and the light to change, softening as evening approached. The gates would be closing soon, but Gabriel was loath to disturb Kassie; she slept so peacefully and he was relishing the feeling of her resting against him. A cool breeze wafted over them and Kassie stirred lifting her head, still fuzzy with sleep, off his shoulder.

"Oh goodness, how rude of me. I didn't mean to fall asleep, but you have the most comfortable shoulder." She smiled slowly, the candid green of her eyes sparkling in the hazy sunlight, making Gabriel's heart pound and he brushed his lips to hers. It was scarcely a touch, yet her whole body pulsed and she could not, for the life of her, prevent a muffled moan. His own breath catching, Gabriel turned her within his embrace and kissed her more deeply, making her forget that if they stayed on this bench much longer they'd likely have to stay inside Pompeii all night. A predicament that may not necessarily have bothered either of them one jot.

Gabriel did remember, however, and broke their kiss, before things got completely out of hand. Taking Kassie's hand, he pulled her up from the bench and, after plonking the floppy hat on her head, slung her backpack over his shoulder and the pair set off for the hotel. They strolled hand in hand along the now empty pathways towards the amphitheatre. Kassie was quite certain that if they looked carefully they would see the ghosts of this place rising with the dusk, going about their business before a wall of hot debris silenced them forever.

By the time they reached the hotel, the rest of the tour group had returned also, a few of whom were relaxing on the terrace with a glass of wine. Gabriel and Kassie joined them, catching up on each other's day before they all headed off a little while later for dinner, just along the street.

As they finished their meal, Gabriel asked Kassie whether she would like to take a walk? Nodding, she grabbed her jacket and the two left in what they hoped was a nonchalant manner, blissfully unaware of the knowing smiles following them along the street. One member of the group, however, did not look quite so pleased and frowning, took out her phone to send a quick text.

Meanwhile Gabriel and Kassie were strolling through the town, stopping occasionally to admire a shop window — although, to be fair, that was mainly Kassie — neither saying much, content just to be together. Kassie liked that they didn't need to talk all the time, she enjoyed the peace of the evening and was unwilling disturb it with mindless chitchat. Gabriel didn't really care, as long as he was with Kassie.

He'd gone from holding her hand to putting his arm around her, loving that she'd done the same to him, tucking her fingers into his belt. Kassie leaned into him feeling the heat from his body as they walked, knowing that she was losing her own battle to take this slowly. It crossed her mind that she had never in her life done anything risky or reckless and, even though she accepted that this risk was a big huge enormous one, she realised that she wanted it more than she had ever wanted anything.

Of course, she was the one who'd demanded they not rush into anything and if he really did want to be more intimate, she would have to tell him that this was all new to her — awesome, way to look like a naive teenager, Kassie she thought. Nerves overtaking her again, she pushed it aside and decided to just see what happened. She couldn't very well ask him; she'd sound like a wanton hussy, the very idea suddenly seeming hilarious. Laughter bubbled in her throat and as she tried to swallow it down, she made a kind of strangled squawk, causing Gabriel to glance at her askance.

"Care to enlighten me?" queried Gabriel. Kassie shook her head stuffing her hand in her mouth to stop the giggles, which threatened to become a bit hysterical. She put it down to three glasses of wine and too much coffee and by dint of gulping lungsful of air, managed to control herself.

"Maybe one day," she finally managed, hiccuping a bit. Gabriel grinned and coming to a halt in a quiet corner, spun her to face him, kissing her until she almost lost the ability to function entirely. The world around Kassie disappeared, all she could think about was Gabriel and his extraordinary kisses. Gabriel was thinking much the same thing about Kassie. Every time they touched it was as though there was an electrical force around them, sparking responses so intense he feared they might burst into flames.

"Kassie love, I…we need to go back, otherwise I'll have no alternative but to make love to you in a back street in Pompeii." His voice was hoarse and his breathing was ragged, Kassie, in the same state of dazedness nodded, incapable of much else. Holding her close until their hearts resumed something close to a regular rhythm, Gabriel dropped a quick kiss on her forehead before they meandered back to their hotel. Kissing Kassie goodnight at her door, Gabriel indulged in yet another long cold shower in a vain attempt to suppress his ardour.

The coach ride back to Rome the following day was uneventful and, once there, the group was left to their own devices, Gabriel deciding that to try to add more sightseeing after a long drive, was pointless. There was always plenty to do in Rome should any of the group feel the need to fill in the rest of their afternoon. Kassie went to check on her apartment and, just in case she had any free evenings, collected her laptop.

The next several days were an interesting mix of activities. They visited the Borghese Gallery and the Vatican Museum, admiring the various styles of art and sculpture from throughout the ages. They were amazed by the monumental Baths of Caracalla, rapt by the Ara Pacis — Augustus' stunningly beautiful Altar of Peace — and made speechless by the engineering masterpiece that is the Colosseum — where they enjoyed rare access to the underground area and the highest tier. They also explored a few of the churches such as San Clemente and San Nicola in Carcere, where ancient

Roman remains have been incorporated into later structures, with all the layers still clearly visible.

Gabriel continued to court Kassie; inviting her out for a drink, or suggesting a pre-breakfast walk or a stroll in the moonlight and never trying to take their lovemaking any further than kisses, although they were mind-blowing enough. The two started to talk about their lives, their families and their work and slowly they came to know each other. Despite their short time together, Gabriel was certain that he wanted Kassie in his life forever and, although he was reasonably sure that she felt the same way, he knew that it was far too soon to propose marriage, he didn't want to scare her off. So, they carried on as they were, which translated into the pair being in a constant state of delightful anticipation.

Nine

One evening, at the end of the second week of the tour, those who chose to do so — about half of their group — attended the opera. It was La Traviata being performed in the Salon Margaretha; a stone's throw from the Spanish Steps. Kassie often came to this Salon, its informal atmosphere much more inviting than the larger theatres and the productions were excellent. One of the staff greeted her by name as they showed their tickets and she spent a few minutes chatting, catching up on theatre gossip.

"So now you are a regular at the Salon too? How do you do it?" Gabriel whispered, sneaking a kiss on her cheek as he did so.

"Do what?" Kassie replied, batting him away.

"Fit all this in? Two day jobs, a writer by night and a patron of the arts." Kassie giggled at the image this conjured up.

"Patron of the arts, my foot! I just enjoy coming here, it's close to home and I've been coming long enough that the staff know me, so I can always get a seat." She gave him a wicked grin and led the way through to the auditorium. As the opera began, Kassie became absorbed by the music and Gabriel was captivated by the multitude of expressions chasing across her vivid face as the tragic tale unfolded. By the time the performance wrapped up, and the cast were taking their third curtain call to a standing ovation, all agreed that it had been a superb evening and an excellent option for their tour.

It was a reasonably short walk back to their hotel and they were soon saying goodnight in the large atrium. A few headed off to the bar for a last drink, inviting their tour guides to join them, but Kassie was exhausted, they'd had a long day walking around the city and she could scarcely keep her eyes open. Thanking them politely, she declined, as did Gabriel who offered to escort her to her room where, shyly and tired as she was, Kassie invited him for a hot drink.

"Or a glass of wine if you like. I brought a couple of bottles back with me after I'd checked my flat."

"Why thank you, my dear, I would be most partial to a glass of wine." Gabriel bowed, as Kassie pushed open her door.

"How very formal," she said, laughter gurgling in her throat as she went over to the cupboard that held the coffee and tea making facilities, lifting out two glasses and a bottle of red wine. Gabriel opened the doors to the small balcony and they sat outside in the cool evening air, looking out over a city glowing with light. Kassie was keenly aware of Gabriel, who was sitting close enough that their knees touched. It was all she could do to stop herself from running her hand along his leg, while images of what he would look like naked, insisted on materialising in her head, making her heart do weird things. He was asking her a question, but she couldn't concentrate.

Gabriel in the meantime was also struggling to keep himself in check. Kassie's long hair was spilling over her shoulders in a silken swathe and the moonlight illuminated her ivory skin with an almost ethereal glow. God, she was so beautiful, how anyone could ever consider her to be plain was beyond him. As though in tune with his thoughts, she turned in her chair and caught him staring, her green eyes hypnotising him.

"I'm so sorry Gabriel, I missed that, my mind was…" she didn't want to say what her mind had been up to, that whole brazen hussy thing was becoming far too common an occurrence. So, she chose "…elsewhere."

"It doesn't matter, it wasn't important," he said huskily. She held his gaze for long moments, trying and failing to come up with some insightful comment or witty remark. Gabriel placed his half-drunk wine on the little glass table and stood, as though to leave. Even knowing that this is what she told him she wanted, Kassie's heart plummeted. He did not leave, however, rather, he took the glass out of her hand, placing it next to his and pulled her out of her chair and into his arms.

"Gabriel, I…" his lips covered hers and she was lost. Sighing, she pressed against him, fitting herself to his shape, gliding her fingers across his back, causing him to tremble and his kiss deepened. Heat licked through her and she whimpered with need, but just as all common sense began to slide away,

Kassie suddenly remembered that he didn't know. She had to tell him; otherwise she wasn't being fair. It was as though someone had dumped a bucket of cold water over her head and she broke their kiss. Panting a little as she tried to recover her equilibrium — a total waste when she was looking straight at Gabriel's taut, muscular body — Kassie was gratified that his breathing was as erratic as hers.

"What's wrong, Kassie?"

"N-nothing, it's just, there's something you need to know. I know I asked you take this slowly and being courted, properly courted is so wonderful, you have no idea. Only, I think…I really want…without sounding…" Kassie stopped, aware that she was gabbling and chewed on her bottom lip, trying to come up with a less stark way of phrasing what she wanted to say.

"Are you referring back to that whole wild sex thing we talked about last week?" Gabriel grinned lasciviously. Hectic colour flared up Kassie's face as she nodded. As this was probably the last thing Gabriel expected her to say, his mouth fell open. "You are?" She nodded again, her eyes pleading with him not to make a joke. "Really?" He cupped her hot face and kissed her again, feeling their passion escalate. Kassie wriggled free and moved far enough away that he couldn't reach her; he was distracting enough being in the same room.

"Gabriel, please, don't make this any harder." Kassie started pacing back and forth, still unable to come up with a way to tell him without sounding like a complete ninny. There should be a handbook for this. How did one phrase this type of explanation?

Taking advantage of her inattention, Gabriel moved closer, trying to figure out what on earth was happening, confusion running though him. He caught her hand and kissed her palm, a frisson ran up her arm and she knew she was close to throwing the last vestiges of her restraint to the devil. He tried to wrap his arms around her, but she shrugged away, scooting to the edge of the balcony.

"I'm…I've never…it's too…oh dammit." Honestly, she was clueless; it was simple really, she'd never slept with anyone, hell, she'd never even been kissed the way Gabriel kissed her. Why was it so hard to tell him that? Oh God, he would think her pitiful! Twenty-eight-year-old virgins were a rare phenomenon these days, probably on the verge of extinction. Gabriel meanwhile was watching the gamut of emotions flickering across her tired features. He wasn't sure what had caused this reaction, but he meant to get to the bottom of it.

"Kassie?" he made it a question. She turned and he could that see her eyes were cloudy with anxiety. What the heck was going on in that head of hers? "Kassie love, talk to me." She shook her head, her hair swirling about her shoulders like a river of dark gold and he desperately wanted to run his hands through it. "Please sweetheart." Kassie stayed where she was, a shadow against the backdrop of one of most vibrant cities in the world, twisting her hands together in an agony of indecision.

"It's just…I'm not…I don't…" pausing she gathered her courage and tried again, "I don't hop into bed with every guy I kiss, especially not one I've only known for three weeks." She paused again, rubbing her hand over her forehead; lordy she was making it worse, she didn't want to admit how naive she was. "I don't want you to think I'm leading you on, only to pull away at the last minute. It's just I worry that…you might think I…" She trailed off, still unable to enunciate what she wanted to say.

Gabriel walked over to where she stood and ran his fingers up her still warm cheek and into her hair, feeling its lustrous weight.

"I never imagined any such thing, Kassandra and I'm more than happy to let things happen as slowly as you want. I don't wish to put any pressure on you." He slanted his lips against hers and the kiss was all fervour and heat.

"N-no, you don't understand…" she pulled away again, paused and looked up at him. God, he was so tall, it really wasn't fair, she never stood a chance. Taking a deep breath, she finally tossed caution to the winds, "…I don't want to take it slowly…" Gabriel stilled and it was as though the world had stopped. He stared at her trying to process what she'd just said.

"Wait, what did you just say?"

Kassie repeated it; so quietly that he had to lean in very close to hear her. "Oh, my love, your wish is my command." Gabriel cupped her head in one hand, using the other to resume his exploration, his fingers skimming up her body, along her neck, brushing the hollow at the base of her throat. Then, down and down searching out the buttons on her shirt, opening one, then two, before sliding his fingers between the soft cotton and the flimsy laciness of her bra, his gentle caress turning Kassie's legs to jelly.

Kassie had read a few steamy novels, heck her own books included the odd amorous scene, but this…this was on a whole other level, his touch igniting something deep within her. She itched to stroke him, to feel his skin, but her innate shyness made her fingers hesitate, which did Gabriel no good whatsoever. He released her lips and trailed feather light kisses down her throat, feeling her pulse fluttering madly and smiled against her soft skin.

"Oh Kassie, you are divine." He lifted her and, tall as she was, she didn't weigh much at all, carrying her over to the huge king size bed, laying her on the pillows. Kicking off his shoes, Gabriel lay alongside her, gathered her close and, although both remained, almost, fully clothed, proceeded to discover every part of her. To be fair, Kassie was beset with the most irrational need to rip off all Gabriel's clothes, but still she held back. Sensing something continued to bother her, Gabriel paused in his sublime reconnaissance of her body and leaned up on one elbow, twining her hair though his fingers.

"Come on, Kassie, give." He let his fingers continue their journey, noticing that Kassie's face was flushed and her eyes were dark with desire and he felt his heart hitch. "Seriously, love what is going on in that muddled head of yours?" She smiled slightly but it seemed as though she was withdrawing again.

"Gabriel, you need to understand. I've never done this before." She took another deep breath. "Any of it." Gabriel slowed his fingers and held her gaze.

"What precisely do you mean by 'any of it'?" Gabriel asked, gently.

"Exactly what you think I mean. Until two weeks ago, I'd never even been kissed like this, I don't know what to do, how to behave. I've never been touched in the way you touch me and I've never…" she put her hands to her face, "…oh bloody hell…I haven't…gone all the way." She choked on the last part, dropping her eyes, humiliated beyond reason. Why, oh why did she let herself get sucked into this? Gabriel was a man of the world and presumably used to partners who knew what they were doing, knew how to please. She was such a fool.

Gabriel was silent, a strange sensation running through him. He couldn't believe that he would be her first; at least he hoped he would be her first. If he was honest, he half suspected that she was inexperienced, her reactions when they kissed were not those of someone wise in the ways of intimacy, but that she hadn't even gone this far, was a revelation. Forcing his attention back to the woman lying almost under him on the bed, he peeled her hands away from her burning cheeks and, reading her face, leaned down to kiss her tenderly.

"Oh, Kassandra, you have no idea how much this means to me." Her eyes flickered back to his, questions in their emerald depths. "To be the one to teach another how to make love is a gift few receive and I am honoured." She gawked at him.

"Huh?"

"I love that you have never been with another man, that you don't know what to do, that we can learn together. Knowing I am the first to caress your skin, to kiss you this way sets my blood on fire." She giggled at that, she couldn't help it, he looked so intense. "Hey don't laugh, I'm being serious."

"So, you won't mind if I ask questions? I just don't want to seem like an idiot."

"You are not an idiot and to be honest, if you didn't ask questions I'd start to worry." He winked at her, his eyes crinkling in amusement.

"You might regret that." She grinned, relief pouring through her. That was it; he knew everything. Well not quite everything, but that could wait. She wasn't ready to share that yet. "So, if I was to do this…" unbuttoning his pale blue shirt and trailing her fingers down his chest, "…that would be okay?" Gabriel groaned, tensing under her fingers. "What about this?" Exchanging her fingers for her lips, his skin hot under her cool kiss.

"Urghhhh…" was all he managed and dragged her against him, re-capturing her mouth and kissing her as though he would never stop. Heat spiralled through his body, as he teased his fingers under her shirt, stroking her downy skin and somehow her top ended up on the floor. Gabriel pulled back and raked his eyes over her willowy form, his hands following his eyes.

"You are so beautiful," he breathed in awed tones as Kassie tried to cross her arms over her body. "No, please don't hide yourself, not from me." He swept his fingers over her curves and hollows, lazily swirling over skin that was tingling at his touch. Lovingly, he palmed one of her breasts, the wispy material no barrier to his large hand. Kassie shuddered and a soft cry escaped her, as his lips took over where his hand left off, teeth nipping at the sensitive flesh.

"Gabriel, oh God." She arched into him, needing to feel his skin on hers and Gabriel knew that it would be easy to take this further, much further but he didn't want to, not tonight. Well, yes absolutely he did, but he wanted to take his time and it was late, noticing as he glanced at the clock by the side of the bed that it was well after midnight and they had a full schedule the coming day.

"Kassie," his voice was gentle, "Kassie, much as I would be delighted to take you now, I would much prefer for us to enjoy a slow seduction tomorrow evening. Would that be okay?" Kassie stared at him through heavy eyes, momentarily confused until, seeing her bewilderment, he repeated it, adding, "we have a busy day tomorrow and it's very late."

"It's not because, you don't want me…now you know?" her whispered query caught his heart.

"No, you kook, but it is because you are innocent that I want us to take our time. Making love is one of the most pleasurable pastimes and there is no point rushing it." Her eyes held his and he saw tension lurking there. "Trust me love, we will have the whole night not just a couple of hours and I am already imagining how enjoyable it will be to spend all of it leading you astray." He dropped a slow wink and Kassie relaxed, moving against him, her arms wrapping around his warm body, her head nuzzling into his neck.

"That sounds sublime," she murmured and kissed the pulse at the base of his throat, feeling a quiver run through him, "but please stay a little longer, I rather like lying next to you." Gabriel kissed the top of her head.

"I'm not going anywhere," he replied and tucked her snugly against him. Kassie started to say something else, but without warning, safe in Gabriel's arms, she fell asleep. A low laugh rumbled through Gabriel's chest as he drew up the bedding over them both and within minutes had joined her in slumber.

Ten

The next morning, Kassie's alarm on her phone chirped at what felt like a very ungodly hour, but was actually 7am. She surmised that she must have slept badly, for it seemed that she was trapped by an inordinate amount of bedclothes. Struggling to kick them off, she yelped in shock, as a deep voice rumbled from near her head and, what she thought were all bedcovers, was partly Gabriel.

"Gabriel!" she squawked. "What on earth are you doing here? You stayed the night?"

"Certainly looks that way. Good morning to you too. Aren't you just the best sight to wake up to?" Pulling her against him and kissing her soundly. Kassie chuckled softly and tried to free herself, but he simply tightened his hold and carried on. Giving up, she sank into his embrace, feeling the now familiar heat coil around her.

Several minutes later, she murmured. "We have to get up, the coach will be here at nine."

"That gives us two hours, plenty of time." Ignoring her protests, Gabriel resumed his kiss until both were breathless. After making sure Kassie was quite wide awake, he re-buttoned his very crumpled shirt and slipped along to his own room to shower and dress, leaving Kassie the unenviable task of getting her unruly thoughts under control.

Slightly less than two hours later, the group, nicely fed and ready for anything, climbed into the coach and they headed out towards Tivoli. Today they were visiting Hadrian's Villa — the emperor's vast private retreat, as well as the Villa d'Este — the sixteenth century villa commissioned by Ippolito d'Este II and added to by his successors. Famous for its terraced hillside Renaissance gardens and its profusion of fountains, the Villa d'Este holds a commanding position with spectacular views across the plain towards Rome. Kassie had been to both a few times and loved them equally. Hadrian's Villa was their first stop and before leading them into the magnificent grounds,

Kassie showed them the scale model, commenting that only one fifth of the original three hundred acres was visible today.

The entrance to the villa opens alongside an elegant lake. Referred to as the Poecile, Kassie explained that the lake was believed to replicate the Stoà Poikile, a painted colonnade in Athens, from which the Stoic philosophers took their name and which Hadrian admired greatly. Originally the lake sported a grand piazza and was surrounded by a colonnaded walkway, a way to keep cool on hot days.

Next, she led them through what is called, simply, the building with three exedras — for modern historians are unsure of its original purpose — pointing out that the three small thermae, or baths, were probably available for the use of guests and personnel of the villa. Behind this structure — following the same layout as any Roman house, but in a circle rather than a rectangle — nestles the Maritime Theatre. A pool with an island in its centre, surrounded by graceful columns, this was presumed to be Hadrian's personal haven, its style of architecture testament to the Emperor's love of all things Greek. The group dallied here, coming up with all manner of private things Hadrian might have indulged in, from the sublime to the utterly ludicrous and occasionally rather bawdy, but made for an amusing interlude nonetheless.

Beyond the small baths stands the Great Thermae; an enormous structure that soars over the current ruins and must have been breathtaking when first completed, its domed roofs reminiscent of the Pantheon. From here they strolled to the Canopus, probably the most recognisable part of the villa. A wide canal 119 metres long, lined along the banks with caryatids, as well as statues of Antinous — Hadrian's favourite — who drowned in Egypt. Renowned, in antiquity, for its sumptuous banquets and night-time parties, today the Canopus is a serene space and the group spent quite some time admiring, and photographing, its simple beauty. Finally, they walked back past what would have been Hadrian's main residence, arranged in three sections, all with roofed peristyles or colonnaded porticoes.

Even though only a relatively small percentage of the original complex is on view, Hadrian's Villa is a huge site and the group had been walking around it for some considerable time. Kassie, who had talked herself nearly hoarse, felt that they'd probably heard enough for now and not wanting to inundate them with too much information, suggested that they potter about at their leisure and meet at the coach in forty-five minutes. That would give them plenty of time to have lunch before going on to the Villa D'Este.

Kassie walked back to the main entrance set in the huge wall that surrounded the villa and found a bench in the shade of two tall Italian pencil pines, where Gabriel came upon her a little later. He had been waylaid by Anna, who wanted to tell him that her granddaughter was arriving in Rome the next day and asked whether it would be okay if she accompanied the rest of the tour.

Gabriel was sceptical, Anna's granddaughter, Monique, was not his favourite person. He very occasionally had dinner with her if she was ever in Rome, more because the family expected him to keep an eye on her than anything else. Unfortunately, Monique tended to assume that it was more than just a meal between friends. Despite him, very tactfully, explaining that he wasn't interested, she continued to bombard him with emails and phone calls, most of which he ignored. The thought of her joining their tour gave him a headache and he had the feeling she might just cause trouble.

Pushing it aside for now, he sat next to Kassie who gave him a sunny grin.

"That was comprehensive," he commented, taking her hand and linking their fingers.

"I know maybe a bit too comprehensive." She shrugged, almost apologetically. "You really need a whole day, there's just so much to see here, but I think I covered the main parts. If I could be bothered I'd walk back down the Canopus, but its so relaxing just sitting here in the shade, nobody else about." Unconsciously, she rested her head on his shoulder, her long plait falling across his shirt and Gabriel was struck by how natural it was, how comfortable they were together. He leaned his head against hers and they sat in tranquil silence listening to the sounds of the villa, the breeze drifting through the trees surrounding the lake, the distant melody of the birds and the lazy hum of insects. Even the muted chatter of tourists, wafting towards them, wasn't loud enough to disturb the peace.

"This is so lovely," Kassie murmured, "I could stay here all day."

"Maybe you and I could come back here before it gets too cold, bring a picnic and spend the day, just the two of us, without needing to drag fifteen other people along with us." He felt her nod, but did not see her secret smile. Despite his words in Pompeii and regardless of what she hoped they might share later, part of her, the rational, logical part kept insisting that this was ephemeral, that at the end of the tour he would vanish out of her life like the dawn's mist in the autumn sunshine. She had almost accepted that it was probable and would in no way regret anything that had occurred, but it made her feel warm inside to think that maybe, just maybe, they had a future.

Too soon, it was time to move on and they met the group back at the coach. After a light lunch, they ventured into the Villa d'Este and, the group was enchanted. The frescoes, the fountains, the gardens and the view, it was a masterpiece and Kassie knew this would keep them entertained for a good couple of hours. Once into the gardens there was no need for a guide, everything was clearly marked and to be honest the details were more of a bonus than anything else. Kassie strolled around with two of the couples, Jenny and Bill, Harry and Claire, who plied her with questions that had little to do with the water features and more to do with her and Gabriel. She gave nothing away, but her expression when she talked about Gabriel was enough to convince them what they already suspected. Their guide was head over heels in love with their organiser and for their part, they could not be happier.

Harry and Claire — who, as Kassie suspected, had known Gabriel for a long time — had confided to him, the previous day, that they were sure their Miss Winters was succumbing to his charms, so it looked as though his plan was on track. Gabriel had grinned and said he hoped so too, but begged them not to say anything to Kassie, he didn't want her to be apprised of his intentions quite yet.

Blissfully unaware, Kassie chattered away artlessly, steering their conversations away from herself and back to the job in hand, her delight in being able to share her love for the villa apparent. On the terrace, high above, Gabriel was watching her walk through the gardens; hearing her laugh at something Claire said, his heart doing that peculiar jolt as he noticed the sultry sway of her lissom figure as she moved. As he gazed down at Kassie, he ran his mind over what he had prepared for that evening, his thoughts causing a wicked smile to curve his lips.

The warm afternoon began to wane and although not constrained by anything other than the time the villa closed, Gabriel knew that they needed to think about setting off back to the city before the evening traffic got too heavy. His reasoning had nothing at all to do with wanting to spend as much time as possible with Kassie.

They arrived back just as the dazzling sunshine started to mellow into the golden light so typical of these late summer evenings. The group spilled out of the bus, sleepy after a long day in the warm fresh air and the gentle rocking of the coach as it sped into Rome. They thanked Kassie for her patience, to which she replied that it had been her absolute pleasure and she was looking forward to the coming week. All went their separate ways and Gabriel caught up with Kassie as she boarded the lift.

"Miss Winters," he began, all very polite, "I wonder whether you might like to accompany me to Osteria del Sostegno for dinner this evening?" Kassie grinned at such formality.

"That sounds quite agreeable, Professor St Germain. At what time?" she replied.

"I will collect you in an hour."

"I'll be ready." She giggled at his serious face. He walked her to her door and as she opened it, pulled her close for a quick hard kiss.

"Just a taster," he murmured, leaving her flushed and breathless. Kassie stared after him as he went into his own room, her stomach full of butterflies. If you don't get a grip Kassandra Winters, she instructed herself, you'll not be able to eat. Taking herself in hand, she had a longed for hot shower, taking the time to massage in some body lotion scented with her favourite perfume. Drying her hair properly, she pulled and twisted until it was in an intricate French pleat, leaving one or two tendrils to trail down her neck.

Eschewing her usual jeans and t-shirt, Kassie teamed a pair of wide culottes in black chiffon with an emerald green silk top. A plain gold chain around her neck, and flat black ballet pumps completed her outfit. She grabbed her black clutch bag, slipping into it her phone and room key, as well as a few euros and credit card — just in case and she was ready.

Promptly on the hour, there was a quiet knock and she opened the door. Gabriel sucked in his breath when he saw her — tall, elegant and refined. He was so glad he'd decided to wear his smart, dark charcoal suit, over a crispy white shirt, open at the neck giving him a slightly rakish look. Kassie's mouth fell open and she just stared at him, unable to speak. Dear lord, he was far too bloody handsome, she was doomed.

"Are you ready, love?" He smiled.

"As I'll ever be," she muttered, tucking her hand under his proffered arm. The restaurant wasn't too far, about a ten-minute walk and they took their time, talking about this and that, their conversation light and relaxed. Arriving, they were ushered to their seats and given a menu. A bottle of champagne miraculously appeared and Gabriel poured them a glass each, the chilled effervescence sparkling in the soft light from the candle in the middle of the table.

Gabriel picked up his glass, waiting for Kassie to follow suit before saying quietly. "To us, may this be the beginning of everything."

As they clinked their glasses, Kassie couldn't tear her gaze away from Gabriel and had the most absurd desire to cry. Blinking fiercely — she never cried and anyway it would ruin her carefully applied makeup — she forced back the tears and took a gulp of champagne, making herself cough as the bubbles caught the back of her throat. Hell, she groused inwardly, I can't even get this right. She glanced back at Gabriel whose lips were twitching with mirth.

"Have you quite finished showing off?" he asked pointedly. Kassie was about to tick him off for his cheek when she noticed his blue eyes crinkling in the most appealing fashion. Sticking her tongue out at him, she picked up the menu and perused the delicious offerings contained therein. Gabriel merely chuckled at her childish antics and took advantage of her concentration by resting his hand over hers and rubbing his thumb across her wrist. It was one of the most sensual things she had experienced and took all she had to ignore him.

"What are you fancying?" she asked and then wished she hadn't, as the look her gave her could only be described as smouldering. "Stop it, or we might as well have stayed at the hotel."

"Would've been fine by me," he growled. Kassie spluttered with laughter and squeezed his hand, which was still over hers.

"This was your idea Gabriel, so please, let's enjoy the evening. We've got a free day tomorrow, there's no rush." She realised what she was implying and blushed, dropping her eyes and returned to studying the menu with interest. She took another sip of the champagne hoping it would calm the butterflies that had resumed their wild party in her stomach.

Taking pity on her, Gabriel asked whether she wanted a starter, which she didn't saying she'd prefer to order pasta then maybe a dessert. Gabriel frowned a little; it wasn't much food, although the pasta dishes could be very filling. Unexpectedly he was reminded of Professor Hardwick's words and, once again contemplated the damage they may have done to Kassie's self-esteem. He decided to revisit this topic on another day, not tonight, tonight was for seduction.

Eleven

Kassie chose the tagliolini with porcini mushrooms, while Gabriel plumped for fusilloni with eggplant which when they came were mouth-wateringly delicious and Kassie's choice was enough for her. Gabriel knew it would not fill him up, so he ordered the chicken cacciatora, persuading her into a red chicory salad with avocado and parmesan, to keep him company. This latter dish was an antipasto, but the owners were unfazed by the odd request of their customers and both meals appeared on their table after a suitable break. They continued the easy conversation they'd begun on the way to the restaurant, sharing amusing anecdotes about misadventures with tour groups. Gabriel tried to draw out Kassie on her writing and although she told him snippets, she still refused to divulge her pseudonym.

"Please Gabriel, don't push me. I promise to tell you when I'm ready. It's been my secret world for so long that it's hard to let anyone else in. No one knows, not even my family and I'd like to keep it that way, for just a little longer." She beseeched him with her eyes and he knew it would be unfair to press her.

"Okay, but I'll find out sooner or later, so get used to it, madam," was all he said, trying to look intimidating, but only succeeded in making her chortle with mirth. "Hey, that's my scary look."

"Hahahaha, I've seen scarier bunny rabbits," she gurgled, receiving an affronted glare that made her giggle even more. "Oh, Gabriel, I do love you." Shocked at herself for making such an open declaration, Kassie clamped her mouth shut, wishing she could retract her words, her face flaring bright red with embarrassment.

"I-I'm, sorry, I shouldn't have, I didn't mean…" Faltering, she fiddled with her fork, pushing the few remaining parmesan crumbs around her plate. Gabriel's hand found hers again and, gently removing the fork, lifted her hand to his lips, kissing the inside of her wrist. Kassie shivered at the emotion in his expression, heat coiling through her. "Errr…is it warm in here or is it just me?" she asked, trying to break the tension.

"Oh, it's not just you," he replied, his voice so low it was more like a purr. "Would you like dessert?"

She stared at him and shook her head. "Not really," she whispered.

"That's what I hoped you'd say." He signalled for the bill and after finishing the last of the champagne they paid, thanked the patron for a lovely meal, and left. Gabriel walked them past the Pantheon, its floodlit splendour protected by the ebony darkness that shrouded the edifice in mystery.

"I'm sure if we stood here for long enough we would see the spirits of ancient luminaries walking through this place," Kassie said as they stood for a moment admiring the regal facade. Gabriel put his arm around her and as he bent to drop a kiss on the top of her head, she turned towards him and he brushed her lips instead, the light touch full of promise.

"I'm sure that if we stood here long enough I might become one of those spirits. I need you so badly I think it might just kill me if we're not back at the hotel in five minutes," he breathed in her ear.

Kassie giggled, she couldn't help it. "S-sorry," she stuttered, "nerves." She heard a laugh rumble through his chest as they turned towards their hotel. They managed to get back without Gabriel dropping dead from desire, although he did feel moved to comment that it was touch and go. Gabriel took her to his room and as they walked in Kassie stopped in her tracks, astonishment holding her motionless. Music played in the background, classical arias she thought, and dotted around the room were several candles, currently the only light. A bottle of champagne — goodness she was already a bit tipsy — was cooling in an ice bucket and, on the bed, a single yellow rose, her favourite flower.

Had anyone else done this, Kassie would have thought it corny in the extreme, but in this moment with this man, all she could think was that it was perfect.

"How did you know?" she questioned quietly. Gabriel raised an eyebrow, quizzically. "About the yellow rose?" Nodding towards the bed.

"Ahhh, I have my sources and they will remain undisclosed." He smiled mysteriously. "Would you like some more champagne?"

"I think I'd better," she said, accepting a cool glass, the bubbles tickling her nose. She swallowed a mouthful in a very unladylike fashion, hiccuping a bit. She was trembling now but she didn't know whether it was with nerves or anticipation.

Gabriel was watching her a smile playing about his lips, knowing exactly what was going on in her head. She wandered the room; glass in hand, picking up the rose to breath in it's subtle perfume, smoothing the already pristine white sheets, tidying the already tidy desk, glancing out of the window upon a view that never ceased to captivate her. Gabriel joined her at the balcony doors, cracked open to let the evening breeze drift into the room and put his arm around her. He felt rather than heard her sigh and as she relaxed against him, he stroked her back, a seemingly unconscious gesture, but one that lit a spark in Kassie's stomach, effectively banishing the butterflies that had returned to undermine what little composure she had left.

Gabriel removed the fluted glass from her, suddenly nerveless fingers, placing it on the table next to them. Turning her to face him he brushed his lips to hers, then leaned back and held her gaze. His eyes had darkened to midnight blue and Kassie felt herself drowning in their inky depths. She reached up and smoothed her fingers through his unruly hair, even so light a caress sending shivers down his spine. They just stared at each other, breath quickening, hearts thrumming, enraptured.

"Kassie." Gabriel broke the spell, his voice not quite steady

"Mmmm," she murmured, blinking hazily, her graceful fingers tracing his jaw line and down his throat.

"Kassie, I…" Gabriel gave up and dragged her against him, kissing her with an almost desperate passion. Kassie responded instantly, opening herself to the onslaught, clinging to him as the little spark smouldered and heat licked through her. Gabriel's hands were weaving their sorcery over her body, cool against her heated skin. Frissons of desire were rippling through her and she moaned, needing more. Gabriel's searching fingers found the buttons on the back of her top, slowly unfastening them, until he could peel it off her shoulders, the silky material whispering to the floor.

"Oh God, how did I get so lucky?" he sighed reverently, kissing the creamy skin of her shoulders, trailing his lips over her collarbone and down to the rise of her breasts. Meanwhile, Kassie was fumbling with the buttons on Gabriel's shirt, trying not to tear the material in her haste. Eventually she managed and gasped as it slid off his broad shoulders. She had seen a hint of him the previous night, but this was something else. She splayed her hands across his broad chest, tangling her fingers through the smattering of dark hairs, feeling him tremble as she grazed his nipples.

Somehow Gabriel removed her trousers and gossamer fine underwear almost without Kassie being aware and suddenly she was naked, the breeze from the open window giving her goose bumps. She shivered and Gabriel gathered her close, his hands caressing her, teasing and tantalising, unleashing a myriad of sensations that cascaded through her so fast it made her head spin. Hoping to give him the same pleasure he was inflicting on her she began to explore his body, her tentative gestures sending Gabriel's heart rate into overdrive.

"Gabriel," she gasped as his warm hand brushed up her chilled back. "Please, it's not fair."

"What isn't, love?" nuzzling her neck while simultaneously unravelling her carefully arranged hairstyle.

"You are entirely too dressed."

"Well, I'm sure we can fix that," he grinned, shrugging out of the rest of his clothes at which point Kassie just gawked.

"Oh lordy," she breathed, her face flushed, her long hair now tumbling over her shoulders in a silken mass. Hesitantly she reached towards him, smoothing her hands over his trim hips and down to his thighs

"Kassie," he groaned, as her fingers brushed against him. He tried to pull her close.

"Shhhhh, what's your hurry?" she asked, a saucy grin on her face as she pushed him away. "Don't rush it you said, we can take our time you said — well let me take my time." Tracing the taut lines of his stomach and his muscular chest, over his shoulders and down his back, his chiselled physique again reminding her of a Bernini sculpture. For some unknown reason, that pleased her. "I swear you are the personification of Jupiter," she purred deep in her throat, quite astonished at her brazen behaviour, but unable to stop herself. She felt his chest rock with laughter as Gabriel trapped her inquisitive hands behind her and drew her against him, their bodies slotting together so completely it was as though they were two halves of the same whole.

The smouldering fire burst into flame and Gabriel, forcing himself to take this slowly, bent his lips to Kassie's. His mouth moved over hers, languorously, letting their passion build, drawing her even closer and feeling her quiver against him, her movements threatening to destroy what little self-discipline he had left. Never relinquishing her mouth, he guided her backwards towards the bed. Laying her on the deluxe white sheets, he moved to lie alongside her, his hands resuming their dance, roving across her satiny skin, following with his lips. Craving every inch of her, his hands and his lips left nowhere untouched, causing Kassie to writhe underneath him, sending jolts of desire through his body as electricity sizzled between them.

Kassie's restless fingers described a tortuous journey over his body, thrilling every nerve, before coming to rest over his upper thigh. She wanted to stroke him, to caress him, but her innate shyness made her hesitate.

"Tell me what to do, Gabe," she whispered. He halted his delicious exploration and lifted his head. Her eyes held his, emerald on sapphire and for a split second he couldn't speak, her expression of absolute trust made his heart miss a beat — several actually — and his knees turned to water.

"Just go with your instinct, love." He managed huskily as she encircled him, massaging the muscle gently, feeling his pulse throb in response. Gabriel grunted and recaptured her lips, his hands gliding down her graceful form, finding her centre, his seductive fingers drawing her irresistibly to the brink of the precipice. Her breath coming in short bursts, Kassie was almost crying out for him to take her and just when she thought she might be the one to die, he flicked her over the edge. Certain that she had splintered into a million shards of light,

Kassie was quite surprised, when everything stopped spinning, to find she was still in one piece. She had the oddest notion that she was floating and clung to Gabriel, fearful that she might fall.

"How…what…how?" she stuttered weakly. Gabriel didn't speak, he simply resumed his heart stopping kiss; fondling her, rekindling her desire until she felt the flame within blaze with the brilliance of a thousand suns as, finally, he claimed her as his. The pain she knew to be inevitable was sharp but brief and before she really had time to register it, her body was consumed by the most wondrous sensations as Gabriel began to move within her. She curled her legs over his, arching her back to welcome him in further, and so in tune was the cadence of their bodies that it was as though they had been making love for a lifetime.

Gabriel could not believe how Kassie made him feel, he burned for her and knew he would never get enough of her. His reactions when she was in his arms were primal and instinctual and as they surged towards the peak together, her spontaneous abandon shook him to his core. A tidal wave of ecstasy burst over them and Gabriel felt a strange elation suffuse his being; she was his, after all this time, she was his and he wanted her to remain so, for the rest of their lives.

Twelve

A cocoon of euphoria surrounded Kassie; nothing in her wildest imagination could have prepared her for this. As the world came back into focus, she realised that she was wrapped in Gabriel's arms and he was still kissing her.

"I'm sorry I hurt you, love," he murmured, his lips grazing across her eyelids and the tip of her nose. She snuggled closer, kissing the hollow of his throat.

"You didn't," she assured him, in a rather shaky voice, her breathing still erratic. "Thank you, Gabriel."

He looked down at her, "What for?"

"For caring enough to teach me, not just take me." His chest constricted and he kissed the top of her forehead.

"I love you, Kassie." She sighed and he felt her settle against him. Her fingers began to carve swirling loops over his chest, swirling out over his nipples and down to his lower abdomen. He shivered and, abruptly, she halted.

"I'm sorry, I can't seem to stop touching you," she admitted, shyly. "My fingers have a mind of their own. It's as though they need to absorb the imprint of your body."

"I didn't want you to stop, love; that wasn't a shiver of discomfort, well maybe it was, but not in the manner you're thinking." She glanced at his face and he winked, a wicked smile played around his mouth. Good grief, he was so bloody handsome. Her breath hitched and she leaned up to kiss him, her lips an invitation. Her body moved sinuously over his and, starting with his mouth, she took a long time to discover every part of him. He kept trying to pull her back up, but she just held his hands, effectively preventing him from accomplishing his goal. Eventually, unable to take any more, Gabriel rolled her under him and pinned her with his body.

"Have you any idea what you're doing?" he growled hoarsely, between fevered kisses.

"Research," she gasped, as his fingers teased over her skin.

"My turn," was all he could manage as he began all over again. Kassie, who was quite certain her whole being was fusing with his, gave herself over to the exquisite torment he was wreaking and let go.

Much later, as they lay together, bodies entwined, hearts slowly returning to something akin to a normal beat, they began to talk about life after the tour. Gabriel knew he wanted to marry Kassie, but still believed it far too soon to pose so huge a question, even after what they had shared tonight.

"I don't know how I'm going to be able to maintain any kind of composure when I'm being your tour guide." Kassie said, leaning up on elbow, her hair trailing all over his chest.

"Haha, maybe I should absent myself for this last week, take the pressure off," Gabriel replied, twining his fingers through her tousled locks and pulling her head down for a kiss. She studied him in the dying candlelight, wanting to hold this moment in her heart forever. She was sleepy now, but her body was still tingling and she knew it wouldn't take much for the embers lurking deep within to burst back into flame.

"Maybe you should. Then I wouldn't be distracted and want to do this…" kissing his chest, "…and this…" inquisitive fingers stroking down his length, "…and this." Lips chasing after her fingers, her hair tickling his now very sensitive skin. Gabriel shuddered, his heartbeat going berserk and his breathing becoming ragged.

"Enough," he grunted. "You will be the death of me." Kassie lifted her head and smiled a singularly sweet smile that crept into his heart and made it eternally hers. He caught her to him and proceeded to make slow and tender love until, finally exhausted, they fell asleep wrapped together — passion cooled for now, but not entirely quenched.

The next day, they didn't leave Gabriel's room. He ordered room service and between meals, a refreshing shower or two and the odd nap, they simply resumed where they'd left off the previous night.

As dusk fell and rather out of the blue, Kassie made a suggestion. "How do you fancy a walk?"

"Sounds rather lovely — now?" Gabriel, paused in his latest exploration and searched her face, she nodded, her eyes a little glassy from his ministrations.

"If that's okay. I feel as though I need to stretch my legs and get some fresh air." She hesitated, wondering whether she was implying that she was tired of being with him, "not that I'm complaining about the air in here, it's just…" she didn't get any further. Gabriel suddenly slanted his lips over hers, kissing her until she forgot all about a walk, and fresh air and pretty much everything else, then just as suddenly he stopped.

"Stop second-guessing yourself, Kassie. I know what you mean and I believe a stroll past the Pantheon is just what this Professor ordered." Her face lit up and she grinned, saying that she'd best just go back to her room and find some more appropriate clothes, as everything she had worn the previous evening was still lying in a rumpled heap on the floor.

"Don't be long," he growled as, grudgingly, he let her go.

"I'm borrowing your bathrobe," she announced gathering up her things and eventually locating her handbag, under Gabriel's suit. Digging out her room key, which she waggled in triumph, she made for the door, only to be prevented from leaving by Gabriel who intercepted her for another kiss.

"I'll only be five minutes," she giggled.

"Far too long in my opinion, make it three," he demanded running his fingers provocatively down the front of the bathrobe.

Kassie gulped. "Okay," she whispered and, reaching up for another kiss, was gone.

Four minutes and fifteen seconds later, Gabriel was banging impatiently on her door. She let him in and before she could say anything he kissed her again.

"Gabriel, I've barely been out of your sight. If this is what you're like after three minutes, what are you going to be like when we have to go back to our regular jobs and we're living in separate flats?"

"Don't! Oh, and it was four minutes fifteen seconds."

"Don't what? Go back to my job. I have to, I have r…"

"Don't go back to your apartment." Kassie turned slowly, halfway through pulling on a jacket and stared at him.

"Well that's crazy! Where would I live?" Bewildered, she cocked her head so she could read his face

"With me." Kassie's jaw dropped, everything went a bit wonky and she staggered backwards, putting her hand out to steady herself thinking she might fall over. Gabriel caught her and tucked her against him.

She gazed into his incredible eyes. "With you?" she breathed. "Are you…isn't it…are you?" She shook her head and tried again. "Why?"

"Because I can't bear the thought of you not being with me every evening when I get home, of not having you next to me when I wake up each morning. Sharing my life, my world, with you is all I can think about and knowing that at the end of this week, you'll go back to your apartment, cute though it is, is something I don't wish to contemplate."

"You want us to live together?"

"Yes." Without warning Kassie's legs gave out and she sat down. Since there was no chair or bed near her, she decided that the floor was eminently suitable. Gabriel crouched next to her, taking her hand in his and stroking her palm.

"Isn't this all a bit sudden?" she asked quietly.

"Not for me. I've been waiting to ask you this probably since the first and definitely the second time we spoke." She lifted bewildered eyes to his.

"The second time we spoke? What in my office? That was only two weeks ago."

"Even if that was when I meant, when you're in love I'm not sure time makes any difference, but no, it wasn't then, it was the day before you left uni." Kassie stilled and gaped at him.

"Y-you've wanted…you've k-known…?" For some completely inexplicable reason, Kassie felt a solitary tear run down her cheek. She brushed it away, she didn't cry, she hated soppy women who cried. Gabriel nodded.

"Yes, since the day I ran into you along that corridor. I've already told you that. Why don't you believe me?"

"Telling me that you think you might have been in love with me since then is one thing, to ask me to move in with you is another matter entirely. People fall out of love Gabriel, what if this doesn't last?" Her words were like a cold shower and he stood up, walking away.

"Do you think you will fall out of love with me?" he demanded. Kassie watched him, wishing she hadn't spoken.

"No," she spoke so quietly it was scarcely a whisper, "whatever happens, I will love you forever." He turned back and, folding his arms, regarded her contemplatively. "I'm sorry, Gabriel," she continued in her reserved way, "I was thinking it more likely that you would tire of me." His face reflected his shock. She shrugged, unhappily, spreading her palms in entreaty, "Look at you, you are a successful, clever, sought after academic who just happens to be the most handsome man I've ever met. Then there's me, not much in the looks department, of average intelligence and working in administration — not exactly partner material, am I?"

"Kassie, honey, you have to stop putting yourself down. You are breathtakingly beautiful, your body bewitches me, your mind challenges me and I love you more every passing hour. I couldn't stop loving you even if I wanted to, which I don't. The only reason I mentioned living together was because I thought if I asked you to marry me after less than two weeks together it would do your head in."

"Y-you want to m-marry me?' she squeaked, her voice rising several octaves.

"Of course I do, you goose! Surely you don't think all this was just so I could get you into bed — intoxicating though that is?" She blushed, not really knowing how to respond to that. "Come on." He put his hand out and, as she grasped it, pulled her up, straight into his arms. "No more nonsense. You're mine Kassandra Winters never forget that," he growled the words sending shivers up and down her spine and, melting against him, she let herself believe for a moment that this might actually happen.

A little while later, they were walking through the streets towards the Pantheon, it was a coolish evening, both were glad of their jackets. They were half way through September and there was a hint of autumn in the air. They chatted as they walked, relaxed, friendly banter that seemed to come so easily to them. Gabriel treated them to a gelato from a kiosk near the Pantheon, which they ate while leaning against the low wall that surrounds the edifice. Then they decided to have a glass of wine, the evening sliding away in a most delectable fashion.

As they talked, Kassie realised that this was how their life would be. Enjoying each other's company, discussing their respective days, light and laughter and love. She knew that it wouldn't be all wine and roses, she was no one's doormat, but, if — if they had a difference of opinion, the thought of making up afterwards sent little shockwaves through her and without thinking, she moaned.

"Kassie, are you okay?" Gabriel sounded concerned.

"Mmmm. Oh, I'm just fine," she replied. Her words, warm like a tropical breeze, dripped with longing and were so unlike her normal tones that Gabriel spun on the wall they had returned to sit on and looked at her curiously.

"What on earth…?" A gentle smile played around Kassie's lips as she explained her inadvertent exclamation, making him chuckle appreciatively. As he listened, Gabriel realised that she was beginning to see them together, as a couple, in the same way he did, but this in no way prepared him for her final comment.

"So, yes, I cannot think of anything I'd rather do than live with you."

Stunned, he stared at her, completely lost for words.

"Gabe…?" she said hesitantly, "Gabriel, talk to me."

His heart was thudding and his head felt as though his brain had just detached itself, and he had to force himself to concentrate.

"Please would you mind repeating that? I want to be sure I heard you correctly." Kassie grinned, mischievously and repeated it, her hand on her heart as though swearing an oath. Gabriel could not prevent the beam of delight that almost split his face.

"Oh Kassie, you have just made me the happiest man in Rome, maybe even the world." He swung her up, off the wall and into his arms for a very passionate kiss.

"Gabriel, there are people about," she sputtered, trying to wriggle out his grasp. He refused to let her go.

"We're in Rome, love, this is beneath their notice!" She giggled and gave up the fight, sinking into his embrace, loving the feel of his arms around her and of his lips on hers. "I believe this calls for further celebration," he said after finally standing her back on her own two, rather wobbly, feet. Pulling out his phone, he made a quick call. "Come on, champagne awaits." Grasping her hand, he set off back towards their hotel, quelling an absurd desire to sing at the top of his lungs.

Thirteen

As they arrived in the atrium of the hotel, Gabriel went to see whether there were any messages. The clerk handed him a piece of paper. Kassie watched as Gabriel unfolded and read it, a frown creasing his face. Scrunching it up in his hand, he shoved it into his pocket and came back to where she was waiting.

"Is everything okay?" she asked.

"What…oh yes, fine. Something's come up at work, which I may have to see to, but that's for tomorrow. Tonight, is for us." He took hold of her hand and they made their way to their rooms.

"Mine or yours?" he asked, a little distractedly.

"How about mine," Kassie suggested lightly. He nodded and, saying he'd just go and fetch the champagne that should have been delivered, disappeared into the adjacent room. Kassie was nonplussed; whatever was in that note seemed more important than a mere work problem. Determined not to let it spoil the rest of the evening, she dismissed it and went to freshen up in the bathroom. Gabriel was back within minutes, bringing with him the champagne and a bowl of strawberries.

They drank the whole bottle and ate all the strawberries and made love several times. On the surface, everything seemed blissful, but for the life of her Kassie could not get the expression on his face when he read that note out of her head. It was as though he knew something was about to change, something that might affect them and, whether he realised or not, was distancing himself. Needing to bring him back to her, she decided to tell him about her other self, the secret part of her that no one else in the whole world knew about. Gabriel was cradling her against him, his hands gently stroking her skin, his lips brushing her cheek when she said, very quietly,

"Chloe Archer." Gabriel's hand stopped mid-stroke and, puzzled, he turned her in his arms to face him.

"Who?"

"Chloe Archer is my pseudonym." Gabriel ran his fingers through her hair, smoothing it back from her face, noticing how red her cheeks were.

"What made you decide to tell me?" he curled his eyebrows inquiringly.

"I'm not sure. I didn't want any secrets and if I'm going to be living with you, you'll find out anyway," she shrugged, "just seemed the right moment." He kissed her nose and her mouth and then leaned away to stare at her again.

"Thank you my love. I am very honoured that you trust me enough to share that. I promise to keep your secret. And it's not if you're going to be living with me, it's when." She smiled and as always it touched his soul. The contents of the note niggled at him, but he pushed it aside, he would deal with it tomorrow. Cupping Kassie's face, her kissed her tenderly, the inevitable passion flaring into incandescence and for a little while longer it was just the two of them.

The next day, when Kassie awoke, Gabriel was gone. Perplexed, she glanced around the room, not quite sure what she was looking for. It wasn't as though there was anywhere he could hide and the thought that he might, made her chuckle. The shower wasn't running, so she presumed he must have gone back to his own room. Trying not to read anything into it, other than the fact that they had a busy day ahead and both needed to get ready, Kassie dragged herself out of bed and began her morning routine.

For no reason that she could think of, she was unwilling to go down to breakfast, so rang for room service and while she was waiting, opened her laptop, to check for any emails. An hour later, she was in the atrium, the rest of the tour joining her bit by bit. Today they were going to the Castel Sant'Angelo. Originally Hadrian's mausoleum, it was converted into a papal fortress in the sixth century and, in 1527 was to where Pope Clemente VII retreated, during the Sack of Rome.

Kassie had suggested that they walk to this museum, it wouldn't take much longer than half an hour and there were plenty of sights to see on the way. They could stop for a coffee and lunch without feeling that they were in a rush. When it came time to set off, there was still no sign of Gabriel. Kassie tried to call him, but his phone went straight to message bank. She left a message and then sent a quick text. After several minutes when she couldn't decide what to do, her phone pinged. 'Unavoidably delayed, will meet you there. Love you, G x'. Unsure why she should feel unsettled, Kassie turned back to the group and plastering a bright smile on her face chivvied them out into the sunshine.

Gabriel didn't meet them for coffee, nor did he manage to make it to the Castel. He did text once or twice but as none of his messages clarified what had happened, Kassie just ignored them and continued as though she knew exactly what was going on. One or two of the group appeared to be uneasy, but didn't elaborate and Kassie had no intention of prodding them further.

It was late afternoon when they arrived back at the hotel, and as they walked in there was a flurry of movement and a diminutive creature flew across the polished marble flinging herself at one of the group.

"Gran, here I am! Oh, isn't this fabulous. What a marvellous hotel and this city, oh Rome is utterly divine. I always feel at home, I'm sure I could live here." The words tripped out of a red lipsticked mouth and long glossy black hair billowed around the figure, which was wearing a smart dress and a pair of the highest heels Kassie had ever seen. Anna hugged the girl to her before pushing her away to run a grandmotherly eye over her. Turning to Kassie she said

"Kassie, this is my granddaughter Monique, she'll be joining us for the remainder of the tour." Kassie groaned inwardly, of course she was, weren't they just the lucky ones. Smiling politely, she shook the girl's hand feeling like a giantess, even wearing her flat shoes.

"Pleased to meet you Monique, I'm so glad you're able to accompany us. Does Professor St Germain know?"

Monique's answering smile didn't quite reach her eyes and she seemed to be assessing Kassie as she gushed, "Oh yes, I spoke with him this morning at length and we sorted out everything. It's ages since I've seen Gabe, I can't wait to catch up on his news. I've several messages from his family."

Kassie felt her own smile slipping and before it disappeared completely, said she was looking forward to catching up with her more the next day and politely excused herself. As she headed for the lift, she heard in bell-like tones.

"Gran, who is that lanky thing and what's she doing with our group? Gracious, she's all legs." Kassie didn't hear the reply, but she felt her cheeks burning. Escaping into the cool of the lift, she pressed her head against the mirrored walls and tried to regain her equilibrium. Oh hell, it was going to be a long week.

She didn't join the rest for dinner; she just couldn't face them, well Monique, and sent her excuses. Ordering room service she sat at the desk and worked on her book while she ate. The novel was nearly finished and she was quite happy with the results so far. She was far away in another time when she was brought back to reality by a repeated knocking. Calling that she'd be just a second, she closed her files and shut the lid of the laptop, before letting in a very tired looking Gabriel.

"Sorry I'm so late Kassie. Did everything go okay today?" he asked kissing her gently and stroking her cheek.

"Yeah, I'm just…never mind. How about you? You look exhausted"

"It's been one of those days. All of my units for this semester are completely f…" he paused and amended it to, "…a complete dog's breakfast and it's taken all day to sort out. I'll have to go back in tomorrow too. Sorry love, I know I'm supposed to be with you but do you think you can handle them on your own?" He sat down; running his hand through his hair in frustration, as ever making it stick out at all angles. He looked ridiculously cute.

"'Course," she said, "don't worry about us, we'll muddle through. I missed you though." She moved behind where he was sitting and began to massage his neck. Her cool fingers kneading into the knots in his shoulders, bending to kiss him on the top of his head as she did so. Gabriel sighed a long, tired sigh and rested back into her hands.

"Oh, that is so good, I might keep you."

She smiled and kissed him again, feeling her heart quicken. "I might stay," she replied, nonchalantly.

He glanced at her through the mirror, noticing her slightly tight features.

"Why didn't you join the others for dinner, Kassie?" a hint of concern in his tones.

"I wanted a bit of time alone. No, that's not quite true, if I'm being brutally honest, five minutes of someone called Monique at the end of a long day was more than I needed, so discretion being the better part of valour, I ordered room service."

Gabriel frowned.

"You know she's joining us for the rest of the week?"

Kassie nodded. "She did tell us. Anna is her Gran."

"Yes, I know, Anna mentioned that she might come along, but as I hadn't heard any more, I assumed it hadn't fallen into place. Looks like I was wrong."

"Seems she knows your family too, something about messages from home," Kassie remarked casually. Gabriel shifted uncomfortably.

"Her family have known my family forever, my mother and her grandfather are second cousins or some such thing and they don't live far from us. We grew up together, well in a manner of speaking. I'm about ten years older than Monique; she's closer to my sister in age. Monique and her brother were in our house so often it was as though they lived there."

Kassie listened to Gabriel, but her mind wandered back to Monique's face when they were introduced. What had Anna been saying and why should that bother Monique? What twenty-two-year old joins a tour of people all as old as her grandmother? Something wasn't quite right. She set it aside for now and concentrated on the man in front of her.

"Want a glass of wine or a beer?" she asked, making as though to go to the fridge. He caught her hand.

"No, thank you. What I want is you," he replied swinging her around onto his knee. Laughter bubbled from her lips, as he ran his hands into her hair, undoing the loose knot she had twisted it into and drew her face close for a kiss. Suddenly it was no longer sweet and tender it was fierce and hot. Clothes flew in all directions, lips clashed, limbs entwined and Gabriel scorched a path over Kassie's body, until she was begging him to take her. It was a frantic melding, more an explosion than a slow burn, but neither cared. They had only been apart for a few hours, yet it felt like days and the force of their passion had increased tenfold.

Sometime later, panting hard they rode the vortex back down to earth and within minutes, wrapped together, fell asleep, too tired even to turn out the lamps. Kassie woke during the night, relieved to find Gabriel was still there, next to her. It had bothered her that he had left that morning without waking her and this business with Monique had unnerved her, although she couldn't put her finger on quite why.

Carefully getting out of bed, so as not to disturb Gabriel, Kassie turned out the lamps and opened the balcony doors a fraction, allowing a little fresh air to drift through the room. As she slipped back beneath the sheets, Gabriel grumbled something and pulled her to him, curving his body around hers and tucking her head under his chin. Kassie wrapped one hand over his and rested the other on his thigh and seconds later was back in dreamland.

It didn't seem as though she'd been asleep long at all when her alarm went off. Groggily she reached out to shut it up, only to knock her phone on the floor.

"Dammit," she hissed, scrabbling about trying to find and stop the far too jolly ringtone.

"You alright there?" a sleepy voice asked from underneath layers of bedding and Gabriel's head peered out, squinting in the early morning light. He was presented with the most delicious vision of Kassie — naked, bending off the bed trying to find her phone — which was still singing away — long legs rising to her very shapely behind. She finally grabbed the offending article, stopping the sound and as she came up back onto the bed, her hair spilled around her reminding Gabriel of a mermaid.

She bestowed on him a cheeky smile and moved to kiss him. He dragged her against his body and ignoring all protests, which to be fair died away rapidly, made tender yet fervent love to her until both were quite sure they didn't care about tours or screwed up units or anything other than each other.

"Well that certainly woke me up," she gasped, snuggling up to him, moulding herself to his shape. "Can you see what time is it?"

"I really don't care," Gabriel replied, trailing his fingers down her spine, feeling her shiver, loving that he could do this with hardly a touch.

"Okay for you to say, but I have a tour to sort out so, much as I would prefer to lie here all day and let you continue what you're doing, I'd best get up." She stretched up and kissed him warmly, smoothing her hands over him, letting her body tell him what shyness still held her back from articulating and just when he thought she was going to stay, she slid out of bed.

"Hey, that's just cruel, you little minx." He complained. She winked and crooked a finger, disappearing into the bathroom and turning on the shower. Gabriel needed no second invitation and shot after her, Kassie's morning routine taking a little longer than usual.

Fourteen

After a snatched room-service breakfast, Gabriel said he'd try and meet them later and rushed off to the university. He was frustrated that this was interfering in his plans with Kassie, but he knew she'd be fine. Today it was the Forum and Kassie was more than comfortable managing large groups through the site.

She sauntered downstairs to the atrium and made herself comfortable on one of the sofas until the rest of the group joined her. She hadn't been waiting long when Monique wobbled over to her. On yet another pair of spiky heeled sandals that probably doubled as a weapon. Oh great, thought Kassie, Miss Perky is first down; boy do I get all the luck. Kassie however was nothing if not professional and she gave no indication of her own feelings merely asking whether Monique had slept well. The young woman prattled on about her room and the luxurious bedding and the fabulous bathroom and so on and so on until Kassie had enough detail that she would recognise Monique's room in a line up.

"Are you coming with us to the Forum, Monique?" Kassie asked, when the girl finally took a breath. Monique nodded, so Kassie suggested, tactfully, that she might prefer a pair of shoes with a lower heel as the ground was very uneven and the last thing you needed on holiday was a sprained ankle.

"Good plan, Kassie, I'll be back in a few. Don't leave without me, will you?" Kassie grinned at her and promised. Maybe she wasn't so bad; maybe she was just overly enthusiastic. Nothing wrong with that was there? The rest of the group appeared in dribs and drabs, asking where Gabriel was.

"The Professor is going to be tied up at the University again today. There has been some kind of academic snafu, one that requires his attention, so I'm afraid it's just me." Monique who had just re-joined them frowned a little at this, the gesture marring her pretty face. For a split-second Kassie thought the girl was angry, but it was gone so quickly that Kassie presumed she had imagined it. "Come on then, let's be off, we'll be walking there, it's not far." Chuckling as she spotted Monique's expression of horror, "honestly, Monique, we don't walk quickly and it's only about ten minutes away." The girl relaxed and Anna said something to her in undertones. Monique huffed a bit, but pulled herself together and the group set off.

Four of the group — Harry, Claire, Jenny and Bill — strolled along with Kassie, asking about the Forum. Just as they passed the Capitoline Museum, they came to Trajan's Column and those imperial fora situated on the opposite side of the Via dei Fori Imperiali to the main Forum. Kassie paused here, pointing out that in antiquity the column had been painted in gaudy colours, rather like an ancient comic strip and would have been read easily from the two libraries, one Greek and one Latin, which originally stood either side.

She went on to explain that it had been dedicated to the honour of Trajan in AD113, adding that not only is the column a narrative sculpture depicting the wars with the Dacians but it has also provided modern historians with invaluable information regarding the Roman Army. The carving illustrates — in astonishing detail — their weapons, armour, ships, equipment, troop formations, medical treatment and logistics. Even allowing for the fact that the column was also excellent propaganda, these details have been substantiated in other ancient sources. The men of the group were intrigued, and they spent quite some time studying the carvings discussing the ingenuity of the architect — presumed to be Apollodorus of Damascus — and the skill of the sculptors.

Meandering slowly past the five imperial fora, Kassie clarified their purpose. Built between 54BC and AD113 — with restorations, additions and modifications continuing through until late antiquity — these fora were important, not only as civic, juridical and social spaces, but were also architectural manifestations of the wealth and power of the emperors who commissioned them. Then they reached the Forum. Purchasing their tickets, Kassie ushered them down the short path to the Via Sacra, the main route through the Forum and asked where they would like to start.

"We can either go up to the Palatine and start there, or over that way to the Arch of Septimius Severus, I think it's probably best if I take you through quite quickly and then let you wander about on your own. I'll be here so that you can ask questions, but standing around and listening to me prattle on doesn't give you much time to explore. There is so much history, that it could take all day just to do the Palatine and you know how I go on." She smiled, letting them see that she realised how enthusiastic she could be.

They chose the Arch and followed Kassie as she led them through a detailed, albeit condensed rendition about the ruins. This lasted until lunchtime, when they found a convenient trattoria and inhaled some very tasty pizzas, then back into the Forum. Once she had given them a quick overview of the buildings on the Palatine, Kassie chose one of her favourite benches, overlooking the House of the Vestal Virgins and told the group they had an hour to themselves.

Checking her phone, Kassie noticed Gabriel had sent a text, 'This will take all day, sorry sweetheart. See you at dinner xx.' Practical enough to know his hands were tied, Kassie still felt bereft. She could argue with herself all she liked that he could not have known this would happen, but it still rattled her. Surely there was someone else who could sort out this problem? He was the visiting professor for goodness sake. What was the admin department doing? Wasn't it their job to fix unit glitches?

Knowing that all this was doing was winding her up didn't help either. After turning it over and over in her head and getting nowhere, she finally resolved to forget about all it, not show that his lack of attendance bothered her in any way at all and be her usual professional, friendly self. She was helped in this endeavour by the multitude of questions from her group and she joined them as they congregated here and there throughout the site and spent the remainder of the afternoon happily lost in the world of ancient Rome.

Later, back in her room at the hotel, Kassie showered and changed into more comfortable garb before joining the rest for dinner, all except for Gabriel and Monique. No explanation was forthcoming for Monique's absence and Kassie had to assume that Gabriel was still at the uni. She'd received no further updates from him and tried not to let this bother her. She didn't own Gabriel; she wasn't even sure they were officially a couple — although maybe these things were just accepted these days. They were now more than a little intimate though, he did seem to be courting her and he had called her 'his girl' — it was bit confusing really.

Not one for going to pubs or night clubs — as she found large social gatherings overwhelming — Kassie hadn't been part of the typical dating scenes so beloved of her contemporaries and thus had no clue about the rules. She didn't feel that she had any right to demand Gabriel's attention, or question his whereabouts, her ingrained lack of confidence feeding this reticence. Following her own advice, she looked to all intents and purposes as though she was enjoying the evening, doing a creditable job until, just as she was excusing herself from the table, Gabriel came into the restaurant with Monique, looking as though she was about to strut along a Milan catwalk, hanging off his arm.

Kassie gaped at them, feeling her cheeks blanch, then flush with hectic colour. Get a grip, she instructed herself, no one else knows; don't let them see how this is affecting you.

"Look who I ran into as I was coming back from my walk!" Trilled Monique. Walk! Kassie thought, uncharitably, dressed like that — unlikely. "We've had the best evening. We ate at the most divine little place, just along the road, so quiet and cosy." She shot a veiled glance at Kassie who swallowed tightly, and forced herself to appear unmoved.

"Oh, how lovely. There are so many delightful little eateries around here." Claire, having noticed Monique's expression, intervened. "So nice that the two of you could catch up." Monique smiled sweetly and then nudged Gabriel, nodding towards Kassie.

Against his better judgement, which he really should have listened to, Gabriel broached the subject on his mind.

"Miss Winters, Monique was upset that you cautioned her about her attire this morning. I really don't think it's any of your business what she wears, and to suggest that she wouldn't be able to join you if she didn't change was not your call." As soon as the words left his mouth, Gabriel knew he'd made a mistake and that Kassie would never do any such thing, but Monique had seemed so distressed about it earlier. Dammit, Gabriel, he chided himself; you really should not let Monique do this.

Momentarily rendered speechless, a dangerous glint appeared in Kassie's eyes; one that had either of her brothers been around would have warned the cause of said glint to apologise immediately or suffer the consequences.

"I do apologise, Professor." Coolly impersonal now. "I merely suggested to Monique that four inch stilettos were perhaps not the best footwear in which to stroll around the Forum, owing to the likelihood of rolling one's ankle on the uneven ground." She flicked a suspicious glance at Monique. "However, thank you for reminding me of my place, far be it from me to suggest the sensible option. Moreover, there was certainly no suggestion that she would not be able to join us. Monique must have misunderstood." Kassie held his gaze, her eyes chilling to a frosty sea green. Gabriel started to speak but she was in no mood and interrupted. "So now that's cleared up, I'm off to my room. I have a few things to do before morning. I hope you enjoy the rest of your evening and I'll see you all bright and early." She smiled around the group, vaguely aware that some of them were looking at her with worried expressions. Ignoring this, she glanced back to Gabriel and glowering at him, spun on her heel and hurried over to the bank of elevators.

"Kassie!" She heard Gabriel call her name but as the elevator doors opened, she saw that Monique had grabbed his arm and, with the most childish pout, begged him to get her a glass of wine, effectively preventing him from following her. With a helpless glance at Kassie, Gabriel let himself be dragged over to the bar, just as Kassie almost fell into the lift, her haste to get away making her more clumsy than usual.

Once in her room, Kassie went out onto the balcony and leaned against the railing, staring out over the city with sightless eyes. Was this all it took? Her anger faded as old anxieties raised their ugly heads. It was like seeing tedious repeats on television. She was okay until someone better came along;

someone who was beautiful, who dressed like a model and knew all the right things to say to keep a man interested. She had thought Gabriel was different, that he meant what he said. Maybe he had, maybe he'd forgotten how stunning Monique was. Well, she supposed, it was better to find that out now. It might have been less galling had she not given her heart, her soul and her body, not to mention confiding in him things she had never shared with anyone, but — hey those were the breaks.

Straightening her shoulders, Kassie retreated into her room and deliberately forcing everything else to the back of her mind, settled down at her computer. She was soon engrossed in the activities of her ancient hero, who weirdly, was looking more like Gabriel every day. She registered that her phone pinged a few times, but she ignored them and, much later when a soft knocking interrupted her, she chose to ignore that too. He had to be kidding! Did he think it was okay to spend the evening with another woman and then expect her to sleep with him? Not a chance, buddy.

Kassie worked long into the night and when she finally did go to bed, sleep eluded her. She tossed and turned, her mind working overtime, her heart slowly breaking. When her alarm went off she felt as though a steamroller had flattened her. These next two days were dedicated to city tours and she needed to be on top of her game as there was a lot to cover. Today they would be starting at the top of the Spanish Steps and although easily accessible on foot, Gabriel had organised the coach to drop them off, as they would be doing quite a bit of walking. For once, Kassie was thankful not to have to walk.

Checking her messages, there were several texts and voice messages from Gabriel. She read the texts and listened to his voice mails; most begged her to answer the phone or at least text him back. He was sorry about this evening blah, blah, blah. Yeah, so sorry that it took you until — she checked the time of the first message — 9:30pm to remember me. One, from this morning, was rather more formal; he would not be available for the rest of their tour. Kassie's heart cracked a little more. The problem, although solved had uncovered several more issues and it was unlikely he'd get any free time in the next few days. The start of the new semester was looming and academic timetables wait for no one.

Kassie texted him back thanking him for the update, confirming that of course she'd handle the tour and maybe she'd see him before the group all went their separate ways. Just after she'd hit send, her phone rang; it was Gabriel. Knowing she couldn't avoid him forever, she answered.

"Kassie love, are you okay? Why have you been ignoring my calls? I'm sorry about last night, I shouldn't have spoken to you like that in front of the others." Unwilling to haul him over the coals for his behaviour the previous evening, Kassie was quiet for several seconds while she collected her thoughts.

"I'm fine, Gabriel. I was just tired and I had my phone on silent. I'm sorry too; maybe it's better this way. It's a real bummer that you're going to miss the last few days, but we'll muddle through." She paused, her lips were trembling and she needed to get her emotions under control.

"Kassie?" She could hear the concern in his tones and it made it worse. "Are you sure you're okay?"

"Yep, it's all good. I'll check in with you later. Don't want to keep you from your busy day." She tried to infuse a cheery note into her voice but she wasn't sure she'd succeeded. Gabriel was nobody's fool. She ended the call without giving him chance to say anymore, tears pouring down her face. Come on, Kassie she chided, you're a big girl; shit happens; deal with it. There could be a totally innocent explanation for the whole thing, don't jump to conclusions. Despite knowing that this was unlikely — she might be naive but she wasn't that gullible — Kassie pushed it all aside and got on with her day.

From the Spanish Steps, they wove their way to the Trevi Fountain, through the Piazza di Pietra where the Temple of Hadrian once stood, its surviving wall of eleven, fifteen-metre-high, Corinthian columns now the facade of a bank. Then Kassie led them along narrow streets full of all manner of interesting shops to the Pantheon. She knew she had to be careful here, for she could wax lyrically about it all day. In as concise a fashion as possible, she clarified that this was believed to be the third incarnation of a temple first built by Marcus

Agrippa in honour of Augustus' — although, at the time he was still Octavian — victory at the Battle of Actium in 27BC.

Going on to point out that the Emperor Hadrian, who retained the original inscription commissioned it around AD120-5. Kassie explained that, originally, it was dedicated to 'All Gods,' until it was reconsecrated in the seventh century as a Christian church and has remained thus. Concluding that the Pantheon was also the resting place of several famous Italians, including Raphael, Vittorio Emmanuel II and Umberto I, which probably accounted for its remarkable state of preservation.

She went onto describe, briefly but in detail, the elegant engineering of the building. Pausing for breath, she noticed amusement on the faces of most of her group as well as, bizarrely, several others who had stopped to listen.

"I'm sorry," she said, grinning. "I know I get carried away, but this building is just so remarkable. For me, this one edifice captures the essence of ancient Rome and to be able to stand on the same floor where her Emperors stood is a privilege I do not take lightly." She blushed as she spoke, aware that she probably sounded a bit bonkers, but the growing crowd around her clapped enthusiastically. One or two even came up to thank her, saying that they had never heard it illustrated so eloquently. Her own group laughingly pulled her over to one side teasing her gently about her passion for the structure, before sauntering across the piazza to enjoy lunch at one of the cafés.

Appetite filled, they walked along to the Piazza Navona, where most of them wanted to check out the market stalls. Kassie was happy to let them; Gabriel and she had ensured that these two days could be adjusted to suit the whims of the group. Kassie herself, preferring to shop when she was on her own, enjoyed a coffee while the group ooh'd and aah'd over the multitude of arts and crafts, spending money like it was going out of fashion. Retail therapy complete, they strolled past the Largo di Torre Argentina, housing the remains of four republican temples, the ruins of Pompey's theatre and currently home to the famous cat sanctuary.

Kassie brought the group to a halt on the little pathway between the Portico of Ottavia and the Theatre of Marcellus. They were tiring now having done a lot of walking and standing and more walking. Monique was beginning to look quite petulant and Kassie had no desire to deal with childish tantrums from that young lady.

"I think we've done quite enough for today. I know you've walked for what seems like miles today; we've a similar schedule tomorrow and then there's Ostia, yes, I know — more walking." There was a collective groan making Kassie chuckle. "Well you can't say the itinerary wasn't clear on how much we were fitting in. I promise we'll take it slowly tomorrow and I'll finish earlier so you can enjoy some free time. I'm heading back to the hotel, anyone coming, or are you happy to wander about a bit longer?"

It was about half and half. John, Ella, Jenny, Bill, Tony and Hugh said they wanted to have a stroll along the Tiber to see the Pons Aemilius — the oldest stone bridge in Rome — while George and Lillian, Walter, Dot, Penny and Tom said something about treating themselves to a gelato. That left Anna, Monique, Harry and Claire; the latter two apparently assuming the role of Kassie's guardians as lately, they rarely left her side when they were out.

The five chattered aimlessly as they walked back to the hotel. Monique did go on bit about her so-called date with Gabriel the previous night and let it slip, deliberately or otherwise, that she was meeting him for a beer that afternoon, when he finished work. Kassie bit her lip and refused to be drawn, but her pale face did not go unnoticed by Claire who was determined to get to the bottom of Gabriel's behaviour. This was not what he'd told them he was up to and she was very perturbed. If he carried on like this, he'd lose her.

Fifteen

Back at the hotel, politely declining Harry and Claire's invitation to join them for a drink, Kassie returned to her room, where she stayed for the rest of the night. She managed to finish her book and set it aside to start re-reading it the next evening, before sending it out for editing. Although she self-published her books, she knew they needed to be proofed; one of her colleagues at work did it as a side line and at a substantially reduced rate compared with most of the professional editors, whose charges were well beyond her limited means. Accepting that they might not be quite as polished as works released through publishing houses, Kassie had a loyal following of readers who seemed to like her novels and her sales continued to tick over nicely.

As always, she found it hard to let a story go, but she already had an idea percolating for the next one so she didn't feel too torn. Making sure it was properly saved and backed-up, Kassie turned off her laptop, had a quick shower and tried to sleep. She had sent a few texts to Gabriel during the day, but had received no reply, not even an acknowledgement and it was playing on her mind.

She knew he was probably very busy, but a brief message took less than five seconds. Tonight, she hadn't heard from him at all, no texts, no calls, no knocking her door, nothing; the lack of which, merely confirmed her suspicions. She realised that at some point she would probably have a meltdown, almost certainly in front of a whole crowd of people, but now, she just felt numb.

The next day, she escorted her charges around on the last part of their city tour, this time to some of the most beautiful of the nine hundred churches in Rome, including San Giovanni in Lateran, Santa Maria Maggiore and — within the Santa Maria della Vittoria — the Cornaro Chapel. They did avail themselves of public transport for it would have taken them a long time to walk between the churches. By early afternoon they were churched-out, trailing wearily back to the hotel. Monique whinged all the way complaining about her sore feet. Kassie closed off her mind and barely made any conversation at all.

Again, she had done the right thing, texting Gabriel to update him on their day, still nothing; it was as though he'd dropped off the face of the planet. She'd tried to call, but his phone went straight to voice mail and as a last resort she'd emailed him, nil, nada, zilch. Presuming that he would get in touch when he saw fit, Kassie tried to keep a cheerful face on things and neatly sidestepped the group's concerned questions. Claire was about at boiling point though, and had left Gabriel several, extremely vexed, voice-mails telling him that Kassie was utterly miserable and he was behaving very badly.

Again, unable to face the rest at dinner, Kassie stayed in her room, working on her initial edits. She found it too hard to concentrate and, giving up, tried to get some rest. Sleep remained elusive, however, and she spent most of the night sitting on the balcony, wrapped in a blanket, thinking about the mess her life had become. Three days ago, she had been happier than she could have ever dreamed possible and in less than twenty-four hours it had all come crashing down around her. She was so confused. What had she done that would cause Gabriel to ignore her like this? She had given him everything he'd wanted, she thought he returned her feelings, he told her he loved her, she told him she felt the same. Her heart ached, her head ached and as the pearly light of dawn painted the Eternal City in its luminescence, she was no closer to an answer.

Standing in the shower she tried to wash away the fuzziness, she needed her wits about her for they were going out to Ostia. Thankfully Gabriel had organised a coach for this tour, as although the site was easy enough to get to on public transport, it would make it another long day.

They met at the entrance; Monique joined them and for once was wearing a sensible outfit and flat shoes. She was chatting with Anna describing her evening with Gabriel, another beer that led to dinner. Kassie's head started to spin and she worried that she might faint. Taking several deep breaths until the darkness receded, she clenched her jaw and ushered them onto the bus. Harry said something to Anna who glanced at Kassie and mumbled something back, before shrugging her shoulders and pointedly ignoring both Harry and Claire.

Kassie had given up caring; she would get through today and leave the tour that evening. She could bear it no longer. It might be cowardly, but she didn't think she could face Gabriel now; it was better just to slip out of his life. He'd forget her soon enough. Forcing herself to smile, she took the group through the ruins, explaining that, although it was now a long way from the present mouth of the Tiber, throughout antiquity, Ostia had served as Rome's major port, even after the construction of the new harbour at Portus about three kilometres west.

She gave them as interesting a tour as she could muster, but she had lost her spontaneity. Her delight in all things ancient had disappeared and despite her best efforts to the contrary, she was listless. Her face was pale and pinched and, even under her sunglasses, it was clear that she had dark shadows under her eyes. Tactfully, the group did not draw attention to it, but most were very concerned, thinking she must be sickening for something. Monique on the other hand gossiped away garrulously, asking inane questions and throwing out comments about Gabriel without a care in the world. Kassie was hard pushed not to slap the young woman; it was only her determination to remain as professional as possible that stopped her.

As they were walking back to the bus, Kassie paused by the spot where she had first seen Gabriel since that day at uni, it was only about six or seven weeks ago, yet she felt as though it had been a lifetime. Lost in daydreams she didn't hear or see the others talking between themselves and by the time she came back to earth, they had moved on. Back in the car park, Monique, who had gone on ahead, came hurtling down the steps of the coach waving her phone about.

"Kassie, Kassie, Gabe's been trying to ring you, apparently one of his colleagues knew we were coming today and left something for him at the gift shop. Some book or other that he'd promised to loan him." Kassie frowned. Oh, so now when it suited him, Gabriel needed her! Charming! Why hadn't he contacted her directly? A question she posed to Monique who replied carelessly. "He said he's been trying but he remembered that you put your phone on silent when you're doing tours."

Kassie yanked her phone out of her bag and saw that there were several texts and two voice mails about said book.

Feeling somewhat resentful that Gabriel saw fit to ask her to collect a book when he couldn't be bothered to answer any of her other texts, she said, "Okay, hang on, I'll just go and get it. Please would you stick this in the coach?" She indicated her backpack. "Saves me lugging it all the way back there." Sending a quick text to Gabriel confirming that she'd got his message and was going to collect the book, she tucked her phone back into the inside pocket. Closing the zip on her bag, Kassie handed it to Monique who nodded, grasping it with her free hand and scooting back up the steps, nearly tripping over George in her haste.

Kassie waved at the others and pointed at Monique assuming she'd tell them where she was going and shot back up the long path to the ruins. She recalled that day again; Gabriel had been talking to two other people, maybe they were well known here, a fact that was confirmed when she appeared at the gift shop, explaining to the lady behind the counter that apparently, there was something for Professor St Germain.

"Oh yes, for Gabe," responded the attendant, pulling out a bag from under the counter and, smiling, handed it over asking Kassie to say 'hi' to the professor. Taking the bag, Kassie thanked her and hurried back to the car park. Ten minutes later, hot and bothered, she arrived back where the coach had been parked to no sign of it or her charges. Flummoxed, she stared around, as though the coach was hiding under a bush or behind a tree and would just pop out when she called.

Panic began to curl through her, as she stood motionless for several minutes trying to work out what the hell had happened. Dammit, her phone was in her backpack, in the coach. What the hell? Why on earth would they leave her here? She'd only been gone twenty minutes or so. Had there been an emergency, which had prompted the driver to rush off without her?

Fighting the urge to cry, she absolutely refused to cry, Kassie rather lost her head. It was easy enough to get back into Rome, and thankfully, she had a few coins in her jeans pocket, but it was being left behind that upset her. After everything she'd done for this group over the last few weeks, this was how they repaid her? The anger that had begun to burn the previous evening reignited, pushing away her distress and she realised her meltdown was imminent.

She stomped down the road and over the bridge to the train station and sat on the platform, stewing for ten minutes or so until the train pulled in. Arriving at Ostiense, she walked over to the metro and, about an hour after leaving Ostia, was back at the hotel. The others were already there and as she entered the lobby, they looked up and smiled, seemingly no one was in the slightest bothered that she hadn't been on the bus. Her anger was now bubbling, but she couldn't take it out on those who looked as though they had no idea what was going on.

Monique was sitting on the arm of Anna's chair flicking her hair back, her bell like tones echoing around the space. She was saying something about Gabriel and shopping for engagement rings but when she saw Kassie she clammed up.

"May I please have my backpack?" was all Kassie said, her voice cool, trying to pretend she hadn't just heard that last bit. He was getting engaged to Monique? Oh hell — and he hadn't had the guts to tell her — bloody awesome! As Monique handed over the backpack, Kassie added, "I suppose you thought that was a great joke, leaving the tour guide behind." There was a sudden hush, as the others paused in their conversations to listen. "What would you have done had there been accident, or one of you had fallen ill? The insurance that covers you on these tours is invalidated if there is no tour guide." Kassie was trembling with rage now, her meltdown inevitable.

"Oh, come on, it was just a bit of fun, don't get so shirty."

"Just a bit of fun, just a bit of f…" Kassie clenched her teeth, determined not to scream and rant in front of all these people, never mind the staff of the hotel. "Please excuse me, I need not to be here."

She nodded to the rest of the group and had nearly made it to the elevators when she heard Monique say, petulantly. "Seriously it was just a lark. God, she's such a drag. I cannot for the life of me understand why Gabe bothered with that bet? Seduce her in three weeks? He must be batty!"

Kassie turned slowly and made her way back to the group. A few of them were frantically trying to hush Monique but she was in full flow now and went on heedlessly, "Honestly, she's got nothing going for her, can't take a joke, boring as anything — all that blabbing on about ancient stuff — and she's not even pretty...what?" suddenly noticing the expressions on the faces of those around her.

"I beg your pardon, Monique," Kassie said, amazed at how calm she sounded. "Did I hear you correctly? Did you just say that Gabriel made a bet that he could seduce me?" At least having the decency to blush, Monique squirmed uneasily on the arm of the chair and stared at Kassie, who turned her attention to the others. "And you were in on it?" There was a flurry of voices as they all started to speak over each other, consternation clear in their tones.

"No, that's not how it was..."

"Please, you need to understand..."

"It wasn't a bet..."

Kassie raised her palm and waited until they'd quietened down.

"Thank you," she said with no small amount of dignity. "I have been honoured to escort you on this tour, although, now I'm not entirely sure why you're here, if not to aid and abet Professor St Germain in his quest. Thank you for listening to me prattle on about sites and venues that you're all probably far more expert in than I. I hope you all have a safe journey home." She walked quickly over to the elevator where, thankfully, there was one just about to go up.

Arriving in her room Kassie flung everything she had into her case, with little regard for order. After making sure the room was as tidy as it could be, she sat at the desk to compose a letter. It was one of the hardest things she'd even written and she swore she could feel her heart finally shatter, as she signed her name at the end.

Sealing it in one of the hotel envelopes and printing Gabriel's name neatly on the front, she gathered her belongings, took one last look around the room and left. Dropping the letter and the book at reception, she was almost at the doors when Claire, who had been lurking near the pot plants, hurried over.

"Kassie, please don't go, it's not what you think. Just talk to Gabe, he'll be so upset."

"Yes, I imagine that finding out your plan has been scuppered must be quite upsetting. I'm sure he'll get over it. Thank you, Claire, I appreciate you waiting for me and sticking up for him, but I really don't think I want to see him ever again." Kassie's voice was icily formal. Claire ran her eye over the young woman whose face was white and drawn and who looked utterly devastated. Holy hell Gabe, Claire thought, you've royally blown it.

"Okay, but promise me you'll consider letting him know where you've gone."

"I've left him a letter, Claire. He knows where I live, although I doubt he'll bother to find me." Kassie's voice was empty, flat — she had nothing left. "Please, I have to go. Tell him I…" she paused, "never mind it no longer matters." Kassie smiled sadly and walked out.

Tapping her foot in frustration as she watched the young woman walk away, Claire pondered her options, wondering where on earth Gabriel had been these past few days. She was about to go and find Harry to see what he suggested when she spotted Anna and Monique lounging in the bar. Marching over them, Claire demanded to know what the dickens was going on. Neither was particularly eager to talk, but Claire persisted until, finally, they capitulated. It appeared that Anna had always hoped Gabriel would marry Monique and when she realised that he was falling for Kassie, decided to see whether her granddaughter could change his mind. Monique, who wasn't remotely in love with Gabriel, still thought him quite the catch and was happy to fall in with her grandmother's scheme.

"Have you any idea the damage you've done to two, if not three lives, Anna?" expostulated Claire, who had known Anna for years and never expected this from her friend. "Monique here has created a rift so wide I doubt it'll ever be bridged. There is no way Gabriel will forgive her — or you for that matter — in a hurry and where you got the notion that he would marry Monique anyway is beyond me! Now, I am going to sit here until Gabe comes in, assuming he does come in, since I haven't heard or seen anything of him for three days, at which point I intend to tell him everything and you can fill in the gaps. You," jabbing her finger at Anna, then including Monique in her wrath, "both of you knew what his intentions were. A bet indeed! What a cruel and thoughtless thing to say. I'm ashamed of you Monique, I presumed your mother had brought you up better than that." Claire was furious and, to be fair, grandmother and granddaughter did look suitably chastened.

Not that this was of any help to Kassie.

Sixteen

It wasn't very long after Kassie's departure, when a very weary looking Gabriel strode into the hotel and over to the reception desk to check for messages. Claire, who was sitting on one of the sofas scattered around the atrium hoping she would catch him before he went up to his room, saw the clerk hand Gabriel a book and a slim white envelope. Puzzled he turned it over and over, trying to work out who it was from, then slid his finger underneath the flap and drew out the single sheet therein.

He stared at it, ran his fingers through his hair and stared again. Abruptly he sat down, his head not understanding what his eyes were reading,

Dear Gabriel,

I wonder whether you expected your experiment — to take a plain, introverted, twenty-eight-year-old virgin and seduce her would be so successful? I don't know why I'm surprised, I should never have been so gullible as to believe someone like you could ever love someone like me, but I thought you were different. I thought you were one of those wonderfully, genuine, old-fashioned gentlemen and I think I am more hurt by discovering that I was wrong than by falling for your act.

Well, you must be very pleased with the result, I'm sure you have been endlessly entertained knowing that not only did you manage to seduce me, you managed to make me fall in love with you too. Top marks Gabriel.

It would have been bad enough had you played your game as a confirmed bachelor, but that you did this while apparently on the verge of becoming engaged was not only unbelievably cruel but also utterly disrespectful. Moreover, the fact that your blushing bride took such delight in being a part of your charade speaks volumes about your relationship and her character. I guess it serves me right for trusting you to be an honourable man.

Under the circumstances, I do not feel that I am the most suitable person to continue as your tour guide. There are only two days left anyway, so I scarcely think you'll miss me. Neither am I comfortable accepting any

payment for my services, as it seems they were acquired under false pretences.

Gabriel, as I write this, images of the last couple of weeks keep running through my head and truly, they have been the happiest of my life, so I suppose I should thank you for that. I don't regret anything that happened between us, you made me feel more beautiful and cherished than I ever imagined possible, despite it all being a lie. Hopefully at some point in the future, I'll be warmed by those memories, but now, all I feel is betrayed.

I wish you a lifetime of joy with Monique; I can honestly say you deserve each other.

Kassie

Claire approached him and as he heard her footsteps, Gabriel glanced up, his face a tormented mask.

"What the hell happened today, Claire?"

"I told you that you needed to be careful, Gabe. She's a gentle soul and desperately in love with you. You haven't been near her in three days. What the hell were you doing?" Claire demanded, rather snippily it must be admitted.

"Didn't Kassie tell you?"

"She mentioned something about uni and that you'd be unavailable for the rest of the tour, but surely you could have seen her at the end of each day?" Claire replied in exasperated tones.

"Well, that was the first problem, the admin department had managed to delete all three of my units and we had to try to retrieve them, then when that didn't work, I had to reload everything. Total nightmare. But then Mum had a fall and I had to drop everything to rush home. I left Kassie a note telling her where I was. You know we have no mobile reception out there and in all honesty, I thought she'd understand." Gabriel explained, half apologetically, half dismayed.

"So, you couldn't pick up the landline? Gabe you're an idiot! You are so smart with anything academic, but when it comes to people you are hopeless. Kassie believes you spent the last two nights with Monique, for that is what she's been telling us." Gabriel started to interrupt. "No, you will hear me out young man." Gabe smiled sheepishly; Claire and Harry were virtually family, he had known them all his life and had trusted them and the others with his plan, believing they all supported him. Claire went on to tell him what Anna had done and then that Monique had managed to abandon Kassie at Ostia, somehow persuading the coach driver that she had been held up and would get home under her own steam.

"Then when Kassie came in, Monique was gas-bagging about you and engagement rings. Kassie must have heard, the whole bloody hotel heard, but all Kassie did was tick her off about leaving her behind. Then, as Kassie was walking away, Monique proclaimed to all and sundry, in her usual clarion tones, that she couldn't understand what it was about her that had prompted you to lay bets that you could seduce her in three weeks. Kassie heard and questioned her on it and although we tried to tell her it wasn't like that, she was too upset and now she's gone."

Gabriel was appalled. This wasn't how it was supposed to go. Where was his letter to Kassie? No wonder none of her messages made sense; she'd had no idea where he was. Minutes ticked by while Gabriel just sat, trying to get his head around what Claire had told him.

"How's Isabella?" Claire asked breaking the silence, her tones rather more solicitous, worried for her friend.

"She's okay," replied Gabriel distractedly. "She fell off a ladder while trying to wash the windows, the loon. Thankfully the neighbour heard her yell and drove her to the local hospital; she's broken her ankle and, obviously, will need to rest up. Dad's home now though, so I could come back here, I just hope I'm not too late. Damn it all, I wish I'd tried to call her, she sounded weird on the phone when I spoke to her, the day before yesterday, but then I got the news about Mum and everything else went out of my head."

"Gabe," Claire said gently, "you left her to finish the tour on her own. Yes, I expect it was unavoidable but that doesn't mean she found it easy to accept or, after everything else that's happened, even believe. Then you spend the evening with another woman, a very young and very beautiful woman. I don't suppose you bothered to tell Kassie what that was about did you?" Gabe stared at her. "Worse, Monique kept tossing out the fact that you also spent the last two nights with her.

What do you expect Kassie to do, wait around for you to rub her face in it?" She paused and saw that her words were getting through.

"I know you love Kassie, Gabe, but your behaviour these last few days hasn't really attested to that has it?"

"I have to go after her, I need her to know the truth. She thinks it was all a joke? Oh God, Claire, I can't lose her."

"Well go get her, Gabe." He stood and was about to leave when he saw Anna and Monique watching him from the bar. He stalked over, his face like thunder.

"I am ashamed to think we are related and that either of you could pull such an awful stunt. You Anna, you knew it wasn't a bet and to drag Monique into it, what were you thinking? Monique! Really? You are twenty-two years old; time to start behaving like an adult. Never mind the rest of it, what do you think might have happened to Kassie if she hadn't had enough money to get back here from Ostia? You thoughtless little idiot." Gabriel could feel his temper rising and bit down on the rest of his words. "It's a good job this tour finishes the day after tomorrow, you've done more than enough damage." Raking his hand through his hair, which was now sticking out like a haystack, Gabriel turned on his heel and left.

While all this was unfolding, Kassie was trudging home slowly, feeling as though her whole world had crumbled. Her romantic side was telling her what a prize nincompoop she was, the first man who shows her any real affection and she goes and falls in love. Stupid! Stupid! Stupid! Well — the sensible part of her countered — he did say he wanted to marry you, so your behaviour wasn't totally without merit. She might have known he had a fiancé, of course he had a fiancé — well an almost fiancé — he was so handsome and sexy and tall! Oh, God why did he have to be so damn tall? Funny though, he had never struck her as a man who would string a woman along, he always seemed so honourable, decent and old fashioned; someone she could trust. Didn't say much for her judgement did it!

Serves you right for daring to dream, Kassandra Winters she admonished herself. Who would want some plain, shy, twenty-eight-year old virgin, with tendency to plumpness, anyway? She had been kidding herself. Recollections of their time together kept flickering through her mind like a silent movie and she knew she would not be able to forget him, neither would she love anyone else — not the way she loved him, those few short weeks would have to last a very long time.

The walk home was taking ages. She didn't think the hotel was that far from her apartment but she was finding it inordinately difficult to put one foot in front of the other; the narrow street leading up to her building seemed to stretch out forever. She should have bought something to eat, but the thought of food made her stomach roil. She couldn't remember the last time she ate a proper meal, or any food of substance. She probably should get on to that. Wearily she pushed herself on, wishing she'd thought to come by taxi.

Eventually, Kassie reached her apartment building and as she glanced towards the doorway, a burly figure detached itself from the shadows. She paused, frowning warily. Who on earth was that? For a split second she felt a trickle of fear, then she shook her head, it wasn't even dusk yet, unlikely anyone would be attacking people in broad daylight, right outside her flat. Hesitating, she realised that the figure looked familiar and, as he walked towards her, she recognised her older brother.

"Adam?" astonishment laced her tones. "Adam! What are you…how did you …when did you?" Kassie stood stock-still and gawked.

"Haven't seen you for two years. Least you could do is give me a hug." Kassie dropped the handle of her suitcase and flew into his arms, bursting into tears as she did so.

"Oh, Adam! How did you know?" Sobbing helplessly.

"Hey, Kass! What the hell is going on? Didn't expect to see you in such a lather, your emails are always so full of how much you're loving it here." Kassie tried to get herself under control, mumbling, "I'll tell you when we get inside. Oh, it's good to see you; you have no idea how good. So sorry I lost the plot like that, it's been a rough couple of days." Collecting the abandoned suitcase, Adam put his arm around his sister, noticing that she looked quite unwell, and ushered her into the hallway of her building.

A little way down the street another figure stood, motionless, a bleak expression on his face. She hadn't mentioned that she had another man in her life, yet this man was obviously close to her. He had tried to catch up with her and had run most of the way, desperate to talk to her, but she had been too far ahead of him and her desolate bearing tore at his heart. He had to explain, he had to tell her that it was all a misunderstanding. She was walking away, out of his life.

Not again.

He'd sworn he wouldn't let her go again. Who was this man? It was odd; Kassie did not seem to be the sort of girl to have two men on the go at the same time. She didn't seem artful enough to keep something like that a secret.

Unwilling to confront her tonight — especially as she obviously had company — and sighing with the futility of it all, Gabriel St Germain turned and walked away.

Meanwhile Adam had managed to get Kassie into her apartment, where he sat her down on the sofa and then went to fill the kettle. He switched on the lights and opened the balcony doors, the fresh air ruffling the curtains and cooling the room, which seemed rather stuffy, having been closed for so long. Kassie had started crying again and Adam was beginning to question whether she would ever stop. Kassie never cried; she was always the stoic one. In fact, he was sure that this was the first time he had ever seen her cry and it bothered him.

"Come on Kass, you'll make yourself ill if you don't stop. Surely it can't be that bad."

"S-s-sorry Adam," she stuttered, making a huge effort to stem her tears. "You were the l-l-last p-person I expected to see and y-you're here j-just when I-I really n-n-needed a friendly f-face." She burst into a fresh bout of sobs and Adam, came to sit next to her, drawing her into his arms and rocking her gently.

"Well, I don't think you'll start feeling better until you've told me the whole tale."

"I'm not s-s-sure I can. I-I've m-made a complete mess of everything."

"Am I to assume that all this has to do with a man?" Her brother hazarded a guess, not all that astutely. Kassie nodded, scrubbing at her face with the soft, white handkerchief Adam handed her. Taking deep breaths, she steadied herself and after a while started to feel less miserable. Adam made them both a strong cup of tea, commenting that Mum always said tea was the best drink over which to solve a problem, making Kassie smile just a little. As they sipped the brew, Kassie started to talk, falteringly at first, then it all tumbled out. She told Adam everything, well except those two blissful nights, that part she skipped over very neatly. Her brother, however was no fool and had always been able to see straight through her, filling in the blanks without much effort.

"Are you sure this is what you think it is?"

"What else am I supposed to think? She was very clear about their relationship and in the short time I saw them together, he didn't make any effort to come and tell me what was going on." She paused, conveniently forgetting that he had knocked on her door that first evening — late though it had been, and heaved a huge sigh before continuing.

"Thing is, he told me he loved me. He pursued me, he courted me, he took me out for the most amazing dinner and toasted us as a couple. He also said he wanted to marry me, although to be fair, he didn't actually propose. I believed he meant it and now I find out that it was all a game. He even said he thought I was beautiful, no one has ever called me beautiful, so I expect he was lying about that too."

Her voice was so wistful that Adam felt his chest tighten, he squeezed her shoulder, but said nothing, realising that she had more to add.

"He didn't seem like the others. I would have never…done what I did, had I known he is about to marry someone else. What was I, some last fling? Regardless of whether this whole thing was a bet or whatever it was, why did he take it so far? I'd be devastated if I thought the person I intended to spend my life with sle…played around. It was just that for once I dared to hope…" she halted. It was too humiliating to tell her brother that she believed in happily ever afters and had been stupid enough to think it might have been her turn.

Adam heard the pain in her voice and the anger that had begun to simmer as her tale unfolded, bubbled over. How could some man do this to her? What a cretin.

"I think that maybe he and I should have a little chat," he growled but Kassie shook her head.

"Just leave it Adam, it's not worth it. He'll have forgotten I even exist by now. Monique — that's her name — is gorgeous, long, jet black hair, grey eyes, slim, like a model you know but quite petite, all sparkly and confident, the complete opposite of me — I can't compete with that. When she was around, he barely noticed me, so it baffles me that he bothered at all…it's all too confusing. Oh, my head hurts."

Kassie slumped and it was all she could do to hold back more tears. Her head was throbbing and her whole body felt as though she'd been used as a punching bag.

"I think I'll go to bed, which reminds me, the spare room is made up." Suddenly registering that she had no clue how long Adam had been in Rome. "I'm sorry Adam, I'm so caught up in my own nonsense and I forgot to say hello properly. How long have you been here? How did you get in and where's Julia?" she said, referring to Adam's wife.

Adam chuckled and said it was of no matter, adding, "Emilia, your wonderful protector, gave me your spare key, after I proved we were related, and Julia is at home. I had business in Milan, so said I'd come check on you. I took a few days of holiday and don't fly out 'til Wednesday." Kassie nodded absently and said goodnight, traipsing into her room. She left her unpacking for the next day, and since getting changed seemed too hard, simply lay on her bed fully clothed, hoping to find some solace in sleep.

Seventeen

Despite being overwrought and exhausted, as had become her pattern, Kassie didn't sleep that night or the night after that and then just stopped trying. Adam would find her, every morning, sitting on her balcony, cup of tea in hand, watching the sunrise. If he hadn't seen her in different clothes, he would have sworn she never moved.

Gabriel — who, of course, hadn't forgotten her — called round several times but so far Adam had refused to let him in. Gabriel would not be put off and kept trying; he sent texts, he left voice mails he even wrote actual pen to paper letters, leaving them under her doormat. Kassie ignored all of them, turning off her phone and leaving the growing pile of letters on the table by the French windows. Adam was impressed with Gabriel's persistence but had to respect his sister's wishes.

Eventually, after numerous thwarted attempts, Gabriel had had enough and the two men faced off on the front porch of Kassie's apartment building. They circled each other like the gladiators of antiquity; both itching to flatten the other for completely different reasons; but suddenly, Adam noticed the same agony in Gabriel's eyes that he had seen in Kassie's. His bunched fists fell to his sides and he leaned against the door jamb, arms folded.

"What the hell did you do to Kassie?" Adam demanded, furiously. "She tells me you laid bets on her?" Gabriel glowered at him, still with no idea who he was.

"Who the hell are you to ask me?"

"I'm Adam, her brother! Who on earth did you think I was?" The fight went out of Gabriel, relief flooding him that this man wasn't also chasing Kassie's heart.

"I thought…I saw you the other day." Gabriel got a grip, "I didn't mean to hurt Kassie…" indignantly, "…at least I hadn't intended to. Oh damnation, it wasn't supposed to go like this. I can't believe she would think…" Gabriel's voice trailed off, he sounded defeated. "I just need to talk to her to tell her that she got it wrong, that it got all twisted." He appealed to Adam who continued to glare at him, his demeanour giving nothing away. Kassie's brother however knew that this had to be sorted out or his sister would become ill. He debated with himself and then came to a decision.

"Look, give me a few minutes. There's a café down the hill there." He pointed in the general direction of a colourful canopy under which stood a few tables and chairs. "Go and order two coffees and I'll join you shortly." Gabriel's look of gratitude was enough to convince Adam that there was more to this story than Kassie knew and he was determined to get to the bottom of it. As Gabriel walked towards the café, Adam went back into the flat, he could hear the shower running and called through that he was just nipping out and did she need anything. He heard her cheerless 'No' and telling her he had the spare key, dropped the latch and left.

Ten minutes later Gabriel and Adam were sitting with a coffee each, the aromatic scent of the roasted beans wafting out from the interior of the café, soothing both men's agitation.

"Right, I think you need to tell me everything, from start to finish, because at the moment all I want to do is grind your face into dust." Adam's words were scathing, but his expression was more encouraging. So, after a fortifying gulp of his espresso, Gabriel took a deep breath and told his side of the story.

"I first met Kassie two years ago. I'd just been having a confab with her professor — man called Hardwick — whom I had approached to see whether he thought Kassie would be suitable for a project I was working on relating to my Ancient History courses. This wasn't the usual the touristy stuff; I was hoping to set up a couple of intensive units that would be held at certain ancient sites and to be included as part of an undergraduate degree. Two or three week courses, covering Roman and/or Greek history, which would be run during the long vacation. It would give classics students the chance to discover, study and absorb the art, architecture and history of some of these places in situ rather than from a distance." Gabriel paused and considered his next words.

"Hardwick told me that he believed Kassie too introverted to be able to hold the attention of the students. That she lacked the charisma required. He also said he thought her plain, rather ungainly and a bit on the plump side — I think those were his words. I admit to being surprised and quite offended on Kassie's behalf, he seemed overly judgemental, not to mention inappropriate. Besides," he mused, almost as an aside, "I fail to see how anyone can call her plain, she is quite astonishingly beautiful."

Adam knew then that Gabriel loved her. Kassie was his sister and he too loved her dearly, but he would have described her as pleasantly appealing with an understated elegance; beautiful was not the first word that sprang to mind when he pictured her. As he forced himself to concentrate on what Gabriel was saying, Adam's outrage eased a little and he started to think there might be some hope for the pair.

Gabriel was still clarifying how they had met. "Maybe a year or so prior to this, I'd observed Kassie presenting on the Pantheon and none of Hardwick's aspersions applied to her — she was captivating. If I thought about it hard enough, I probably fell for her then, but didn't realise until much later."

Gabriel went onto explain how he'd knocked Kassie flying as he rushed out of the professor's office, then that he'd run into her again the next day.

"When I asked her about her studies, I worked out that she must have heard Hardwick's comments for she gave me short shrift." He grinned at the memory, as did Adam, knowing that Kassie was never backwards in coming forwards. "She didn't give me the chance to ask her about the units and stomped off in a bit of a huff. The next time I saw her was about two months ago, out at Ostia, when she was escorting a group of visitors. She told me she was working for Discover Antiquity — a tour agency — and an idea started to percolate, one that I'd had to put aside for two years.

"Tour groups?" queried Adam, suddenly having an inkling were this was going. Gabriel nodded.

"As luck would have it, I have several family and friends who spend much of the summer in Italy. It didn't take me long to contact them to find out whether they'd be interested in a three-week tour of ancient sites, in and around Rome as well as Pompeii and so forth." Adam nodded, his interested piqued.

"I told them that there was someone I wanted to come along as the tour guide, that she was someone I cared for, someone I really wanted to spend time with, away from our normal everyday lives to see whether she felt the connection too. There was no bet, all I'd said was that I hoped three weeks would be enough for her to know I was serious." Gabriel paused again and drew a deep breath, determined not to shirk his part in all this.

"It was all going well, the more time we spent together the harder I fell for her and it seemed she felt the same way. Then several things happened at once and I know I should have handled each one quite differently. Twenty-twenty hindsight is a wonderful thing isn't it?" his tones ironic. "First, I had a note from the university regarding three of my units that had somehow gone to hell in a hand basket. I could not in all conscience leave them to try and muddle through; they'd have made it worse. I had to help fix things up. Then Monique arrived and I really didn't need her coming. Anna, that's her grandmother, had mentioned she might join us, but I'd kinda hoped she'd forgotten. Monique's always been a bit of an imp, I don't think she's malicious, just thoughtless, but she went too far with this plan of Anna's."

Gabriel went on to explain about his mother's fall and that Monique had made it sound as though he'd been with her every evening, when in fact he'd been miles away at the family home.

"Yes, I know I should have told Kassie that I was having a drink with Monique, but it never occurred to me that it could be misinterpreted. To me, Monique is like a kid sister, I've never had a romantic thought about her. All we talked about was family gossip. Of course, I had no clue what Anna was hoping for, so that just went from bad to worse. Then I had to go help my mother, who'd had a fall. It all happened so quickly and since I'd anticipated being back that evening I didn't tell anyone what had happened. Didn't think it'd be necessary. Typically, I ended up having to stay 'til my Dad got home and by the time I got back to the hotel, I find that everything's gone pear-shaped and Kassie thinks I'm some tosser out to make her an object of ridicule. I know I screwed up over not calling her from Mum's but the thing is, I left her a letter telling her what had happened and that I'd had to go to help and presumed she would realise that I'd been held up. She mustn't have got it; can't work that out at all."

Gabriel stopped, obviously confused. Moreover, there was only so much he wanted to tell Kassie's brother, some of it was far too personal and was between Kassie and him. Despite this being a conversation he never thought he'd be having, Gabriel took a breath and laid it out for Adam.

"I love her Adam, I love her more than I can express in words and I need a chance to talk to her, to tell her what happened." Gabriel studied the impassive face of man sitting across from him as he spoke, thinking he discerned a slight softening of his scrutiny. Would he help?

"Let me think about it. Kassie is a wreck; she's not sleeping and she's barely eaten. She's taken an indefinite leave of absence from both of her jobs and did mention that she might leave Rome altogether. Something about libraries and archives; no clue what that's about, but maybe you have a better idea." Gabriel knew exactly what that meant, but didn't think it quite the right moment to explain it to Adam. He dragged his attention back to Kassie's brother who was still speaking. "I don't know whether you talking to her will make it worse or better. Give me your mobile number and I'll text you later."

The two men chatted for a little longer then Gabriel stood to leave, putting out his hand to shake Adam's in a gesture of appreciation. For a split second, Adam hesitated, then shook the proffered hand firmly, recognising that Gabriel was not the man Kassie believed him to be. Circumstances had conspired to create this debacle and although Gabriel should have handled some of it far better, his intentions were honourable and it was clear how much he loved Kassie. The man looked haggard, almost as haggard as Kassie did, about which Adam was secretly, very pleased.

As they parted it began to drizzle with rain, the sky had been clouding over while they'd been talking and the wind had picked up. Gabriel tucked up his collar and hurried away down the street and Adam went to see how Kassie was doing. His sister scarcely acknowledged his return; she certainly hadn't noticed that he'd been gone for over an hour and that he hadn't brought anything back with him. He made them a coffee and sat next to her on the sofa.

"Kassie sweetheart, have you had anything to eat yet today?" She shook her head.

"I can't face food, the thought of it turns my stomach." Her tones uninterested.

"You need to eat, Kass. How about I whip up a nice Spanish omelette? You know mine are the best in the world." He smiled at her persuasively and she acquiesced, responding with a hint of a smile. Adam banged about in the kitchen and soon the smell of frying onion, peppers, potatoes and carrots permeated the small flat. Kassie's stomach rumbled and she realised, with some surprise, that she was quite hungry. She couldn't remember when she had last eaten but then neither could she remember what day it was, so it might not have been that long ago. She knew she needed to pull herself together, but found she couldn't be bothered. Maybe tomorrow.

Kassie managed to eat a little, not nearly enough, but Adam forbore to comment. After lunch, she went back to her seat at the window, watching the rain, the grey of the afternoon suiting her mood. If she went outside she could cry and no one would know, and maybe the rain could wash away the pain. Adam mentioned that he was going to pack, as he was leaving the next day. That was weird, thought Kassie, that meant it was over a week since she'd last seen Gabriel and nearly that long since she'd left the tour group. It felt both fleeting and longer than several lifetimes.

Suddenly she felt constrained and needed to get out, to feel the rain on her face and the breeze in her hair.

"Adam!" she called through to the spare room. "I'm going for a walk, I won't be long."

"Give me five and I'll come with you," he replied, but when he came out of the bedroom, she was gone. "Bloody hell, Kass," he groused, "why'd'you go without me?" Nothing he could do, so he made another hot drink and opened his laptop to check for emails. There a few business ones, which required a response, as well as a lovely long one from his wife. After dealing with anything work related, he settled down to read and reply to his wife's news; then they began to chat online, Adam becoming so engrossed that he forgot all about his sister.

Meanwhile, Kassie had strolled down to her favourite building. She hoped it would make her feel better, lift her spirits as it always did. She stood within it's cool interior, willing the peace she craved, and usually found even amid a crowd, to descend on her. It was not to be. Not today. Her head was full of pictures and feelings and sounds and Gabriel.

She could not shut him out and, unbidden, little things about those last few days were starting to gnaw at her; things that now she thought about them, more or less objectively, didn't ring quite true. Even if Monique had been with him, why hadn't she, Kassie, seen or heard from him. Surely, if he'd been in the hotel she'd have spotted him, or the others would have done and he'd have replied to her texts and emails — wouldn't he? She frowned — and what about this bet? That seemed so out of character. What had Lillian said? — 'it wasn't like that,' so what was it like? What had Gabriel done or said that made Monique believe there was a bet? Kassie couldn't answer any of it. She would need to talk to Gabriel and she didn't think she could do that, not yet, maybe not ever and, at the end of the day did it really matter? It wouldn't change anything.

As she left the monument, Kassie scarcely noticed that the rain was coming down rather more heavily. She walked over to the steps of a building opposite the Pantheon. Undergoing renovation there was no chance that she would be in anyone's way so she could just watch the world go by undisturbed. Brushing a few leaves off the steps, she sat on the top one — the leaky porch overhead offering scant protection — leaned her head against the stone doorframe and let her mind wander.

Eighteen

Several hours later, a loud banging on the front door disturbed Adam. Glancing at his watch, he realised that it was after six and that as far as he knew Kassie hadn't come home. Odd! He opened the door to a drenched Gabriel, who was shaking the water of himself, much like a wet dog.

"Gabriel, what do you want? I haven't had a chance to speak to Kassie yet; she went out after lunch."

"And she's not come back yet? It's freezing outside; the wind is biting and its pelting down." Frowning.

"Oh, she'll have found herself a coffee shop to wait it out, don't worry about her" Adam waved his hand distractedly, wanting to go back to the online conversation he was still enjoying with his wife.

"Hang on," pulling his mobile out of his pocket, "let me see whether she'll answer her phone." Gabriel punched in Kassie's number and both were startled to hear her phone sing its chirpy little song from under a heap of papers on the table by the window. Gabriel walked over and lifted the pile, noticing as he did so, that it was his letters. There was her phone, lying next to her purse. "So, she's got no phone, no money and, knowing Kassie, no jacket. Where on earth would she go on a day like this?" Gabriel asked, troubled. Adam shrugged,

"No clue, but she'll be home soon, stop fussing. She's a big girl and I'm not her keeper." Even as he said this, Adam realised that under normal circumstances Kassie was very sensible about such things, but the circumstances were far from normal right now and any chance that she might be thinking straight was highly improbable.

"You do realise how awful it is out there?" Gabriel repeated, flicking through the letters, all still sealed. "She hasn't read any of my letters," he said pensively. "I thought she might have at least read them."

"Neither did she tear them up and throw them out, so it's not all bad. Give her time, Gabriel, she's barely clinging on to her sanity, reading them might well have pushed her right over the edge." Gabriel conceded Adam's point but it hurt just the same. Then, recognising that he was being more than little self-centred, headed back out.

"Okay, I'm going to look for her, you stay here and if she comes home, just send me a text so I know she's safe." Adam, who had no intention of going anywhere, nodded and went back to the computer, updating Julia on what had just happened and suffered his wife telling him off because he hadn't registered that his sister was still out.

Gabriel hurried along streets that were running with water, trying to imagine where Kassie might be. Glancing at his watch he saw that it was coming up to 6:30pm, most of the free sites would be closing soon and unless Kassie had some coins in her pocket, she wouldn't be able to buy a hot drink or get out of the rain. He had been walking for quite a while and was just passing the cat sanctuary when he remembered her love for the Pantheon. It would be open still; maybe she had taken shelter there.

He increased his pace and long strides saw him at the back of the immense monument in less than five minutes. He walked quickly around to the entrance and scanned the interior for any sign of Kassie. It was quiet; there were not too many people within, but no Kassie. He frowned, uncertain now. This had been his last possibility; if she wasn't here he had no idea where she might be.

He turned and let his eyes rove around the piazza in front of him and just as he was about to give up, a dark bundle caught his gaze; something against the doorway of a scaffolded building. More a shadow within a shadow, but it was out of place. Maybe it was just a bin bag, but Gabriel wasn't about to presume anything. Quickly, he walked over and saw that it wasn't a bin bag. A huddle of a person, soaked to the skin and fast asleep. It was Kassie.

His relief was so great, his legs went wobbly and he almost fell, rather than crouched, down in front of her.

"Kassie," he spoke in low tones not wanting to frighten her, "Kassie love, come on we need to get you home." She didn't respond. While he waited to see whether she would come round, he texted Adam to let him know, asking him to organise towels, blankets and, if he could find one, a hot water bottle. Kassie hadn't stirred. "Sweetheart, wake up." He took her hand in his, she was frozen. He shook her gently. She mumbled something and, shivering, pushed herself closer to the doorpost but didn't wake. "Kassie," he said, more forcefully, "Kassie, please you must wake up." He sat next to her and shifting her on the step, pulled her against him, placing his jacket around both of them so she would feel his body heat.

Kassie felt really peculiar. Her head felt as though it was full of cotton wool and her body didn't seem to be behaving properly. There was a weight over her shoulders that she tried to shrug to off, to no avail; she shrugged again and this time she felt a hand stroking down her arm. Panicking, she struggled, but the arm held her close to a body, a very warm and comforting body. Wait! A body! That couldn't be right, she'd been on her own. She felt a scream bubbling up.

"Let me go," was what she tried to say, fear coursing through her, but it sounded more like "Lermpho." Her chilled lips were unable to form the words.

"Kassie." The voice was smooth and rich, like dark chocolate, and so dearly familiar, that she knew she must be imagining things. Oh, dear lord, she was going mad. Awareness began to seep in, and she realised that she was very cold, well most of her was, her left side seemed slightly warmer, but she couldn't work out why. A light finger turned her head and she tried to open her eyes, but they were too heavy and she just wanted to sleep. "Kassie." She felt the word rumble through the body and it took her all her will power not to relax back against it. Forcing her eyes open, she blinked and her gaze collided with a pair of deep blue eyes, full of anxiety and if she was not mistaken love — she shuddered and blinked again, positive now that she was hallucinating.

"G-Gabriel?" Disbelief laced a voice, which squeaked her question several octaves higher than normal

"Yes love, I'm here and whether you like it or not, I don't think I'll ever be letting you out of my sight again." He stared down into her beautiful green eyes, seeing misery and pain and his heart clenched.

140

"Am I d-dreaming? H-how are you here? How d-did you know where I w-was?"

"No, you're not dreaming. I remembered that you said the Pantheon always helped you feel better, so I thought it worth try. Kassie, I'm so sorry I hurt you. Please believe me when I say that I love you with all my heart and when you're warm and dry, I'll tell you what happened."

Kassie watched his lips moving, but struggled to comprehend his words, everything was hazy.

"I-I th-think I'm c-cold."

"I know sweetheart, we need to get you home. If I help, do you think you can walk?" She shivered violently as she tried to stand, but her legs buckled and she dropped back on the step.

"G-give me a m-minute," she whispered, her teeth chattering. "M-my legs don't want to w-work. I m-might have been s-sitting for a little w-while." Understatement of the week, thought Gabriel, a 'little while' could well have been four or five hours.

"It's okay, love." He rubbed her legs vigorously, trying to get warmth into them, to get the blood circulating, but could see that Kassie was falling asleep again. With no other choices, he swung her up into his arms and began the walk back to her apartment.

"You c-can't carry me all the w-way," she stammered, her head falling against his shoulder.

"Watch me." He replied dropping a kiss on her head. She weighed nothing, despite her height — she was far too light. Damn it all, what had he done to her?

"I'm s-sure I c-can walk, l-let me walk," Kassie said, wriggling to get down.

"Hush," he admonished, settling her back into his arms. Duly chastised and completely befuddled, she hushed and snuggled her head under his chin. The rhythm of his stride lulled her back to sleep and she had no recollection of getting home, of being peeled out of her wet clothes, of being wrapped in huge fluffy towels and then, once dry, of being tucked into bed with a hot water bottle and covered with enough blankets to melt the ice caps.

While Gabriel dried himself off, he explained to Adam where he'd found her and that as far as he could tell she'd fallen asleep there, possibly, hours previously. Adam made a hot meal and although they would have preferred Kassie to have something too, she was too deeply asleep and they decided it was better to let her rest.

Gabriel refused to leave her and Adam had given up worrying about it. The pair were adults; they could sort it out. Gabriel's face when he carried Kassie in was enough to tell Adam that the man was devastated at the thought that his behaviour might have contributed to this.

Despite their quick actions, it became clear that Kassie had caught a chill. During the evening, her breathing became harsh and rasping and her cheeks were fiery red. She tossed and turned, shoving off the covers when she was suddenly hot, only to tremble with cold minutes later. Gabriel sat up with her for most of the night, talking to her quietly, making sure she didn't get overly warm or cold, keeping her fevered skin cool with a damp cloth.

Adam took over around dawn insisting that if Gabriel wanted to look after Kassie, he needed to get some rest too. Gabriel, however, did no such thing, merely rushed across the city to his own apartment to stuff an overnight bag with anything he might need. In the event, he managed a few hours of sleep, knowing that Adam had a midnight flight to catch, but by late morning, Gabriel had become concerned enough about Kassie to call in a favour from Jack Watson, a doctor friend he knew through the University, who agreed to call around during his lunch break. When he arrived, Kassie was restless and although couldn't wake up enough to talk to Jack, the doctor asked both men several pertinent questions and soon diagnosed what was wrong.

"Yes, Kassie's running a fever, Gabe, and no, this is not necessarily because she was cold and wet for a prolonged period. More like that if — as Adam says — she hasn't been sleeping or eating properly, her immune system is slightly compromised, leaving her vulnerable to infection. The drenching simply exacerbated it. Just keep her warm, hydrated and comfortable. Have you some menthol?" Adam said he thought they did, "it will alleviate her breathing, either rub it into her chest, or if it's in liquid form find a way to heat it, the scent will permeate the room and have the same effect. No need for antibiotics, regular painkillers will suffice if she needs them — paracetamol, or better still, something like Lemsip. You've got my mobile if you need it?" raising an eyebrow at his colleague. Gabriel nodded

"Thanks, Jack, I really appreciate you coming out."

"No problem, just look after the lass," he said, then, as Kassie started tossing again, "I'll leave you to it." Nodding at Adam who also thanked him, Jack disappeared down the stairs. Adam hunted about in the bathroom cabinet finding both the Lemsip and the menthol, while Gabriel boiled the kettle. Spotting an aroma oil burner with a tea light under it, Adam poured a few drops of the menthol into the diffuser and lit the candle. Almost instantly the scent drifted through the room and, after a few moments, Kassie's breathing seemed to ease. They managed to get her to sip nearly all the hot lemon drink and both men stationed themselves at either side of the bed until she settled.

"Thank you, Gabriel," Adam said quietly as they walked through to the small living room about an hour later. "I was going to change my flight, but I reckon you've got it covered. I think I can leave tonight knowing Kassie is in good hands." Gabriel smiled wearily.

"Thank you for trusting me with your sister, Adam. It means a lot," he replied

"Just make sure we're invited to the wedding," Adam grinned winking at Gabriel whose jaw dropped. "Well, you'd better make an honest woman of her or I'll be back to finish that thumping I believed you so richly deserved." Gabriel chuckled

"I promise," he said and the two shook hands. Adam went to finish his packing and Gabriel, to sit with Kassie. Adam left in the early evening, Kassie mumbled a goodbye to her brother, but neither man could be sure she was fully aware that he was leaving. Gabriel repeated the cycle of treatment; Lemsips, plenty of water, trying to get her to eat something —

anything, keeping the menthol going, and sitting by her bedside, holding her hand and talking to her.

Kassie, meanwhile, barely woke, unaware that in her fevered state everything that had happened, all her heartache and anguish, spilled out in garbled mutterings. With this and what Claire had told him, Gabriel managed to piece together much of the sorry tale, wishing he'd had the sense to realise that this might happen.

In between keeping an eye on Kassie and snatching the odd hour of sleep, Gabriel tried to distract himself by searching for her books online. Once he'd found them he downloaded the e-versions and began reading them while he watched over her. She was good, really good. All the stories were set in ancient Rome, gentle mysteries with a little romance on the side. Her characters were entertaining, the plots not too convoluted and the romance was sensuous without being gratuitous. If the reviews were anything to go by, Kassie had gained a solid following of readers and it wasn't hard to see why.

Gabriel gazed down at her flushed face, mulling over how she had changed his life. This woman who possessed his every thought. This woman who had enslaved him with her astonishing eyes and that glorious body. This woman whose humour, sincerity, perception and empathy not to mention her impromptu bouts of temper — no one wanted an angel — had stolen his heart. This woman who meant everything to him. God, he hoped she believed in second chances.

Nineteen

It was three very long days and nights before Kassie began to feel less wretched. She was aware that people were around her, but she couldn't wake up enough to ask what was going on. Her head seemed too heavy to lift off the pillow, her body ached and she was unutterably tired. Memories kept flitting in and out of her consciousness, but she couldn't hold onto them; they confused her and what she could recall was painful. Deciding that it was all way too hard she stopped trying, content to let oblivion swallow her, its darkness a balm to her weary soul.

Sometime during the afternoon, four days after Gabriel had carried her home, Kassie finally stirred. As she came to full wakefulness and tried to work out where she was, she realised that someone was holding her hand. Her movements disturbed whoever it was and a face swam across her vision.

"Kassie?" It was him. How was he here? Her brow creased as she tried to concentrate, but the cotton wool in her head was too thick. "Kassie, can you hear me?" She couldn't tell him; her voice wouldn't listen to instructions. She shook her head trying to banish the wooziness but that just made her feel dizzier.

"Can't." It was all she could force through dry lips. A gentle hand lifted her head and a glass was held to her mouth. Cool refreshing water slipped over her tongue and soothed a throat that seemed parched. She drank the whole glass and as he lowered her head back on the pillows she felt less disoriented. "What happened?" she croaked, trying to focus on him through bleary eyes.

"You fell asleep near the Pantheon and it was pouring with rain. You got soaked and the doctor said because you hadn't been sleeping or eating, you had nothing to fight off the chill."

"Where's Adam?"

"He had to go home, love."

"Oh." She felt a tear roll down her cheek. Adam had left her with Gabriel? She knew that was probably significant but her brain was so mushy that she was unable to pin down why.

"Why are you here? Where's Monique?" She stuttered a bit over this, feeling another tear follow the first one. No Kassie, she reprimanded herself, don't cry, you've cried enough and he doesn't deserve your tears.

"I'm here because you couldn't be left alone while you're so sick, and I have no idea where Monique is, nor do I care." Gabriel wiped her tears away with a soft handkerchief.

"Oh. Well, I'm better now and I don't want to keep you from your very important life, so you can go," she grumbled, somewhat ungraciously, hearing a chuckle rumble through his chest.

"If you insist; although I'm only going as far as the kitchen. I think a hot lemon drink is in order. As I imagine you can barely put one foot in front of the other, you may have to put up with me a little longer."

"Why?" A loaded question and one to which Kassie wasn't sure she wanted the answer, but the ache had returned, the other ache and he was too close. She could smell his aftershave; if she reached out she could touch his skin and it was torture. There was a long silence and she couldn't see him anymore, making her wonder whether she was still asleep and dreaming his presence or he'd left the room. "Gabriel?" she said, slightly panicked, her voice scratchy.

"I'm here, sweetheart."

"Please don't go." She knew she sounded pitiful, but she felt so ill, she didn't care.

"I'm not going anywhere, love, just rest. I'll be back in a minute with a hot drink." She relaxed and dozed again, waking a little while later when a large, cool hand cupped her cheek and his voice informed her that she should try to drink this hot lemon that he'd made for her. Obediently, she swallowed the mixture, it tasted weird, but that was the least of her worries. She still couldn't focus and it was frightening her.

"Why can't I see properly?" she beseeched him.

"No idea, here, let me wipe your face, maybe there's some gunk in your eyes from being asleep for so long." Mortified that he should see her like this, Kassie had no real option but to submit to his ministrations and as he wiped the cool washcloth over her face, her vision did start to clear.

"Thank you," she rasped, trying to push herself up on her pillows. Why was everything so damn difficult? Gabriel helped her, his strong arms surrounding her as he propped her up carefully.

"Better?" He smiled. She nodded.

"What day is it?" she whispered.

"Saturday." What? No way, that couldn't be right. She frowned in confusion, trying to figure out how she had missed so many days.

"I'm sorry, I can't work it all out, how can it be Saturday already?" Concentrating made her feel as though the room was spinning around her, so she gave up. Gabriel explained, again, about her falling ill and that she'd been in bed since Tuesday evening, four days ago, a little concerned that she didn't remember.

"Was it you who brought me home?" she asked, self-consciously. He nodded,

"I'll tell you all about it when you're feeling better. You seem to be having trouble remembering what happened." She stared at him and as he watched, she withdrew, her eyes losing what little light they had in them

"I haven't forgotten much," she said, her hoarse voice dead of any emotion.

"No, maybe not, but all is not as you assumed sweetheart and soon we will talk, but not yet, I don't think you can stay awake long enough." Gabriel's voice was tender and kind and she could feel tears threatening again. Why did he have to be so darned adorable? It wasn't fair. She blinked fiercely. "Hey, don't cry love, it's going to be okay."

"No, it isn't! How the hell can it be okay? You used me for a bet, you're about to become engaged to someone else and you went and made me fall in love with you." Kassie didn't care how that sounded, she would deny all knowledge when she felt better, but she couldn't help it. The words just wouldn't stay inside her. Gabriel chuckled softly. "Don't you dare laugh, don't you dare," she hissed, a cough building as she put too much strain on her vocal chords. Ignoring her protests, Gabriel lifted her against him, rubbing her back to try and soothe the cough before it broke, but it was too late, Kassie bent double with the bout and struggled to get air into her lungs. She was gasping, but every time she tried to breathe, it set her off again until she thought she might faint.

"H-help me," she wheezed, as spots appeared before her eyes.

"Just try to breathe more slowly, Kassie, I'm here, don't panic."

All right for you to say, she thought distractedly, you're not the one who can't breathe. Slowly the spell passed and she began to catch her breath. Gabriel continued to hold her, stroking his large hand up and down her back, it was so calming and she felt herself relaxing against him. No, this absolutely would not do. She tried to pull away, but he just held her more closely and as she didn't have the strength to fight, she stopped trying and suddenly, she fell asleep.

Gabriel held her until he was sure she'd settled properly before laying her gently back on the bed and tucking the covers around her. He ran his fingers through her very tousled hair, brushing the damp strands off her face and unable to stop himself leant in and kissed her lightly on her mouth. Even so brief a touch engendered a response and a quiver ran through her. She sighed his name, so quietly he wasn't certain she had spoken.

"Yes, love."

"Please don't leave me." Unconsciously, she reached for him and he took her hand in his and kissed her palm.

"Never." A hint of a smile twitched at the corner of her mouth and she snuggled further under the bedclothes, pulling him to her. Rather unsure what was going on, but willing to take anything she offered, Gabriel lowered himself gingerly onto the bed, nestling her against his huge frame and pulling the comforter over them both. Seemingly fast asleep, Kassie sighed and wrapped her arm over his stomach binding him to her. He kissed the top of her head and picking up his Kindle, was soon as lost in the world of ancient Rome as Kassie was in dreams.

Kassie slept for another few hours, waking to a darkened room, the only light a dim lamp on her bedside table. She was encased in bedclothes and Gabriel. He was sleeping and she was in his arms. Odd, how had that happened? She remembered something about him staying with her but thought she had dreamt it. Cautiously she turned in his embrace. He looked exhausted. How long had she been ill again? Frowning she tried to remember their earlier conversation but it kept skittering away from her, her head still too fuzzy to hold anything for long. It was very frustrating. She had so many questions, none of which she would likely remember the answers to, even if he told her. Damn it all.

That he was here with her must mean something, that Adam seemed to trust him, even more so. What had the two talked about? Adam had been so upset for her that whatever Gabriel had told him must have been compelling otherwise there was no way her brother would have left her with him. She gazed at his beloved face; noticing the dark circles under his closed eyes, his rigid jaw and that his hair, never particularly tidy, was now a complete mess. She could not help but tangle her fingers through its weight, needing to feel its dark silkiness.

As Kassie watched him, something shifted deep within her soul; her heart saw what her brother had seen. Gabriel loved her, whatever else was going on, Gabriel loved her. A bloom of joy spread through her and although she had no intention of letting him get away with whatever nonsense had been going on, she suddenly believed that her happily ever after was maybe not so implausible after all.

Gabriel's eyes flickered open, disconcerted by his surroundings, his head taking a while to catch up with what he was seeing. He was ensnared by a pair of inscrutable eyes staring at him from a head, tilted adorably to one side, the glow from the lamp reflecting fire into her fathomless green gaze and all he wanted was for those eyes to burn for him.

"Kassie?" he asked quietly. Kassie smiled gently and without pausing to question her motivation, slid up his body and kissed him softly on his cheek, then his nose, then his lips.

He shuddered and his breath caught. "Kassie?" he asked again, rather nonplussed.

"I just needed to kiss you," she murmured, "now go back to sleep."

Like there's any chance of that now, thought Gabriel. He shifted his position, so he could look at her properly. Eyes closed, breathing steady, she was smiling a secret smile and looked so beautiful that it took all his will power not to ravish her right there and then. Only that fact that she was obviously still so unwell stopped him.

"Oh God, Kassie, I don't think you have the slightest idea how much I love you," he whispered.

"I think I could take a wild guess." She surprised him with her hushed reply and, never opening her eyes, she moved back against him, her head coming to rest in the crook of his shoulder, as she pressed a kiss to the base of his neck. "Now, please go back to sleep." Gabriel felt mirth rumble through him and cradling her close, did as he was bid, the two of them soon far away in the land of nod.

Twenty

The next time Kassie awoke it was dawn and she was pleased to note that she didn't feel quite so rotten. It still hurt to breathe, but not as much and although she was still a bit shivery, her body didn't ache. She was desperate for a shower, she felt grotty and was certain that her hair must resemble a rat's nest. She noticed a glass full of water on the table by the side of the bed and leaning across she sipped it, the cool freshness easing her still sore throat.

Even so slight an action disturbed Gabriel, who was still lying next to her, his clothes rumpled almost beyond recognition. Kassie giggled at the state of him, murmuring that he looked as though he'd been dragged through a whole county of hedges backwards. He grinned back sleepily, but was too tired to reply and merely pulled her against him, curving her back against his chest. She fidgeted however, extracting herself from his hold.

"Gabriel, do you think I might be allowed to get up and take a shower? I'm all sticky and grimy, I promise I'll come straight back to bed." Gabriel lifted himself up on one elbow and twirled a very recalcitrant strand of hair through his fingers.

"Only, if you let me help."

"I'll manage, you don't need to fuss yourself."

Gabriel tutted, but all he said was, "All right, Miss Independence, have it your way, but don't say you weren't warned." Kassie scowled at him and swung her legs out of the bed, seeing that she was in her pyjamas. Who on earth had got her into them? She stole a glance at Gabriel who looked the picture of innocence, a clear indication that it had been him.

"Well, I didn't think Adam should do it, so that left me," he said by way of explanation. Kassie's cheeks flared with sudden heat and he chuckled quietly. "I was more concerned with getting you out of your wet clothes than being distracted by the delights of your body, but it was a close thing," he said, wickedly. Flustered, Kassie shot off the bed towards the bathroom, but in her haste, forgot that she was pathetically weak. She had only taken one stride, when her legs refused to support her and, if not for Gabriel's lightening reflexes, would have gone headlong on the floor.

Gabriel caught her and as he lifted her she was trembling and ridiculously close to tears — again. This would have to stop.

"S-sorry, I hate being so feeble," she stuttered, sniffling loudly.

"Hey it's okay, love. Stop apologising and listen to me next time. Now come on, let's get you sorted out." For all the world, as though this was quite normal, Gabriel carried her into the bathroom, setting her on her feet, turning on the shower, while she tried — without much success it must be admitted — to divest herself of her pyjamas. Grinning at her frustrated expression, he slipped her out of them, helping her into the shower, before removing his own clothes and following her in.

"Oh, my," she said, her legs going all wobbly again and this time it was nothing to do with having been unwell. It wasn't as though this was a new sight to her, but after everything that had happened, she was uncertain how to deal with it, especially as she had not expected to see him like this, or in any other way, ever again.

"Come on Kassie. Yes, I can think of nothing better than making love to you in the shower, but you aren't strong enough to stand, never mind engage in those sorts of antics." He winked and she chuckled at his mock salacious expression.

Starting with her hair, he gently massaged in the shampoo, holding her steady while she rinsed it out and then lathered up her shower scrunchie with the lightly scented gel, carefully sponging it over her, letting the powerful jets wash the suds off her body and away down the drain. The heady fragrance of coconut and frangipani swirled around the steamy room and Gabriel knew he needed to get Kassie out of the shower before his body took over from his mind.

For Kassie, to be pampered like this was wonderful, she felt cherished and cosseted, not to mention how sensual it was — her heart rate ratcheting up as Gabriel dried her off. What her head thought her capable of was one thing; her body, however, was a whole other matter and just as Gabriel was helping her into a clean pair of pyjamas, her legs gave out.

"Gabri…" she started to croak, but whatever else she was going to say was lost as, the room became distorted and she slithered to the floor. Gabriel lifted her gently off the tiles and carried her back to bed, kissing her on the cheek as he laid her on the sheets. Covering her up, he left her to sleep, going through the little flat and tidying up.

It was going to be a lovely day, Gabriel opened the balcony doors, breathing in the cool autumnal air, its crisp scent banishing the last of his fatigue. The sun was rising over the roofs of Rome, their colours morphing from soft greys to the warm mediterranean shades, so evocative of this vibrant city.

While Kassie slept on, Gabriel strolled down to the little shop along the street, buying the few essentials he had worked out that they would need. On his way back, he stopped at the café, standing at the counter to munch through two cornetti and gulp down a very strong espresso. Deciding Kassie might be persuaded into something tasty, he bought a crostata — the delicious breakfast tart — filled with sour cherry jam and after adding two take away coffees to his purchases, returned to the flat.

Emilia greeted him as he passed by her open doorway, anxious to hear how Kassie was doing, so he paused for a few minutes to give her an update. Once Emilia had realised what was going on, she had insisted on cooking mouth-watering soups for both Kassie and her very handsome young man, the latter of whom was most appreciative, the former, as yet had no idea, but Gabriel had at least managed to get her to swallow a few spoons full.

During the odd moments that Emilia and Gabriel had spoken, the elderly lady had talked a lot about Kassie, who had lived in the flat above since she'd arrived in Rome two years previously. It was obvious that the two shared a very caring friendship, both looking out for the other. Emilia had confided in Gabriel that she was glad Kassie had someone like him to take care of her as, in her opinion, Kassie needed to be loved. Gabriel had thanked her, confiding that if he had his way, he would be loving Kassie for the rest of his life. Emilia had been ecstatic, promising not to utter a word of his intentions, delighted that he entrusted her with such a secret!

They chatted for several minutes, but aware that the coffees were getting cold, Gabriel excused himself and was soon wafting one of the cups under Kassie's nose, the rich aroma tickling her senses as she slowly came awake.

"Is that coffee?" she asked sleepily. Gabriel nodded and helped her sit up, so she could drink it properly. "Oh, that is nectar," sighing with pleasure. Gabriel handed her a slice of crostata, which Kassie just nibbled at, until suddenly realised how hungry she was and devoured the rest, savouring the sweet crust and the tart jam. "Mmmm, delicious. Thank you. First time I've actual been able to taste anything in ages." Little realising she was giving away just how little she had eaten in the last week or so.

"Glad to be of service, hopefully you'll be able to manage some more at lunchtime." He grinned; pleased to see her colour was less hectic. She was still pale; that was to be expected, but the red flush had faded from her cheeks, which hopefully meant the fever had burnt itself out. "I was wondering whether you might like to get up for a bit, you could sit by the window, if you don't mind being wrapped up in a blanket or six."

"That sounds great, I'm totally fed up with being in bed." Gabriel laughed then; she looked so disgruntled.

"Sweetheart, as you've barely been conscious these last few days, I fail to see how you can be fed up with being in bed." She pointedly ignored that and fussed around trying to disentangle herself from the bedclothes. Gabriel helped her through into the main room as her legs still resembled jelly and settled her onto the large armchair, tucking a huge fluffy blanket around her. He lifted the cushions, so she could rest her head and then asked whether there was anything else she needed.

"No, I'm fine. Are you leaving?" She was worried, as Gabriel seemed to be gathering up his things.

"No, I'm just making a bit of space, so I can do some work. Do you mind me using your table?" She shook her head and he turned his attention to the papers on the desk, immersing himself in academia. Kassie enjoyed just being able to watch him, studying his hands as he jotted things down in a large notebook, her eyes drawn to the muscles flexing along his arms while he was typing. The way he ran his fingers through his hair — clearly an absent-minded gesture — but it was so endearing, especially as it was, once again, sticking out at crazy angles. She watched him for so long that she fell back to sleep, comfortable in the chair and secure in the knowledge that he was close.

Gabriel turned at one point to ask her something, smiling when he realised she was asleep. Her head was pillowed on her hand and her hair, rather more curly than usual, spilled over the arm of the chair; dark eyelashes described smutty curves on her pale cheeks and a slight smile hovered around her mouth. He didn't think he would ever tire of gazing at her; she took his breath away. Even though he knew that they were due a very awkward conversation soon, he believed that she had begun to trust him again — that had to count for something, and maybe he could rekindle the love he was certain he'd all but doused.

Sometime later, Kassie awoke, momentarily confused as to where she was, then realised it was her own living room. She had been dreaming that Gabriel was sitting at her desk working and was therefore not overly surprised to see that it was, in fact, no dream. Gabriel was still there, so completely engrossed in his work that he didn't even notice she had woken.

Content to remain where she was, Kassie, pulled the blanket back up over her shoulders and made herself a little more comfortable in the chair — well comfortable in a way that meant she could see him without twisting her neck. She also knew they had to talk, and she had a vague recollection that he had told her Monique was not and never had been, in his life, but the past few days were so muddled that she couldn't be sure what she had imagined and what was real. She presumed that if he did have someone else more important, he would not still be looking after her, Kassie Winters, in her poky little flat somewhere near the Spanish Steps.

As she observed him, she felt that familiar desire wash over her. She wanted him to hold her, to touch her, to kiss her. She wanted it so badly she was quite stunned that he couldn't hear her body yelling at him to stop what he was doing and make love to her. Her sensible side informed her, less than politely, that she was being ridiculous and was too unwell to indulge in such intimacies, while her sentimental side could not have cared less.

As though aware of her scrutiny, Gabriel turned, smiling a slow, sweet, smile when he saw her watching him, causing a soft pink blush to stain Kassie's cheeks. She lowered her eyes, feeling shy suddenly and heard a low chuckle. A hand stretched across and grasped hers, squeezing gently.

"How are you feeling, love?"

"Better. Well, not fantastic, it hurts to swallow but I don't ache quite as badly. My head still doesn't want to connect with the rest of me, though and I'm struggling to remember anything anybody tells me." Gabriel was concerned about her lack of ability to focus, but he had to hope it would come right as the infection lessened; he made a mental note to check with Jack, just to be on the safe side.

"Do you want something to eat? Emilia has made us some tasty looking soup."

"As long as I don't have to move," she assented. Gabriel went into the kitchen and turned on the heat under the pan, stirring the soup as it warmed through. It smelt delicious and Kassie ate a whole bowlful as well as a soft roll. That was all she could manage though and within minutes of finishing, the bowl still on her knee she dozed off. Gabriel sorted out the pots, leaving them in the sink to soak and went back to his work. Kassie slept the rest of the afternoon away, an indication that she was still far from well and by the middle of the evening she felt dreadful again.

"I think you should go back to bed sweetheart, you're done in," suggested Gabriel, noting that her face was flushed and her breathing had become raspy.

"Must I?" she grouched, frustrated with herself for being so weak. Gabriel persuaded her that she really must and after helping her through to the bedroom brought her a hot lemon drink, settling himself in the chair by her bed. As she sipped the soothing lemon, a thought came to her. "Have you been sleeping in that chair?" she questioned him, curiously. Gabriel nodded, but did not elaborate. "How many nights?" she pressed him.

"Except for last night, only four," he said, carelessly. Kassie gaped.

"'Only,' there's no 'only' about it! Four nights? You must be exhausted, that's crazy! You'll be as ill as me if you're not careful." Her croaky voice squeaking her consternation. Gabriel smiled,

"I'll be okay, I'm tough as old boots and I didn't want to leave you."

"I have a spare room, you could have slept there." Quite reasonably, she thought

"It was fine, Kassie, don't fret." She studied him, seeing shadows in his eyes, the weary cast to his face and wondered whether he'd had any sleep at all.

"How sick was I?" she asked quietly.

"You caught a nasty chill, but your temperature was rather too high and you had a few bouts of delirium. I wasn't comfortable leaving you, even for a short while," he replied in the same quiet tones as hers, but as she searched his face, she realised that he had been very worried.

"I would have been fine, Gabriel. You shouldn't put your own health at risk for me. You have a job and people who rely on you."

"There was no way on this earth that I could have left you, my job can manage without me. What kind of man do you think I am? How could I abandon you here when you couldn't even get out of bed? Especially as it's my fault you're so ill."

Twenty One

Gabriel's anguished words fell into an odd little silence. Elbows resting on his knees, he dropped his head into his hands, his demeanour the picture of dejection. Kassie didn't say anything, his claim not incorrect and it seemed as though he expected her to push him away. She contemplated him, she really wanted to get all this out in the open, but her head was still all over the place and she wasn't sure whether she would remember anything he told her. Reaching out, in much the same way as she had done the previous night, she grasped his hand.

"But you found me and you brought me home and you've been looking after me, with little care for yourself. That's the man I think — I trust — you to be, the man I fell in love with, he just got lost in the murk for a little while. I know there are things we need to talk about, but my brain is so scrambled that I doubt I'll manage to stay awake long enough to discuss this mess, never mind actually recall any of it." It was a huge effort to speak, her voice was hoarse and her chest felt as though there were bands tightening around it, but it had been worth it for the look on Gabriel's face when she told him she loved him.

"You still love me?"

"I never stopped loving you, Gabriel. If I had it wouldn't have hurt so much." She held his gaze and he leaned close, brushing her lips with his. "Please don't sleep in the chair again, I don't think I am capable of looking after you right now." She tried to admonish him, but her words sounded slurred. Gabriel could see that the hot drink was taking effect, her eyes were starting to glaze over and she was slipping down on her pillows. "You could sl…" the last part of her instruction lost as oblivion claimed her.

Resting the back of his hand on her forehead, Gabriel realised that she was too warm and worried that the fever was spiking again. Fetching a damp cloth, he cooled her head and hands, going to rinse it out several times before he felt that he'd managed to regulate her temperature. There was no way he was sleeping in the spare room if she was going to have another bad night. One more night in the chair wouldn't do him any harm.

Kassie's temperature fluctuated throughout the night and it was dawn before she fell into a more settled rest. Gabriel called Jack as soon as he deemed it acceptable, the doctor promising to call around during the day. Kassie never stirred, exhaustion still preventing her natural immunity from fighting the infection. This time, Jack prescribed some antibiotics, more to assuage the symptoms than the infection itself. Gabriel, worried about how weak she seemed and her inability to hold anything in her head, asked his friend whether Kassie should be in hospital. Jack said he didn't consider it necessary — they wouldn't do any more than Gabriel was doing, adding that her forgetfulness was likely the result of fatigue and that it should sort itself out as she began to recover.

It was one day shy of a week since Kassie had fallen ill and Gabriel's academic commitments resumed the following day. Luckily, the previous week had been student orientation and as his attendance had not been required, he had managed to complete any last-minute preparations while Kassie slept. The winter semester, however, had now begun in earnest and Gabriel delivered several lectures every week, Tuesday to Thursday. He was torn though, as it was clear that Kassie still needed him, or needed someone.

Then he remembered Claire and, keeping his fingers crossed, rang her asking whether she might be able to sit with Kassie while he was at work. Claire agreed readily; she and Harry spent a large part of their year in Rome and had a cosy little house just on the outskirts of the city. It was no hardship for her to come and watch over Kassie for the odd couple of hours here and there. Harry said he would accompany his wife, both glad of the chance to see their favourite tour guide again.

Thus, it was organised and a very relieved, Gabriel went back into the bedroom to check on Kassie. Her breathing was harsh and her colour higher than it should be, but he thought she would be okay while he went to get the prescription filled. He left a note on her bedside table, just in case she awoke, before hurrying along the street to the nearest pharmacy. She was still asleep when he returned, so he made himself a coffee and pottered about the flat, making sure it was tidy, opening the windows, letting the fresh air waft through the rooms, the sounds of the city — muffled at this distance — somehow restful.

Kassie finally awoke at lunchtime, asking whether she might get up. Gabriel was agreeable and, wrapped up in blankets, she managed to eat another bowl of Emilia's delicious soup, followed by her first dose of the antibiotics. Gabriel, made a cup of coffee for them both, then sat down to explain that he had to go back to work the next day, but that Claire would be here to look after her. He couldn't decide whether this news pleased her or not, she looked at him while he told her and then simply nodded, accepting that it was so. Gabriel frowned, Kassie was shrinking into herself again, and he couldn't work out why. He reached for her, but she shrugged him away and shuffled, blankets and all, back to her bedroom, needing to put some space between them.

Kassie heard Gabriel tell her about his job and that Claire and Harry would be coming to make sure she was okay, but she was too tired to process it properly and in her dazed state thought he meant that he wouldn't be coming back. Unexpectedly, she felt desolate; she didn't want him to go, but it was clear he couldn't stay, neither did she want him to see her being so pathetic so decided that the best course of action was to go back to bed. She was a grown woman; of course she could look after herself. She was quite capable most of the time and this chill should clear soon, but the thought of not seeing him every day made her want to cry and half way across the room, being wholly unable to stop herself, burst into tears.

Gabriel was there in an instant, cradling her to him while she sobbed, tears cascading down her cheeks like a spring deluge. All the pain, heartache and misery that she had tried to keep at bay over the past couple of weeks spilled over and she wept as though she might never stop.

"Hey love, what's all this about?" Gabriel's voice wrapped itself around her, warmer than the blankets she was muffled in.

"W-why a-are…I d-don't want…w-will you…I c-can't…l-leaving…" coherence, quite thoughtlessly, deserted her and Gabriel, utterly flabbergasted, had difficulty working out what she was stammering.

"Kassie, take a breath honey, you'll make yourself cough. I don't know what you're saying." He held her close, stroking his hand up and down her back, soothing her distress. Kassie rested against him, needing his strength, needing his touch.

"P-Please don't l-leave me," she whispered on a hiccup. He leaned away so he could see her face.

"I'm not going anywhere," he replied, clearly puzzled.

"Y-you said C-Claire is c-coming, th-that you have to g-go." Fresh tears threatened and despite a herculean attempt to stop them, they flooded out, her despair a tangible thing. "S-sorry, useless, i-ignore me." Gabriel ran her tangled words though his head, trying to figure out why she was so upset. Suddenly he understood.

"You think I'm going away for good?"

She stared at him, still hiccuping from the bout, eyes shimmering with more tears, some of which escaped, trailing down cheeks flaring red from the fever that was making her so muddled. Slowly she nodded, pressing her trembling lips together trying to swallow her sobs.

"Kassie, sweetheart, I'm only going to be out for a couple of hours each day. I have to teach class."

She drew a shuddering breath. "Oh," and, feeling a prize idiot for not understanding, burst into tears again. Good grief, Kassie, she thought hazily, you'll need a mop and bucket soon. She felt mirth rumble through Gabriel's chest.

"Oh dear, you are in pickle aren't you," he said, amusement in his voice.

"I told you not to laugh at me," she ground out in fierce tones, which had no effect whatsoever, merely making him chuckle even more.

"Oh, Kassie my darling girl, it's a good job you've got me, I'm not sure anyone else would appreciate the way your mind works."

"H-Have I got you?" she asked, desperately needing his reassurance.

"Always and forever," came the simple and heartfelt reply, which of course, set her off one more time. "Come on love, you have to stop crying, you'll give yourself the worst headache." Gabriel sat down on the sofa, lifting her onto his knee and snuggling her into his arms. She nestled her head against his shoulder and, by dint of drawing several deep breaths, began to calm down, slowly regaining her composure.

"I'm sorry, Gabriel," she said sometime later, "I don't know what's wrong with me. I'm not usually such a cry baby."

"Don't apologise, sweetheart. You have been through the wringer this last couple of weeks and I think your head is still rather befuddled. So, to clarify; I have to go back to work tomorrow, but I'll only be out a few hours each day for the next three days. Claire and Harry will be here to look after you while I'm out and I'll be home by mid-afternoon. I have Fridays and Mondays off, but may need to do some prep work. If it is acceptable to you, I would very much like to stay here until I'm sure you are completely better. After that we'll revisit our discussion about where we're going to live, but not right now, you're not well enough to concentrate on such things. Okay?"

As he finished speaking, Kassie twisted in his arms so she could look into his face. He stroked a cool finger along her hot cheek and down her jaw line, tracing a path to the hollow at the base of her throat. Her pulse fluttered under his touch and her breathing, already unsteady, went haywire.

"O-okay," she whispered, staring into his eyes, hypnotised by their cobalt brilliance. "Maybe I should go back to bed, I can't seem to think straight and I'm of no use to you." Gabriel didn't answer, transfixed by her gaze, his whole body crying out for hers. "Gabriel…?" she asked.

"Mmmmm."

"Did you hear me?"

"Mmmmm. You are never of no use to me." He bent his lips to hers, barely touching them, then he kissed away her tears and kissed her damp eyes and kissed her nose, before returning to her lips, those lips that he could kiss until the end of time. Mindful that she was far from well, he stole one more, very fervent kiss, eliciting a moan from Kassie that sent ripples of desire right through to his toes.

He lifted his head and their eyes locked. Kassie's heart tripped as she cupped Gabriel's face in one hand, smoothing her thumb over his bottom lip, her fingers stroking up into his unruly hair, never relinquishing his gaze. The blanket fell away and Gabriel trailed his hand down her spine, skimming the bare flesh at her waist, making her quiver with pleasure, while at the same time he entwined his other hand through her hair, gently bringing her face back to his.

"Oh God, Kassie," he breathed. It was like a prayer, his words a supplication, his petition piercing her soul and she knew that she needed to convince him, that he needed to know. She thought she had told him the previous evening, but she still struggled to recall what was real and what she had dreamt.

"I love you, Gabriel," she sighed. "Whatever else happens, whatever else we have to deal with, I love you and will do so throughout this life and into the next." Gabriel paused in his delectable quest and stared at her, as though unsure that he had heard her correctly. She smiled slowly, willing him to believe and his whole countenance changed. "I thought I told you so last night, but maybe I imagined it." A frown creased her brow, her concentration slipping again, although right at this moment it had nothing to do with being unwell.

"You did, but your conversations have been somewhat garbled and I didn't dare to hope," he said, drawing her back to him, nuzzling her neck, his lips catching the sensitive skin below her earlobe.

"I really want you to make love to me, but I don't think I have the strength quite yet," she whispered. Gabriel bit his lip — she had turned the understatement into an art form. "If you wouldn't mind though, I'd quite like to take a little longer exploring this whole kissing business."

Gabriel chuckled.

"Mind? Now why on earth do you think I would mind? I do think you might be pushing your luck though, you seem rather woozy."

Before she could reply, he kissed her again, letting the passion build, his hands roving over her slender body, caressing, teasing and tantalising until she was whimpering his name. Kassie wriggled against him, pushing her fingers under his shirt, seeking out his muscles, feeling them tremble. Gabriel's breathing hitched and heat scorched along his body at her touch. Kassie could feel the erratic beat of Gabriel's heart and revelled in the knowledge that it was she who inspired such a response, one that her own heart echoed.

Despite, however, the most ardent of intentions, Kassie was still fighting a nasty infection. One minute she was quite certain she was capable of seducing Gabriel, the next everything went askew. Her head seemed to be disconnecting itself from her body and her limbs felt weightless. Determined to cling onto consciousness, she gripped Gabriel's arms, feeling herself drifting away.

"Gabriel, ugh…head float…" with a long shuddering breath, she crumpled against him, head lolling on his shoulder and would have slipped to the floor, had not Gabriel been holding her firmly.

"Come on, Kassandra Winters," he said, a hint of mirth in his tones, "what did I tell you?" He carried her though to the bedroom, laying her gently against the pillows and, covering her up, made sure she was settled. Then he went through to the kitchen to boil the kettle for a hot drink and, once his heart had resumed its normal steady rhythm, spent the remainder of the afternoon and evening making sure everything was prepared for his first few lectures. Much later, after he'd eaten dinner, after he'd managed to wake Kassie enough to take her evening tablet, after he'd somehow got her to drink another Lemsip and after he'd tidied the already tidy flat, he went to bed.

Tonight, he would sleep next to her, needing her in his arms as much as she seemingly desired to be there. Slipping out of most of his clothes, he climbed in beside her, drawing up the covers and turning her so that her back was against his chest. Unconsciously, she moved against him, moulding herself to his shape and sliding one leg over his.

Gabriel smiled his sweet smile and whispered, "Sleep well, my Kassandra." Within seconds he had joined her in slumber.

Twenty Two

Kassie disturbed Gabriel several times during the night but would never recall doing so. Her temperature flared, making her fretful, causing Gabriel to repeat his actions of previous nights; cooling her body with a damp cloth, encouraging her to sip a little chilled water and, in the early hours, persuaded her to drink another Lemsip. This seemed to work better than anything, as shortly thereafter she had settled into a deeper sleep than she had managed so far.

Concerned that the warmth of his body was exacerbating her temperature, Gabriel decided it would be better if he slept in the spare room, leaving the doors ajar, so he would hear should she need him. When his alarm went off at 7am — he had to be at the university by 9:30am, to set up for his lecture — it felt as though he'd only just shut his eyes. Thankfully, a hot shower and two cups of strong coffee went a long way to clearing his grogginess.

Kassie slept on and, knowing she really needed to rest, Gabriel was unwilling to wake her. He ran, what was becoming a very practised eye over her features; her sooty lashes grazing the soft skin of her still red cheeks, her hair — once more completely dishevelled — splayed across the pillow. She was lying on her side, one arm over the top of the bedclothes and if he wasn't mistaken, one foot peeked out from under the comforter. Her breathing seemed less constrained this morning, for which Gabriel was grateful. Hopefully the antibiotics were starting to do their job.

He ate a good breakfast, not worrying about making a packed lunch; he would buy something at uni. Promptly at nine, Claire and Harry arrived, escorted upstairs by the ever-faithful Emilia, who promised to bring up an Italian stew later. Gabriel thanked her appreciatively and then led his friends into the flat.

"Thank you for doing this, she's still no-where near well enough to be on her own," Gabriel explained, checking to make sure he had everything. Claire assured him it was no problem and, after showing them where everything was and pointing out the café along the street, Gabriel went to see whether Kassie had woken. She looked to be fast asleep, but as he brushed her cheek with his fingers, she opened her eyes and smiled, making his heart do a weird jolt.

"Are you going?" she asked, drowsily, grasping his hand.

"I am just about to. Claire and Harry are here and I'll be back this afternoon. Will you be okay?" She nodded, pulling him close for a brief kiss.

"Thank you."

"What for?"

"Everything." Sleep reclaimed her almost before she had finished speaking. Gabriel smiled down at her and kissed the palm of her hand, tucking it back under the covers.

"Anytime love, anytime." He left her to sleep and thanking Claire and Harry once again, hurried out in to the cool morning.

It was nearly lunchtime before Kassie woke again, but she felt less feverish than she had the previous day. After freshening up in the bathroom, she wrapped herself in one of the blankets and traipsed though to the living area, spotting Claire and Harry sitting on the balcony with a coffee.

"Hi," she greeted them, shyly, memories of her last conversation with Claire leaping into her head.

"Kassie, hello dear. It's lovely to see you, I'm just sorry you are so unwell." Claire sprang up from her chair and came over enveloping the young woman in a warm hug. Harry followed suit and after a moment of awkwardness, the three relaxed into easy conversation, well Claire and Harry chatted, Kassie mostly just listened, her ability to focus for any length of time still lacking. A little later, Claire made them lunch and reminded Kassie — who had forgotten — to take her medication.

The afternoon was mild and despite the older couple's concern that she shouldn't be outside, Kassie preferred to sit on the balcony, enjoying the feel of the fresh air on her skin. Claire did insist on bundling several blankets around her so there was absolutely no risk of her charge getting cold.

"Thank you so much for looking after me. I'm sure I'd be alright on my own, but Gabriel seems a bit worried that I'll do something silly if there's no one to keep an eye on me."

"It's our pleasure Kassie, don't think we mind this one bit. I'm really happy that we get to see you again, I wasn't sure we would after what had happened the last time we spoke," Claire said smiling cheerfully. Kassie flushed,

"I'm sorry I was so abrupt that day, Claire, everything just kind of got on top of me."

"No, you weren't, you were altogether polite even though you were distressed. I'm just glad you and Gabriel have sorted it out.

"We…ll," she said drawing out the word, "it's not really sorted out yet, but I hope it will be soon. I-I…we haven't…since I caught this chill, I can't seem to concentrate for very long and just when I think we might be able to talk, I fall asleep." She shrugged diffidently. "Poor Gabriel, I'm such a bother, especially now he's back at uni." Claire frowned at this; Kassie still didn't seem to think she was worthy of Gabriel's attention. It was as though she was giving him an out, an out that Claire knew Gabriel did not want. It was most peculiar.

"Kassie, you need to understand that you are not and never have been a bother, at least not in the way you're thinking. That you have turned Gabriel's nicely ordered life on its head is a whole other matter and for that we are profoundly grateful." Kassie stared at Claire in puzzlement. The older woman clarified. "Firstly, you need to know that we, that all of us on the tour, have known Gabriel for years, since he was a child."

Unbidden, an image rose in Kassie's mind of Gabriel as a boy, making her smile. Before she became completely distracted, however, she dragged her fickle head back to what Claire was saying.

"We had long given up on him ever falling in love with someone, he's only had one or two short-term relationships and the occasional date. It was always too hard; his work used to take him all over the world, often for long stints and most women aren't prepared to put up with that. He's more settled here and he said that the contract at the university is likely to be extended. He first mentioned you a couple of years ago, this girl he'd met in England, but then nothing and we all forgot about it. Suddenly your name came up again in conjunction with this tour. That's when we knew he was serious." Kassie's ears pricked up, the tour; this was where she would hear about the bet, the mere thought of which continued to upset her. She vaguely recalled Gabriel telling her there was no bet, but it still rankled.

Taking a gamble, she said, "Claire, I know both you and Harry are probably sworn to secrecy over this tour, but please could you tell me. I want to know how Monique came to believe that Gabriel had made some kind of bet."

Her entreaty tugged at Claire and, surreptitiously, she glanced at Harry who mulled over Kassie's request for a moment.

"It's time she was told, Claire, I expect Gabriel will explain anyway, but you can give Kassie our perspective too." Harry smiled at Kassie, leaning over to pat her hand. "I think this might help." Kassie beamed at him and suddenly there was a hint of the old Kassie, the bright vivacious young woman who had enthralled them with her knowledge of and love for ancient Rome.

"Before you start, though, I must warn you there's a decent likelihood I'll either fall asleep during this, or forget what you say, so you'll probably need to tell me again. For some reason, I can't seem to hold onto information. Gabriel's Jack thinks it'll sort itself out, I don't share his faith, but we'll see." Kassie advised them, humour lacing her tones.

"Fair enough." Claire grinned. "So, what would it be Harry?" she asked turning to her husband, "Maybe six, seven weeks ago, maybe a bit longer?" Harry nodded. "Gabriel approached us about a tour he was hoping to organise; one which would take in the sites around the city, but would also go out to Pompeii and so forth. Harry and I have been on a few of Gabriel's other ancient tours and they are excellent. He usually only allows about ten or a dozen at the most, that way he doesn't need any extra guides. He told us that if he could manage it, this tour would require an assistant.

"If he could manage it, what did he mean by that?" Kassie asked curiously.

"Well, isn't it obvious? He wanted enough people on the tour so hiring an assistant would not seem out of the ordinary. That assistant would be you dear." Kassie stared at Claire, nonplussed.

"This was…the whole thing, *everything* was deliberate?" Claire and Harry nodded. "B-but, how did he know I would come?"

"He didn't, but he said he remembered you doing a presentation or something while you were at uni and you really knew your stuff." Kassie flushed bright pink, recalling that horrible day. "He just hoped he could persuade you, that the sites we'd be visiting would pique your interest, oh, and he'd had a brochure made up so you would know it was legitimate, that he wasn't some oddball weirdo." That made Kassie giggle, imagining Gabriel wearing a dirty old mac and carrying a map of Pompeii.

"He kept appearing on the days I was in charge of tours, he said it was because he wanted to see how I handled the different types of questions, whether I actually knew my stuff or had just learned the patter and whether I had the patience to look after an older group. Oh sorry, that's not to say you're old…rather…it's just…I mean…" Kassie clammed up, embarrassed.

"I know what you mean, Kassie, stop fretting," Claire reassured her. "Anyway, he told us you'd agreed to his proposition and then three or four weeks later the tour began and we met you." Claire leaned back, regarding Kassie, wondering just how much she should share. "I knew, that first day, I knew, exactly why Gabriel had fallen in love with you. You shone with enthusiasm; you cared about a group of people you'd never met, dealing with all those intrusive questions about your personal life. You do know we were sussing you out don't you?" Kassie gaped.

"No! I thought you were just very nos…inquisitive." She paused. "Wait, Gabriel was already in love with me…no way that can't be right. He barely knew me, he still barely knows me."

"Well, all I can say is that you must leave a very lasting first impression, because when he discussed the possibility of a tour with us, he told us that there was a certain young lady, one whom he had only spoken to couple of times, but who he wanted to include as the assistant. Gabriel doesn't do things like that; he doesn't pick random people to be part of his tours. He only choses those he trusts. More than that, he said that he really hoped you wanted to be involved, as the twice you had met had been under less than auspicious circumstances and he needed a chance to show you how he felt. It was so unlike him but the more he talked about you the more clear it became that he'd already decided you were the only woman for him." Kassie gulped, pesky tears threatening again. She clamped her jaw together, absolutely refusing to cry, she was worse than a flipping waterfall in flood at the moment.

"I'm sorry, I still don't understand. If this was what he wanted, how did it become twisted into being about a bet that he could seduce me?" She paused, seeing the bewildered expressions on the faces of both Claire and Harry, realising that she needed to explain. "I guess, it's just that I find it hard to believe that he cares for me anyway. I have no idea what he sees in me. Okay, so I might know a bit about Ancient Rome, but that's not enough is it? I don't do well in crowds and I know I'm overly shy. I'm under no illusion about my looks. I'm quite plain you know and bit too tall and, try as I might, I'll never be fashionably thin — I like my food and if that makes me…errr…curvy, then so be it. I'm not about to become a stick insect to fit anyone's ideal image of how a woman should look."

Claire and Harry were looking even more confused.

"Don't you get it? I'm not much of a catch at all. So, when I heard Monique say he'd wagered that he could seduce me, it seemed to fit. What a fun challenge — to find the last person anyone would ever expect you to be with, oh and quite fortuitously here we have an ordinary, naive, reticent and obviously gullible young woman, she'll do. Next, go out of your way to make her feel as though she's the most beautiful woman on the planet and then not only do you manage to seduce her, there's a bonus — bang she falls in love with you — bet won!"

Kassie was trembling, weariness and the emotional fallout from remembering that afternoon overtaking her. "You have no idea how much that hurt," she whispered, "I gave him everything and I mean everything, and then I hear that it was all a joke, that he didn't care for me at all."

"But Kassie, you know that Monique got it wrong don't you? There was never any bet! All Gabriel wanted was for three weeks with you, without all the other commitments that might prevent you from spending quality time together. He wanted to prove to you how much he loves you, hoping that you might just fall in love with him." Claire tried to persuade Kassie.

"I know! In my heart, I know that he loves me and I love him more than I ever believed I could love anyone. The thought of him not being in my life was what made me so ill, but I can't seem to shake my unease. I'm afraid to trust him. Half the reason I got sick was because I hadn't been able to sleep or eat since the day Monique joined us, then I was stupid enough to get soaked last Tuesday. In all honesty, I don't think I cared whether I lived or died at that point. I know that's cowardly and over-dramatic and, as a woman I should not be defined by a man, but I had begun to trust in us. Finally, it seemed that someone truly cared for me and that to him I was beautiful…to him I was beautiful…"

Kassie's voice trailed off, realising that, once again, she couldn't think straight. Her head was pounding, her chest ached and she felt most peculiar.

"I'm sorry, maybe we could talk about this again tomorrow." She stood, swaying, as the floor seemed to be sliding away from her. "Oh, what's happened to the floor? I-I really don't feel very w…" and Gabriel walked into the flat just in time to see Harry catch Kassie as she slumped onto the rug.

Twenty Three

Gabriel took over, as being much taller than Harry, it was easier for him to carry Kassie through to the bedroom. Her skin had taken on a greyish pallor, she was clammy and her heart was beating too fast. Praying that she'd just overdone it, Gabriel made sure she was properly tucked in, waiting until her pulse and breathing settled before going back into the main room.

"Okay, what was that all about?" Gabriel asked, somewhat shaken. Claire told him what they'd been discussing.

"I know you didn't want Kassie to find out about your plan, but I, we — Harry and I — thought it preferable for her to learn the truth from us than go on worrying about this so-called bet. It's still bothering her you know, Gabe."

"I know, I know, but she's been so out of it and then when she's awake, her head is totally muddled. She keeps misunderstanding things, as though whatever we say ends up all jumbled when it gets to her brain," Gabriel said, clearly perturbed. "Jack assures me it's temporary and when the infection clears she'll be back to normal. It is worrying though. When I told her that you were coming to sit with her while I was at uni, she thought I meant I was leaving her for good. Mind you the fact that she was really upset gave me some hope!" He smiled ruefully at his two friends and thanked them for their kindness.

"It's nothing, Gabe, honestly! Kassie is delightful, a little bewildered right now, but just be patient. She loves you as much as you love her, everything else is just incidental. Now," she continued changing the subject completely, "Harry and I are going — same time tomorrow?" she confirmed, raising a questioning eyebrow. Gabriel nodded and walked with them down to the main entrance. Claire gave him a quick hug "She'll come good," she whispered as she dropped a motherly kiss on his cheek. "See you tomorrow."

They waved as they strolled off down the street, hand in hand. Gabriel watched until they were out of sight then he climbed the stairs back to the flat. Emilia followed him about ten minutes later bringing with her the promised stew. Gabriel was very touched and even though he told her that he could manage, the elderly lady shook her head

"Not until my Kassie is better, you don't worry your head." She patted his cheek. Gabriel gave her a quick hug and although she flapped him away, he noticed a smile curve her lips as she shuffled back down the stairs. Grinning, he closed and latched the front door and went to check on Kassie.

She was still asleep, but he didn't think she was any worse than she'd been that morning. Her cheeks were no longer waxy grey, now a much healthier pale pink and, thankfully, not the bright red they had been. She was warmer than he would have liked, but not overly so. He just had to hope that her funny turn was because she'd been out of bed for too long. He sat with her for a little while but she showed no signs of waking, so he went through to the kitchen, spooning out some of the steaming stew into a bowl and devouring it; it was so delicious that he went back for seconds. Then, checking his schedule for the next day ensured all his notes were prepared. Satisfied that he'd done all he could he closed and locked the balcony doors, sorted out the kitchen and main room and went back into Kassie's bedroom with a cup of tea.

Picking up his Kindle he was soon engrossed in the deeds of Laurentius, Kassie's ancient detective and his sometime assistant Mariana. He had been reading for a good hour when something made him glance across at Kassie. She was awake and regarding him with an enigmatic expression, he risked a smile, not sure how she would react after Claire's revelations of earlier.

Kassie, who had been awake for a little while, was enjoying being able to observe Gabriel unnoticed, studying his features in the soft lamplight. Her head was swimming slightly but at least she could remember the conversation she'd had with Claire and Harry. One thing was certain, Gabriel and she had to clear the air as there were way too many threads dangling, some of which threatened to become rather large knots.

As she gazed at him, she felt that warmth coil through her, like wisps of smoke from a dying autumn bonfire, cobweb fine but under the right conditions, powerful enough to spark a new blaze. He must have sensed her watching for he turned and smiled, but guardedly making him seem vulnerable and exposed, as though he still feared that she might push him away. Little did he realise that she was incapable of letting him go.

"Time for your tablet, love," he said after several moments of silence, his quiet words breaking the mood. "Would you like a Lemsip too?" She nodded, pushing herself up on the pillows so she would be more comfortable. Gabriel disappeared through to the kitchen and she could hear the kettle boiling and the banging of cups, the noise making her smile. They were the sounds of domesticity and homeliness and they were sounds that she yearned to hear every day. Gabriel reappeared with a tray on which were two large mugs of steaming liquid, a fresh glass of cold water and a bowl of something that smelled heavenly. He placed them on the floor, lifting the bowl first.

"Emilia made this, I had some earlier and thought you might be hungry." A low growl emanating from Kassie's stomach answered that question, drawing a chuckle from Gabriel, who held the bowl while she ate. She managed to finish the whole lot as well as the roll that accompanied it.

"Oh, that was scrummy, I didn't think I was at all hungry until I smelled it. Emilia is a culinary genius. Thank you." She grinned up at him, her eyes twinkling impishly. He grinned back, handing her the glass of water and a tablet, which she dutifully swallowed, putting the glass on the bedside table. Finally, he passed her the hot lemon drink, the sharp citrusy aroma clearing her fuzziness somewhat.

"How do you feel?" Gabriel asked when they were both sipping their drinks. Kassie considered his question.

"Not too bad. My head is still a bit weird, sort of floaty, but it isn't pounding like it was earlier and my chest still aches. I'm sick of feeling like this, I beginning to think I'll never get better."

Gabriel chuckled, "It's only been a week, love and I think you might have turned the corner; after your funny turn this afternoon your temperature didn't spike. You did look a bit ghastly for a while, but I think it was more a faint than a collapse."

Kassie frowned at him. "What faint?"

"You don't remember?"

She thought back, recalling the conversation about Gabriel and why he'd chosen her for the tour, then remembered feeling a bit odd, then nothing until about half an hour ago. She shook her head, frustrated.

"No. Claire was telling me about the tour and why you wanted me along and I think I pointed out why a wager seemed to fit." Not noticing Gabriel's look of sympathetic concern, she carried on. "Then I was gabbling on about not sleeping and getting soaked and that I hadn't really cared whether I li…" she stopped speaking, remembering the direction of that conversation.

"Don't worry about it, sweetheart, we'll revisit it tomorrow. I walked in to see you slithering onto the floor, but I think it was more because you'd been up for quite a long time and maybe the discussion you had with Claire upset you." Gabriel said. Kassie stared at him dubiously, fingers clutching at the bedclothes, twisting them in her agitation.

"Gabriel, we have to talk about it. I know it will be difficult, for both of us, but it's lurking at the back of my mind and no matter what I tell myself, it just won't bugger off. I need to hear it from you." Kassie reached for his hand as she spoke, interlacing her fingers with his, feeling the pressure of his thumb on her palm. He nodded in agreement.

"I know, love, but you've been so muddled, that I didn't want to talk about it until you were better able to concentrate. I don't want to you to misunderstand anything, it's too important."

"I think I have a better idea after today, but you're right, I'm too tired now, what time do you have to leave tomorrow?"

"Same as today, 9ish, but I only have one lecture, no tutorials, so I should be home just after midday. How about I bring us something to eat and maybe, if it's not too cold, we could sit on the balcony and chat."

"That sounds lovely." Kassie smiled. Gabriel asked whether she'd like another hot drink, which she didn't but he went to make himself one and Kassie took the opportunity to use the bathroom, but by the time Gabriel returned with his cup of tea, she was back under the covers.

Before he could sit down, she reached for his hand and drew him close.

"Now, before all the medication that's in my system takes effect, please would you do me a favour?" Gabriel raised an eyebrow, placing his cup on the bedside table. "Kiss me." He smiled then; his slow sweet smile and Kassie felt her heart thrill in response.

"It would be my absolute pleasure," he murmured. She pulled him onto the bed and as he lay next to her, he wrapped her in his arms, slanting his lips over hers, kissing her until she was gasping. Tangling his fingers through her hair, he cupped her head; scattering butterfly kisses over her eyes and cheeks, making her tremble. At the same time, Kassie's hands found their way under his shirt, undoing the buttons, tracing his muscles, loving the feel of his skin under hers as she wound herself around him, her long limbs securing him to her.

"Kassie," he growled, his voice darkly intense, feeling infinitesimal pulses of electricity crackling between them, turbulent heat prickling right through his body. His hand skimmed under her pyjama top, fingers lightly stroking her creamy skin even as he strove to maintain control. Kassie ignored him, reclaiming his lips and kissing him until he thought the world had stopped spinning. As ever, she ignited in him a wild hunger and he knew he had to be careful or it would run away with him.

"Kassie," he tried again, breaking their kiss, seeing the same desire in her eyes he knew must be in his. "Hell, Kassie, you fainted this afternoon, I…urghhhhh…" as Kassie's inquisitive fingers slid under his jeans, threatening to send him past the point of no return. He grasped her hand, his body shuddering with need, his lips seeking hers, his tongue tasting her velvety mouth, drawing from her an almost primal cry. Dragging air into his lungs, he shifted so she was under him, raising himself over her. She gazed up at him, her incredible eyes enticing him, her hands resuming their intricate pattern across his flesh. She lifted towards him, long hair flowing around her like molten caramel, her lips brushing his chest, cool on his fevered skin.

"Dammit woman, you'll be the death of me." He rolled her over, so they were facing each other, hearing a distinct chuckle as Kassie slid against him.

"I know, but what an enjoyable way to go." She smiled, running one hand through his hair, trailing a finger over his ear and down his throat, resting on the pulse in his neck, while the other crept around his back, delicate fingers stroking languorously up and down his spine from his shoulders to the top of his jeans. He laughed; he couldn't help it. She was such a paradox, demure introvert one minute, provocative siren the next — a puzzle for sure, but one he delighted in solving.

"Come on love." He drew a ragged breath. "Much as I cannot think of anything I'd rather do than make love to you until you beg me for mercy, I think we need to use a bit of common sense. If you promise not to ravish me, however…" he paused while Kassie spluttered her indignation, "…maybe I could share your bed tonight." He winked at her. Kassie punched him in the shoulder. "Hey, no need for violence, you're supposed to be an invalid."

Kassie glared at him, to no discernible effect and then realised she was very tired, evidenced by the huge yawn that suddenly overtook her and the drooping of her eyes.

"Okay, if you must, but to be clear, I'm only allowing this because I might relapse in the night." Her words were languid and as slumber claimed her she moved against him, nestling her head into the crook of his neck. "Just hold m…" her words trailed off as the medication did its job and she was asleep. Amused by her astounding ability to drop off mid-sentence, Gabriel waited until he was sure she was completely settled before getting himself ready for bed. Taking the cups and bowl back to the kitchen, he left them soaking and had one last check of the house.

After making sure that the apartment was all locked up, Gabriel was walking back through the lounge, when he glanced out of the French doors; Rome was bathed in twinkling lights, the view was magical and he was reminded how Kassie loved to lose herself in the night. Going back into the bedroom, he divested himself of his clothes, pulling on a pair of shorts for propriety's sake more than anything and slipped between the sheets. Drawing up the comforter, he tucked Kassie against him, who sensing his presence, sighed and shuffled closer, her hand overlapping his as it rested against her abdomen. The night wrapped around them and everything was peaceful.

Twenty Four

The next morning, the alarm disturbed them both, but for the first time since she had fallen ill, in fact for the first time since the evening Monique had shanghaied Gabriel, Kassie had slept through the night. She awoke to find herself enveloped in Gabriel's arms, her back against his chest and his head resting on hers. Well that was exceptionally romantic! She vaguely recalled asking him to hold her, but had assumed he would only do so until she fell asleep. She turned around so that she was facing him and pressed a kiss to the base of his throat. She felt a tremor run though him and smiled to herself.

"I think it's time for you to get up," she murmured, unable to stop her hands from skimming over his torso. Lordy he was irresistible, she shimmied against him and his arms tightened around her, holding her closer still.

"Think I'll give it a minute," he replied kissing her nose, before capturing her lips in a most pleasurable kiss. "Mmmmm…the best kind of good morning, well one of them anyway," he said as with a last hug he, reluctantly, got up unfolding his impossibly large frame from the bed, leaning in for one more quick kiss and disappearing into the bathroom. Kassie, stretched, smiled and snuggled back under the covers, glad that she didn't need to move just yet and immediately fell back to sleep.

Claire and Harry arrived on time and were pleased to hear that Kassie was none the worse for her antics of the previous day. Gabriel took himself off to work and Kassie herself didn't wake again until mid-morning. Before venturing through the main room, she decided to indulge in a long hot shower, washing her hair and massaging some of her favourite body lotion into her skin. She even got dressed, albeit into loose fitting jogging pants and a sweat top that would have been too big on Gabriel but was very comfortable, and by the time she joined Claire and Harry, she felt almost human.

Claire greeted her with a hug and Harry smiled, commenting that it was nice to see her up and about.

"For the first time in I don't know how long, I feel nearly normal. I just said to Gabriel last night that I was starting to think it would never happen. I do apologise for coming over all nonsensical on you both yesterday, I have no recollection of it at all." Kassie smiled at the couple, who assured her it was nothing to worry about.

"You look much better today, Gabriel mentioned that you actually slept right through the night, something he was inordinately pleased about."

"Poor Gabriel, he must be exhausted, I don't think he's had a proper night's rest since he brought me home. I worry about him."

"Oh, he'll be fine. Does the soul good to care for another person occasionally — it's a great leveller," Harry commented, winking at Kassie. "Plus, it's his penance for not telling you what he was up to." Kassie giggled at Harry's expression and, after Claire made them all a fresh coffee, they fell to talking about nothing of any importance, just the relaxed chatter of friends. During their conversation, Claire broached the subject of the tour, wanting to make sure that Kassie had remembered everything that they'd talked about the previous day.

"Kassie, I know you're probably sick of hearing about this tour now, but there's one last thing you should be aware of, I feel." Kassie looked at Claire, who looked as though she was bursting to share this last titbit.

"I'm all ears. You obviously think it's vitally important." She grinned and Harry chuckled, having a fair idea what his wife was about to disclose. Intrigued, Kassie sipped her coffee, breathing in the full-bodied aroma, very happy that her sense of smell was returning.

"Well it's like this; you know what I told you yesterday, that Gabriel chose us because we've known him for so long, well what we didn't get a chance to tell you, because of that whole chucking a wobbly thing..." grinning at Kassie, who blushed and smiled back, "...is that Gabriel paid for everything."

"What do you mean 'everything'?" Kassie queried, confused.

"By everything, I mean absolutely everything; the hotels, the coach, the entry fees, everything." Claire held Kassie's gaze, "Now does that sound like someone who did this as a bet?" Kassie gawked at Claire, then glanced at Harry who nodded his affirmation. "We all tried to pay our share, even contribute but he wouldn't hear of it. Said it was all on him, that way, if anything went awry, we weren't out of pocket."

Kassie was astounded, it must have cost Gabriel a fortune, he had gone to extraordinary lengths to make this as flawless as possible and bloody Monique had gone and spoiled it all. Well her and the problem with the units and the fact that regardless of anything else, Gabriel hadn't acted very honourably, although — being scrupulously fair — Kassie knew if she had hauled him over the coals straight away she might well have prevented some of the misunderstandings.

"Thank you, Claire, Harry," she said in her quiet way. "I appreciate you sharing this and everything you told me yesterday. I know that Gabriel and I need to resolve this, but it has been helpful having your input — truly. I'm not sure how much of this Gabriel would have told me, he would see it as being brash. I must admit that I have been troubled by those last few days, for with hindsight, much of what seemed to go wrong didn't add up, but I couldn't see beyond my own pain. So, let's hope that after Gabriel has explained himself and I've administered a verbal clip, or six, around his ear, there's still a chance for us." Kassie smiled, an open and unrestrained smile, her lovely eyes sparkling with an inner happiness. Claire pressed her hand

"We hope so too. I cannot think of anyone more perfect for Gabe." Kassie blushed, hurriedly changing the subject and when Gabriel retuned to the flat around an hour later, the three were gossiping away about the beauty of the north east of England and how, having lived there for most of her life, easy it would be for Kassie to conduct tours along Hadrian's Wall.

They hadn't heard him come in, so he took a moment to study Kassie. She was sitting with her back to him, but he could see one side of her face and, although still pale, her colour looked better. Her hair was falling in thick waves over her shoulders, spilling over the back of the chair and glimmering like silk as she laughed at something Harry was saying.

He strode across the small space to the balcony, his footsteps attracting their attention and all three turned and smiled, Kassie's face lit up when she saw him and his heart missed a beat. He wanted to see that smile every time he came home, in fact every time they looked at each other, for the rest of his life.

"Hi, sounds like you three have been having a fun morning." Unable to stop herself, Kassie slid a glance at Claire who grinned conspiratorially, her sly wink at Kassie not unnoticed by Gabriel, while Harry affirmed that they had indeed; and, oh by the way — the next tour Kassie was going escort would be to ancient Roman sites in Britain. Gabriel chuckled and sat down on the sofa, stretching his legs out in front of him, interlacing his fingers behind his head and casually leaning back — the picture of nonchalance.

"That's excellent and you won't need me. I can just to sit back, relax and let someone else do all the worrying."

"Pah, don't think you'll get out of it that easily, my lad," said Claire wagging her finger at him. "Kassie here will need an assistant." Kassie bit her lip to stop herself from chuckling at the appalled expression on Gabriel's face. Claire merely arched her eyebrows at him and the two made good their getaway, saying that they'd be back at the same time the next day. Kassie started to say that she'd be fine on her own, but caught Gabriel's eye and he shook his head imperceptibly, so she let it go.

"I'll be okay, Gabriel," she said, after the door clanged shut behind the couple.

"One more day, humour me," he replied, getting up from the sofa. They stood several feet apart staring at each other, as though uncertain. Kassie ran her tongue over suddenly dry lips, willing Gabriel to sweep her into his arms; Gabriel wasn't sure whether he should, the thought of their upcoming conversation rearing large in his mind.

"Gabriel?" Kassie's hand fluttered towards him, then dropped to her side, her brow creased, "w-what is it?" unnerved by his silence.

"I want to kiss you, badly, but I know we have what will likely be a very uncomfortable discussion looming and I don't want you to think I'm muddying the water," he replied gruffly.

Kassie pondered that for a moment, then asked. "Do you love me, Gabriel?"

"You know I do." A smile tugged at the corner of his mouth.

"Then everything else is just details." She held his gaze, he groaned and in two strides wrapped her to him, lifting her off the floor, her legs went around his waist and she clung to him, their kiss frenzied, heat spiralling through them with an almost unquenchable intensity. It went on and on, neither wanting to relinquish the other. Gabriel carefully lowered them onto the sofa, somehow rolling her under him and still they kissed. Limbs tangled together; hands searched, stroking and teasing, stoking a fire that threatened to become a conflagration.

Gabriel knew he had to stop but at the same moment this thought ran through the mush he now called his brain, Kassie broke their kiss. They were both flushed and gasping, hunger throbbing between them and it would have been so easy to ignore the large pink elephant in the middle of the room and give in to their desires. Sanity, however, dictated that they do no such thing. Slowly they sat up, righting their clothes, now totally dishevelled and Kassie mentioned something about lunch. Gabriel looked at her with such a lecherous expression that she burst into uncontrollable giggles.

"Don't look at me like that, I'm not on the menu." She chortled, using her fingers to comb her hair out of her eyes, while looking around for something to tie up its length. She spotted an elastic band on the table by the window and grabbing it, dragged her wayward locks into a relatively respectable ponytail. Gabriel twisted the heavy length in his hand loving the feel of its weight through his fingers.

"Can't help it, you are just too edible." He grinned, before letting go of her hair and going through to the kitchen to lay out the salad he had brought in for lunch. Kassie made a cup of tea and they sat on the balcony to eat. They talked about mundane matters, Gabriel explained about his work at the university and Kassie gave him more of an insight into her work at the international school. Soon, though, they could avoid it no longer. Armed with fresh hot drinks they made themselves comfortable. Kassie was curled up in her chair, enveloped in a huge blanket and Gabriel had shrugged into a warm jumper and as they sipped their tea, he started to speak.

Twenty Five

"Kassie, before we get into this I want you to understand, to trust, that the last thing I ever wanted to do was to hurt you. In the brief time we have known each other you have become the most important person in my life. I love you so much that when I thought I'd lost you, it tore me apart. That said, this isn't about my feelings, it's about you and your feelings. I screwed up, simple as that. I thought I'd concocted this excellent plan to court you, to spend time together in the hope that you might decide that I wasn't just some crank of a professor who, the second time we met, asked you seemingly random questions." He paused, Kassie was watching him, yet she didn't look angry or even upset, more resigned and he couldn't tell whether that was good or bad.

"Okay, so here it is and I realise that some of this may sound preposterous, but it's the truth, unvarnished, awkward and possibly rather ugly, but the truth all the same." He paused and took a deep breath. "The first time we met, even though I was the one who knocked you for six, you bowled me over. You were glaring daggers at me with those beautiful eyes and I could hardly drag myself away, so I contrived to run into you the following day."

Kassie gaped at him. That had been deliberate? How the hell had he managed that?

"I saw you with your friends and simply waited 'til you left them and walked around the building." He smiled rather sheepishly, answering the question in her eyes.

Kassie was dumbfounded. "I'm sorry. What now? That encounter wasn't accidental?"

He shook his head. "Not even close. I had hoped to be able to talk you into working for me, but you were so mad and I hadn't realised that you'd overheard Hardwick. I'm so sorry Kassie, if I'd had half a clue that you thought I was a party to his prejudices, I would have set you straight there and then.

"You were laughing, I heard you laughing," she blurted out, hanging her head in embarrassment.

"Laughing? No way there was no laughing about you, I promise." Kassie wasn't convinced telling him what she'd overheard and the quiet mirth that had followed. Gabriel thought back, every detail of that day etched in his memory and it came to him. "I diverted the conversation away from you by telling Hardwick about an incident at one of the digs I'd been on, maybe that was what amused us. I did suggest that his comments were less than appropriate though.

"What did he think I was unsuitable for?" she asked curiously. Gabriel went on to explain about the intensive units he had been trying to organise to be held at various ancient sites. Kassie was intrigued and saddened at the same time. She would have enjoyed helping to run something like that; she believed she would be good at it, something she mentioned to Gabriel.

"I agree, wholeheartedly and, although this isn't what we're talking about right now, they are still in the pipeline and if you're interested, I would love you to be involved." Kassie stared at him, the idea running through her head, the pleasure she would get from being involved in such a project, indescribable.

"I would be honoured," she whispered, her face a picture of delight. Gabriel grinned and reached for her hand squeezing it gently. She brought his hand to her lips, brushing a light kiss on his knuckles and then rested both their hands in her lap, absently stroking her fingers over his, as he continued.

"Anyway, I didn't get the chance to tell you about the scheme because you were still obviously mightily cheesed off, so I let you go. Stupidest thing I ever did. I wasted two years wondering about you; where you were, what you were doing, had you found someone who had swept you off your feet. I didn't think about that last part too much, couldn't bear to." Kassie pressed his hand, thinking how easy it was to miss the one thing that's staring you right in the face, not once, but several times.

"Then one day, my luck changed. You were here, in Rome! Not only that, but you walked right by me and apparently recognised my voice. I couldn't believe it, standing there in the sunlight, in the middle of those ancient ruins; you took my breath away. There was no way I was losing you again, but you didn't make it easy, did you? Your agency refused to tell me anything about you until I'd hounded them for days and then all they did was suggest I try the international schools. I don't suppose you have any idea how many photographs I scrolled though on the off chance that'd you'd show up in one of them?" Kassie giggled, imagining his frustration, impressed with his perseverance.

"I can't think why you needed to find me that badly," she mumbled, rather self-consciously. Gabriel stared at her appraisingly,

"No, I don't suppose you can," he said, not going into any further detail. "Finally, after hours of searching, I tracked you down and you know the rest, well up until two weeks ago." Gabriel took a deep breath, this was the hard bit. "So, now we come to the tour. You were incredible, the amount of knowledge you hold and the love you have for anything to do with Ancient Rome is astonishing. You blew me away, you didn't carry notes or guide books, it's all in your head and I am in awe that you can do that. I too have a depth of knowledge, but you bring it alive. They are no longer ruins when you talk about them, they are living, breathing, vibrant places and it is as though you have experienced life in them; you know the people, you are friends with them. It is an extraordinary gift."

Kassie went a fiery red, she had never thought what she did was any different from the other guides. Yes, she loved her history but wasn't that the point? She forced her attention back to Gabriel.

"We got to spend time together, I knew I was taking it faster than I would have liked, but I had thought that it was clear from our few…errr…close encounters…how I felt about you."

"I never assumed anything. I never really expected anyone like you could care about someone like me. It was rather lovely though, you seemed interested in me for my own sake, not as a way to be introduced to my far more attractive friend." Gabriel's heart lurched when she said this. She didn't even sound upset, just accepting.

"How could I not be interested in you? You captivated me the first time we met and continue to do so." Gabriel sounded amazed that she should even question this. Kassie looked at him doubtfully, and he realised that he would need more than that to persuade her. Making a mental note to go back to that, he carried on with his explanation.

"So, there you were winning hearts and souls; the group loved you and it seemed as though you and I were getting closer. When I said that you were beautiful, that I love you and have done so for a very long time and that I wanted it all, I meant it, I still mean it and I still want it all. I would never, ever string anyone along the way you presumed I had because of what Monique said — and yes, I'll get to her in a minute. What kind of man do you think I am?" Kassie held his gaze, her eyes cloudy with uncertainty.

"Don't you see?" she whispered, "I trusted you to be an honourable man; honest and truthful and I believed you when you told me I was beautiful. You are the only person ever to have said that to me, even my own parents, whom I assume love me; have never even told me I was pretty. I gave you everything, my heart my soul and then my body. Then after two wonderful nights, when I started to hope, to dream that there was a chance for me, for us, you virtually disappeared."

"You were called into the university, I accepted that was unavoidable, but to go out with Monique without so much as a call or text to let me know, was just plain rude. I know you tried to get hold of me, but that was later, way later. I was awake when you knocked on my door — in fact I didn't sleep that night at all — but you made me feel like a fool! You had just spent the evening with a young and, stunningly beautiful, woman and then you expected me to welcome you into my arms and into my bed? You needed your head read! Then it was as though I no longer existed. I tried to contact you, so many times that I must have seemed like an hysterical stalker, especially as it appeared that you'd been spending your free time with Monique. Even then I tried to give you the benefit of the doubt only to hear that you were planning to look at engagement rings with her. The final straw was when she bellyached about the bet and everything seemed to fall into place."

Kassie could feel treacherous tears building, but she blinked them back fiercely. She was still holding Gabriel's hand — for which he was very thankful — but now she was gripping it tightly, her distress threatening to overwhelm her; the pain of those few days coming back to haunt her. She sucked air into her lungs and steadied herself.

"I think, had you not seemingly ignored me, it wouldn't have upset me as much, for not only had I let you seduce me, I fell in love with you and to top it off, shared my most precious secret. Then, suddenly nothing and all your wonderful words, your gestures and your sentiments, appeared to be contrived, deliberately planned and to a greater success than you could have imagined. To hear that the man who told me I was beautiful and that he loved me and that he wanted to marry me was all a lie almost killed me. In fact, the day you found me near the Pantheon, I think I'd lost the will to live. I know that's pathetic and a coward's way out, but the humiliation was more than I could bear." Kassie drew a shuddering breath, needing to tell him everything.

"But you did find me and you were distraught, which stumped me. Where was Monique? Why weren't you with her? Unfortunately, I have little recollection of the next few days, much of it is hazy and muddled, but I do remember your constant care and it seemed at odds with someone who only wanted to win a bet and then walk away. Things began to niggle at me, small things that were out of place or didn't gel with the story Monique had wanted us, had wanted me, to believe. Then on Monday, Claire and Harry told me the rest, well not quite all of it, the last little bit they shared this morning and now the puzzle is complete." She lifted their joined hands to her heart; Gabriel could feel the agitated beat pulsing against his skin.

"I need to hear it from you. I need you to tell me how it fell apart, what happened in those few days and why did you not even try to get in touch with me." She paused, irresolute and then decided she was going to let him have the last little bit, or she would regret it. "Gabriel, although now I know differently, at the time, I felt like some cheap prostitute; used for sex, then thrown away. I felt like a laughing stock and, worse, the whole group knew of your plans — this wager — and were party to it. That all those incredible hours we'd spent together were nothing more than a figment of my imagination."

Her tears were falling now, trailing down her cheeks; the torment of those days, the long nights without sleep, the agony of losing her heart only to have it trampled into the dust, clear in her face. Gabriel was aghast, even though he realised there'd been misunderstandings, never in his worst nightmares had he expected it to be this bad. He could only hope he could find the words to save this, to save them.

Maybe love wasn't going to be enough.

Twenty Six

"Kassie, my only love." Gabriel faced her, holding her eyes. "I am devastated that I hurt you so badly. I cannot imagine what you suffered and had I realised what was going on, I'd have left Mum with her neighbour and been back in a heart beat."

Kassie frowned. "What do you mean 'left Mum'?"

Gabriel raised his eyebrows, so Claire hadn't told her everything. He proceeded to explain about his mother's fall and that he'd expected to be back by the evening, but had ended up having to stay for two nights until his father returned home.

"Then when I walked into the hotel, I got your letter and I was floored. Claire was waiting for me and she gave me a piece of her mind, before telling me everything that had happened. I took a couple of minutes to vent my anger at Monique and Anna and then came haring after you. I'd nearly caught up with you, but then I saw Adam — although I had no clue who he was — walking towards you and you threw yourself into his arms. That totally confused me; I couldn't believe the Kassie I knew had two men on the go, yet you were obviously very close to this man. You have no idea how relieved I was when he finally admitted that he's your brother. I think he took malicious delight in letting me think he was your boyfriend."

A hint of a smile tweaked Kassie's lips at the image this created in her head. She was quite chuffed her brother had been so quick thinking.

"I'm sure your anguish was well deserved," she said, her smile taking the sting out of her words.

"It was the day you got drenched before he finally talked to me. I'd been trying to call, text, I even wrote actual letters, but later, when we found your phone underneath them, I noticed that you hadn't read them. Adam and I met down the hill there at the café and I told him what had happened. He said he would talk to you, but when I called round later in the day, you'd gone out and hadn't come back. The rest of that particular bit you know." He let that sit for a moment, knowing the hardest bit was yet to come.

"To go back to the day after Monique arrived. I was coming back into the hotel and she waylaid me, apparently full of gossip from home and did I fancy grabbing a beer. No point including anyone else, this was family stuff. To be honest, I didn't give it a second thought, my head was full of the problems at uni and I presumed it would be half an hour. Next thing I know she's ordered a pizza and more beer. I explained that I needed to get back to the hotel, that I had commitments to the group and she casually flung out that as I had an assistant she would surely be able to handle things. I didn't want her to know about us, not then. She's always been a bit of a nuisance, and I suppose I never think of her as anything other than a pest of a kid, so it never dawned on me that not only did she already know how I felt about you but that she had an ulterior motive. She'd also had a bit of a whinge about you telling her off and she made it sound as though you'd been quite abrupt with her."

Kassie's jaw tightened and he raised his hand, "I know, I know she was exaggerating, but she can do upset for an Olympic sport, so I said I'd have a quiet word."

"Hmmm, you and I may need to discuss what 'a quiet word' means, Gabe." Kassie chastised him gently.

"I'm sorry, love. As soon as the words left my mouth, I realised that you would never speak to anyone in such a manner, but by then it was too late. Everything just went downhill from there. I knew there was something wrong the next morning when we spoke on the phone. Your words were oddly final and I was determined to talk to you when I got back that night. I was half way to uni when the phone rang and it was Mum's neighbour, telling me that she'd fallen and as Dad was away, I had to go to her." Kassie nodded in understanding.

"Anyway, my car was parked at the hotel, so I dashed back to get it and left you a letter at the front desk telling you what had happened and that all being well, I'd be back at the hotel for dinner. Of course, I ended up staying much longer. Mobile phone service is sporadic at best out where my parents live and

I couldn't get a signal. Claire scolded me for not using the landline, but again, I never thought. I presumed you'd received my letter and that you'd realise that if I wasn't back, I'd been held up at Mum's." He stared out over the rooftops of Rome, his mind on the afternoon he'd got back to the hotel and read Kassie's letter.

"Then I get back to find that you believed that everything we'd been to each other was a lie, that I had placed some kind of wager that I could seduce you in three weeks. Your letter, oh God, Kassie, your letter. I felt as though I was being sucked into a black hole. I had no idea what Monique and Anna were up to and was horrified when I discovered the truth. I had been so caught up in the problems I was dealing with, that what should have been obvious didn't hit me until it was too late and you'd gone." Gabriel rubbed his thumb over Kassie's palm, looking her straight in the eyes.

"Stupidly, I had assumed that you would be there, when I was done fixing everything; that you'd wait for me. After all, what difference could a couple of days make? I'd be there at the end of the tour and I hoped you'd have realised by then how much I love you and that you might be open to becoming more than just my girl. Little did I realise what damage can be done in so short a time. The evening I found you drenched and frozen near the Pantheon was one of the worst moments of my life. For a split second, I thought you might have actually died and I would never be able to tell you how sorry I was, or that I love you more than anything in this world and how I hoped I might get the chance to spend the rest of my days proving it to you."

Gabriel trailed off, his voice cracking and as she studied him Kassie was fairly certain there were tears glistening in the uneasy indigo of his eyes. She ruminated over his words. As far as she could see, she had two options. She could accept his explanation, forgive him for his complete idiocy, tell him that it was over that she couldn't trust him and that she wasn't prepared to tempt further heartbreak. Alternatively, she could accept his explanation, forgive him for his complete idiocy — trusting that it was a mental aberration, that the heavens had conspired to create a perfect storm in which, had even one of the factors not happened they wouldn't be having this discussion, and move forward with their lives together.

She believed that he loved her and she knew she loved him. What was the point of being inflexible and righteously outraged if that meant she would miss out on the chance of sharing a lifetime with Gabriel? Wasn't he worth the risk? Wasn't she?

Kassie was silent for so long that Gabriel started to feel panic coiling though him and his heart faltered. She was staring at him, her face expressionless and her eyes unreadable. Had he lost her? Please no, he couldn't lose her. He squeezed her hand, very gently. She looked down at their joined hands, noticing, not for the first time, that his fingers were long and finely sculptured, artist's fingers. Admiring them for a few seconds, she let her gaze travel up his arm; his shirtsleeves were folded back at the cuff, revealing a hint of tanned forearm. Up to his shoulders, so broad, yet there was not an ounce of spare flesh anywhere on his body. Her breathing hitched as she saw the pulse beating in his throat and it was all she could do not to lean over and press her lips to it. Not yet, not quite yet.

Her eyes wandered along his jaw, noticing a shadow of stubble, recalling, absently, that he liked to shave every evening. Onwards past his ear and to his hair, as ever resembling that of a scarecrow. Back down over his huge frame, even seated he was enormous. Kassie, close to six feet tall herself, loved that he was so much taller than her, not just a little bit, a lot. His height made her feel protected, safe, yet for all his size, he had the grace of a jungle cat. She shivered as images of them together teased at her consciousness. No, she could not let him go. In the end, it was quite simple. She loved him, he loved her and — what had she said to him the previous evening? — everything else was just details.

She brought her eyes back to his and he saw warmth kindle in their depths, the empty dark jade brightening into glorious emerald, and he held his breath.

"Gabriel?" it was barely a whisper, his name almost lost on the breeze.

"Yes love," he replied just as quietly. To speak any louder seemed…irreverent.

"Promise me you'll never let me go." Hope sprang in his chest, his heart thudded so loudly he was sure she would hear it.

"I promise Kassandra. I promise to love you throughout this life and into the next and I will never let you go." She sighed, a long drawn out sigh that seemed to release the tension surrounding them.

"Show me." His eyes held hers reading the invitation simmering there. He wasn't sure he'd heard her correctly. "Show me how much you love me." She leaned forward then and brushed her lips over the pulse in his neck, feeling it leap at her touch. Gabriel shuddered and — needing no second bidding — stood, drawing her into his arms, his lips claiming hers with bruising fervency. Her response instant, Kassie clung to him, drowning in his kiss, as her whole body seemed to be dissolving into his. Familiar heat circled them and before the fire that pulsed through their veins became an inferno, Gabriel lifted her, carrying her through to the bedroom where he spent a very long time showing her tenderly, languorously and with an exquisitely ardent devotion, just how much she was loved.

It was another week before Kassie felt as though she had recovered fully, but after that she came on in leaps and bounds and was soon chomping at the bit to be out and about, fed up with being confined to her flat. The strange fuzziness in her head cleared, albeit rather more slowly than she would have liked, but before long she was back to her normal cheerful self. Claire and Harry continued to visit, even though she assured them she was fine on her own. It seemed they liked her company and she enjoyed their easy-going camaraderie, a new friendship blossoming.

During this time, Kassie finally read the letters that Gabriel had written to her before she fell ill. They were letters of atonement, letters of explanation, letters of remorse and, most importantly, letters of love. They were poignant, impassioned, revealing and persuasive and Kassie read them all several times.

They made her smile, they made her cry, they warmed her heart and, although she realised that she should have read them sooner for their contents would have saved her considerable heartache, in some ways she was glad that she had waited. Secure in Gabriel's love for her, she believed she could appreciate them more. Then, as women have done for centuries, she tied a ribbon around them and placed them in a little wooden box for safekeeping.

Gabriel, eventually discovered — after many, *many* conversations with the reception staff at the hotel — that the letter he had written to Kassie telling her that he'd been called away, had ended up in a slot allocated to a different room number and, obviously, never collected. Incredibly, it was still there and Gabriel retrieved it, thankful to prove to Kassie that he had at least tried to do the right thing.

It seemed, also, that Monique and Anna had suffered a crisis of conscience, for Kassie received an email via Claire, in which they apologised profusely for causing her such unhappiness and that they hoped in time, she might forgive their imprudent behaviour. Kassie was still very aggrieved by their actions, but harbouring a grudge only served to hurt her, not them. Even though she stewed over it for quite some time, eventually, her innate generosity came to the fore and she replied with a cordiality she would not have believed herself capable of a month previously.

Both Gabriel and Kassie did occasionally revisit what had happened, but what had been done could not be changed, it was how they dealt with it that mattered and knowing that their love for each other had weathered the storm, they consigned it to the past and let it go.

Epilogue

One evening around a month later, Gabriel came in to find a large pan bubbling on the stove and a mouth-watering smell tantalising his nostrils. Curry! Definitely some kind of curry, oh yum! It was a Wednesday and because Kassie's tours usually finished around three, she was often home before him. She was back at work full time although Gabriel could tell that she still struggled a bit, her energy levels not quite back to normal. She tired easily and, once it became clear she no longer required round-the-clock care, Gabriel had used this to justify staying on at her apartment rather than returning to his own place. Not that either of them were complaining!

Kassie was sitting on the balcony, snuggled into one of his heavy jumpers, a cup of something — which she must have made only moments before as it was still steaming — in danger of being knocked off by her feet, which were resting casually on a cushion on the table. She appeared to be reading, although when he looked more closely, saw that she was fast asleep; her head against the back of the chair, the book open on her lap. He checked the pan, stirred the contents, turned the heat down to a low simmer and then made himself a drink before going over to sit next to her.

After a milder than expected October, the weather had finally changed. The days were much colder now and had taken on a wintry aspect; the sunsets were spectacular though; pale blue afternoon skies morphing into cool pinks and purples, tinged with flashes of orange fire as the weak sun began to set. They both loved to watch the sun go down over the city and, despite the cold, would sit for hours admiring nature's light show.

With half a mind on their dinner, Gabriel turned the rest of his attention to some papers he'd brought home to mark, becoming absorbed in — and in some cases dismayed by — how students chose to explain the intricacies of the Augustan principate. He had been working solidly for about an hour when he became aware that Kassie was watching him. He turned and smiled and she grinned sleepily at him in return.

"Sorry, I don't know what came over me." Still not quite awake, she gazed out over the city, seeing the lights flickering on as the night drew in. "Aaaaahhhhhh…" wincing as she lifted her feet off the table, muscles tight from the awkward angle, "…goodness me, how long have I been asleep? I didn't think I was tired." She yawned prodigiously, making Gabriel chuckle.

"At least an hour, love. No matter, I've got half of these papers marked which is a bonus. Dinner's nearly ready. I turned the heat down when I came in and checked it about ten minutes ago. Looks great!"

"Ha, it's only chicken curry. I turned the rice cooker on too, which should have clicked over to 'keep warm' by now. It'll be ready whenever," Kassie said, smiling her thanks as she stretched out her arms, flexing her body in a bid to get her circulation going again.

"Just enough time to say good evening then," muttered Gabriel, grasping her hand and pulling her onto his knee. She chuckled softly, brushing a light kiss over his cheek.

"Good evening, Professor," she breathed, and everything suddenly quietened as he held her gaze, eyes fathomless in the gloom. Heart thrumming, Kassie squirmed around so that she was sitting astride his legs. Gabriel uncoiled the knot keeping her hair neat and tidy, interlacing his fingers through the luxurious weight as it swung free and, cupping her head, brought her lips to his.

Everything seemed to be happening in slow motion as Kassie fell further and further into Gabriel's kiss; the sounds of the city faded and all Kassie could hear was her own heartbeat. Over these last few weeks, she had noticed that, subtly, their connection was evolving; that there was a gradual strengthening of trust, a solid foundation on which they were building their lives. Now, as they kissed she was aware that the delicious sensations rippling through her were also different somehow. No less acute — their passion was quickly spiralling out of control — but it was as though the love that bound them had, despite the odds, flourished and thrived into something far more enduring. An indissoluble love, whose flame would never be doused.

Gabriel too was aware of this indefinable, yet profound shift. Suddenly it was more than passion and love and sex, it was a lifetime of togetherness, of shared experiences, of laughter and fun, of sad times and joy. He had always presumed that he wanted this, but until this moment he knew he had been playing on the fringes. This woman whose body bewitched him, whose mind challenged him, whose touch could set off a thousand fireworks and whose smile never failed to warm his heart, had reached a part of him no one else ever could and she would be there for eternity.

"Kassie," he said breaking their kiss. His voice sounded frayed, the tumult of emotions threatening to overwhelm him. "Kassie, I need to ask you something." She stared into his face; her eyes cloudy with desire, her fingers teasing under his shirt, sending his heart rate through the roof.

"Hmmmm?" kissing him again, needing his lips on hers.

"Kassie, urrghhhhhh…" as she wriggled on his knee, "…lordy woman, have you any idea what that does to a man?" his voice a low growl. Kassie smiled against his mouth.

"Of course! Why do you think I'm doing it?" she said impishly, fingers now stroking up his back. Gabriel smothered a chuckle as she dropped him a cheeky wink.

"Kassie, please." Something in his voice made Kassie pause, her fingers stilled and she searched his face, trying and failing to read him.

"What is it?" she asked, rather tremulously, a trickle of unease running down her spine

"Although we have only known, really known, each other for a relatively short time and I have no right to ask you this so soon, but I need to, I have to." He paused attempting to get his thoughts in order, or they would just tumble out in a chaotic muddle.

"Kassie, I cannot imagine my life without you. That afternoon in Pompeii when I told you that I wanted it all and when I told you the same thing a month, I meant it. Nothing that has happened since has changed my mind; in fact, it has only served to make me more certain. My beautiful

Kassandra, I love you, you are everything to me and I do not want to waste another moment of our lives together. I want to laugh with you, cry with you, sleep with you and have fun with you, make love with you, adore you and cherish you 'til the end of my days. Please, would you do me the greatest honour of marrying me?"

Kassie gawked at him — okay they had talked about living together and Gabriel had mentioned that he'd wanted to marry her and, of course, she hoped that was still on the cards but this was the last thing she'd expected, especially so soon. As she stared at him though, a peace settled around her, a serenity of mind that she'd never experienced. She already knew that she was irrevocably in love with him and that would never change, the last few weeks had proved that beyond any doubt. Elation flooded through her and she started to smile.

Gabriel was watching her, hoping that with all that they had gone through; the debacle at the end of the tour, her illness and his revelations, which he knew still bothered her occasionally, he hadn't ruined everything. He knew she loved him, but being in love and trusting your life to someone were two vastly different things and he was smart enough to realise that having one in no way guaranteed you the other. He saw the smile curve her lips and his heart leapt, Kassie cupped her hands around his face and looked deep into his eyes, emerald on sapphire, and kissed him. She kissed him until he lost all his powers of concentration and just when he thought he was going to have to take her right there on the balcony she broke away, panting slightly.

"Yes! A thousand times yes!" Gabriel's mouth dropped open in astonishment, she'd said yes, she'd actually said yes. Kassie giggled at his expression; his smile was bright enough to light a small village and he stood, sweeping her against him, carrying her through to the bedroom and proceeded to demonstrate just how happy he was. The curry could wait!

Three Years Later

In the middle of Pompeii's amphitheatre, a tall woman held a group of people in thrall as she explained the complexities of the gladiatorial games. The way the seating arrangements reflected the different levels of Roman society, the pomp and the ceremony, the diverse categories of gladiators and how they fought, and most importantly the combat itself. As she spoke, she wove a tale around them until they could see the crowds sitting or standing, tier upon tier and, hear their roar as they bayed for blood. They could feel the sawdust beneath their feet and smell the fear of the men whose only crime may have been to be a captive from a conquered nation.

She described how those in the audience would enter through the Porta Triumphalis, showed them the tunnels through which the combatants entered the arena and pointed out that those who did not survive their bout were carried out through the Porta Libitinensis, the gate for the dead. She did clarify that although many did die during these fights, it was not as frequent as the movies suggested. Gladiators were an expensive commodity, they had to be nurtured; fed, clothed, housed, trained and kept healthy. None of this came cheaply and thus no lanista — the manager of the school — would want any men under his care to die. Further, many became celebrities in their own right, and there was far more profit to be made from gladiators who managed to avoid death than those who didn't.

As she talked, copious notes were scribbled and photos taken. Questions were flung at her in a constant stream and she answered each one as though she'd never heard it before — which to be fair, in rare cases she might not have done. A little to one side, leaning against the stone wall that, in antiquity separated the arena from the audience, was a giant of a man. His well-worn Akubra-style hat was tilted so that his face was in shadow, but anyone bothering to check would have noticed that his eyes never left the face of the woman who was speaking.

"Okay everyone, that's all for this afternoon. Remember that by tomorrow evening I want a four hundred-word essay on any aspect of Pompeii that we covered this week, on why you find it significant either historically, archaeologically or both. Thanks for your attention guys, I appreciate it…" she grinned waving her arm in a sort of casual dismissal, "…now go — find a beer!" The group cheered at this and went to grab their backpacks that had been scattered randomly around the amphitheatre. She walked over to the tall man, who stood, took her ever-present, yet ridiculously large sun hat off her shining hair, drew her into his arms and kissed her soundly.

"Perfectly presented, my Kassandra," he murmured in her ear when, eventually, he relinquished her lips. Kassie removed his hat, placing it on top of hers and, sliding her fingers through his dark locks brought his mouth back to hers, totally oblivious to the smiles of the group as they trudged out of the ruin.

"Why thank you, kind Sir! Not sure it is quite appropriate though, kissing the assistant," she said, smiling into the deep azure of his eyes.

"It's okay," replied Gabriel, "I know the organiser. He assured me that it was the only acceptable way to thank said assistant." Kassie chuckled, brushing his hair out of his eyes and kissing him again. The familiar heat, never far away, was beginning to coil around her centre.

Trying to distract herself she commented, "This is such a great group, they're like sponges. Makes my job so much easier. By far the best set of students we've had." A little over two years previously, after a *lot* of organising, Gabriel and Kassie had initiated their intensive courses. Held during the university vacations, they organised two or four tours of two weeks each — depending on whether it was the winter or summer break — and they had proved very popular, so popular, in fact, that they had a waiting list. The current one was the last for this summer season. The academic year for the university from which these students hailed, resumed in a fortnight, giving those attending one week's grace between the end of this course and start of their winter timetable.

Gabriel agreed, saying they had been the same for the more technically based lectures he'd taken, covering such topics as the archaeological methods being used to preserve and conserve this most astonishing of sites.

"Want to stay a while?" he asked, knowing his wife's penchant for being in Pompeii when the crowds started to leave. She glanced at her watch, they still had a good couple of hours before they'd be required to leave and, grinning like a child who'd just been told ice cream was for dinner she replied, eagerly. "Could we?"

"Glad to, this way I get you to all to myself." He took her hand and they left the amphitheatre meandering slowly along the Via dell'Abbondanza, chattering about the group and the upcoming semester and what days Kassie would be conducting tours around Rome. Kassie still worked for Discover Antiquity, but she had long resigned from the International School, three jobs had proved too much and she preferred the tours to administration. It also freed her up to spend more time on her books, the romance in her newest release bearing a striking resemblance to the rather rocky start her relationship with Gabriel underwent.

They reached the Forum and by tacit consent — and as they did every time they visited Pompeii — went to sit on the same bench where Gabriel had told Kassie he loved her three years previously. Gabriel bought them a coffee each and while they sipped the rich brew Kassie started to speak, then stopped, tried again and then stopped. She bit her lip and fidgeted on the seat. Gabriel was astonished, this was so unlike his normally unflappable wife that he started to feel quite concerned.

"What is it, love?" he asked quietly, brushing her hair off her face with his fingers, cupping her cheek in one of his huge hands. He brushed her bottom lip with his thumb, staring into her incredible eyes.

"It's just…well, I wasn't sure…but then this morning I thought…so I checked twice…showed the same…" she trailed off, coherence, as ever when she got agitated, running for the hills.

"Hey, it can't be that bad, what's got you in such a tizzy."

"I think I might be going to develop a tendency to plumpness," she said, deliberately reminding him of their first meeting five years previously.

"Huh?" was Gabriel's less than eloquent response, raking his eye over her statuesque figure, making her blush as he dropped a lascivious wink. She giggled and shoved him in the shoulder. "I think you need your eyes testing, sweetheart." He ran his hand up her leg, over the curve of her hip, letting it rest on her waist. "Nope, you are just right." She grinned at him, knowing she had to clarify her comment, and with a deep breath, she started to speak, the words spilling out so fast Gabriel had to ask her to repeat them slowly.

"Did a test. I'm pregnant. I think about three months. I need to see a doctor. We haven't planned for this. I wasn't sure…" she paused uncertain now. They had been married for nearly three years, their wedding taking place not long after the ill-fated tour during which they could so easily have lost each other. A small ceremony — just family and a few friends — held in the little village in the north of England where Kassie grew up. Afterwards, they had honeymooned in Tuscany, a short yet blissful week, before they were both straight back into their busy lives.

Shortly before their marriage, Kassie had moved in with Gabriel. He owned a stunning apartment in the Aventine district, with spectacular views and she loved it. It was large enough for them and several children should that occasion arise, but they'd never discussed it. Kassie wasn't even sure she was maternal; she liked that it was just Gabriel and her, that they could up and leave to conduct one of their tours or go on holiday when it suited them and that they only had to consider each other. She'd also assumed that as they didn't take precautions and that she hadn't fallen pregnant, it probably wasn't going to happen. Now everything was about to change and Kassie had no clue how Gabriel would react.

"Wait, you're telling me that you think you're pregnant?" Gabriel finally getting her garbled words sorted in his head. She nodded, still chewing on her lip; her husband meanwhile was trying to curb a huge bubble of happiness that was threatening to burst out of him. "Kassie, my beautiful Kassie, we're going to have a baby?" She nodded again, a slight smile curving her lips, relieved at the joy in Gabriel's face.

"I've never really thought about children, I didn't really want to share you and I like that we're not answerable to anyone except each other, but it's weird…" she paused, and Gabriel raised a questioning eyebrow, taking hold of her hand. "…I'm quite excited. This child will be part of you and part of me and it feels so perfect." She hesitated worried that she sounded overly sentimental.

"Kassandra St Germain, I didn't think I was capable of loving you any more than I already do, but this, your news has proved me wrong." He kissed her then, slowly, drawing her into his embrace and running his hands lazily across her body, the world around them fading into insignificance. The passion that had defined their early romance had never lessened, merely deepening as their relationship matured.

"I think maybe we need to go back to the hotel. This calls for a celebration," Gabriel murmured in her ear, fluttering feather light kisses down her neck.

Kassie shivered at his touch.

"I find no fault in your suggestion, but it can't involve champagne," she replied pertly, squeezing his thigh, delighting as he caught his breath. As they stood, throwing their cups in the bin, gathering their hats and backpacks, something about the scene in front of them tickled at the back of Kassie's consciousness. She rolled it around for a few minutes when suddenly it came to her.

"What did you say to that group?" she asked Gabriel.

"What group, love?"

"That group of people, they were standing here the day you told me you loved me. You had just been kissing me and they clapped. You shared something with them that you refused to tell me. What was it?"

Gabriel smiled at her, dropping another, very satisfying, kiss on her lips and said, "I told them that you were the most beautiful girl I'd ever met, that we were in love and that I intended to spend the rest of my life with you." Kassie just gaped at him.

"You did not!" She was astounded. "How could you possibly have known that?"

"How many times must I tell you, my Kassandra, that I knew you were the girl, the woman for me the first time I met you. I loved you then, I love you still and I will love you until the stars fall out of the sky."

"Oh, Gabriel," Kassie sighed, warmth fluttering through her, "I love you too, always and forever. Now what were you saying about going back to the hotel?" She moved against him, fitting herself to his enormous frame, tempting and tantalising, her nearness intoxicating. Gabriel growled, the sound rumbling through his chest.

"Come on, minx, let's go before I take you here in the middle of these ancient remains and finally give those ghosts something to talk about." Kassie chuckled, sliding her arm around his waist, as he draped an arm over her shoulder, hugging her to him. They strolled unhurriedly along the pathway, past the palaestra and the amphitheatre, out of the ruins and into the rest of their lives.

Once Upon An Earl

As we all know love has a habit of striking at the most inopportune moments and that sometimes fairy tales happen when we least expect them.

Giles Trevallier, 5th Earl of Winchester − tired, cold and very wet − was lamenting his decision to try to outride the storm. Escaping from the hustle of the city, Giles was looking forward to a few months of peace and quiet, while he managed his vast country estate. Now all he wanted to do was to get home, change into dry clothes and sit in front of a roaring fire with a hot meal and a large tumbler of whisky.

Fate, however, had other ideas and was about to intervene in the guise of a bedraggled female, who literally dropped at the Earl's feet, soaked to the skin and more dead than alive; her sudden appearance turning his neat, orderly and, to be honest, rather boring existence completely upside down.

Waking, briefly, in an unfamiliar room and in the arms of a very tall and dangerously handsome stranger no less, the young woman has no memory of who she is or how she came to be there. Under the tender care of the Earl's household, she slowly starts to recover, eventually recalling that her name is Willow, although everything else continues to elude her.

Following discreet enquiries into his unexpected guest − whose face haunts his every waking moment, Giles is shocked to discover that she is rumoured to be responsible for a fire that destroyed her family home and that her father's body is presumed to be one of those recovered from the ashes. Suddenly this most respectable Earl is faced with the possibility that he is harbouring a criminal.

While trying to unravel the mystery surrounding her, Giles realises that he is falling hopelessly in love with Willow, who unbeknownst to him is fighting similar emotions. And as with anything involving the heart, a thoughtless word or gesture has a tendency to thwart even Fate's best-laid plans.

Have Willow and Giles any chance of a happy ever after or will all manner of obstacles, such as misunderstandings, whispers of scandal, secret documents and foreign agents force them apart?

To Unlock Her Heart

Relief seemed at hand when, after suffering a year of abuse at the hands of the Duke of Aldwych, Grace Aldeburgh was caught with him in an extremely compromising situation. Instead of rescue, Grace was shunned by her family, ignored by her friends and ostracised by Society. Now, rarely leaving her home Grace has accepted that it will be years, if ever, before she is free of the stigma attached to her name by the duke's heinous actions. To shield herself from further pain, Grace locked away her heart, burying it so deeply that she wasn't sure it could ever be found.

Out of the blue, Grace is granted a boon. She inherits a house in the tiny village of Oak Stanton, a place where nobody knows her and, Grace wonders, whether this is her chance to start afresh; a new life far away from her tormentor, and the malicious whispers of the *ton*.

Arriving in Oak Stanton, Grace becomes acquainted with Giles and Billie Trevallier, the Earl and Countess of Winchester, and Theo Elliott ~ the doctor for this little hamlet ~ their warm welcome, a balm to her aching soul.

Theo knows of Grace and is intrigued to meet the woman whom Society treated so harshly. A budding friendship between the two soon blossoms into something far more enduring but, for them to have any chance at happiness, Grace knows she must share her darkest secret with Theo, expecting that once it is revealed, he too will condemn her. Theo, however, is no fair-weather suitor and, already irrevocably in love with Grace, is resolved to be the man to unlock her heart.

Unfortunately, just as a fairy tale ending seems within reach, a chance encounter precipitates a chain of events that will have tragic consequences. Determined to reclaim what he considers his prize, the duke has one of his henchmen follow Grace, tracing her to her new home and jeopardising her longed-for happiness. After a failed kidnap attempt, the duke's quest culminates in an acrimonious confrontation with Grace and suddenly the reason for his venal pursuit of her becomes agonisingly clear.

The Pomegranate Tree

Hannah's Heirloom ~ Book One

After receiving an ancient ruby clasp from her long dead grandmother, Hannah Wilson decides to visit Masada, supposedly the place where this gift was given to one of her ancestors. Travelling with her is Max Vallier, her best friend, who was already going to Herod's fortress in the desert, as part of an archaeological excavation team.

Once there, Hannah is disturbed by strange visions. Visions, which seem to revolve around the AD66 attack by Zealot rebels, on the Roman garrison based at the fortress.

As her two worlds begin to entwine, Hannah realises that she is experiencing the events of the past as they unfold, events that so far she has only dreamed about. Pulled into the ancient world, she tends to three Roman soldiers who survived the attack, but who are now captives. Back in the modern world, she finds artefacts that tie her to her ancient counterpart. Meanwhile, her relationship with Max takes an interesting turn, but just as they admit their feelings for each other, a tragic accident tears them apart.

Fate intervenes and Hannah slips into the world of Ancient Masada. There, away from all modern trappings, she must rely on her wits and instincts to deal with the demands of her alternate life. A life in which she, an unmarried Hebrew woman, is a healer — a trained physician, fighting to keep alive the men under her care. This life becomes more complicated as she realises she is falling in love with one of the Roman soldiers, a love that could have deadly consequences.

Unsure whether she will ever be able to return to the modern world, Hannah accepts her destiny, rising to the challenges of life on an isolated fortress and, believing that she has a chance to save those she loves by using the knowledge she has brought with her from two thousand years in the future. The knowledge that, eventually, Jerusalem will fall and, that those escaping the city will make their way to this outpost, followed by an avenging Roman army intent on destruction.

Will Hannah escape? Will she ever see Max again, or is she doomed to die along with hundreds of others as Masada falls - and what does any of this have to do with an ancient ruby clasp?

Echoes of Stone and Fire

Hannah's Heirloom ~ Book Two

Pompeii was once a bustling port nestling under a forbidding mountain. Then in AD79, the mountain erupted, smothering the town under a thick blanket of ash and volcanic debris, leaving it lost for centuries. Now, rediscovered and a world-renowned heritage site, archaeologists from across the globe yearn for an opportunity to uncover the town's past. Some things though, are best left alone - revealing the secrets hidden beneath the stones could prove perilous.

Eighteen months have passed since Hannah and Max left Masada, Herod's isolated fortress in the Judaean desert. The place where just as they admitted their feelings for each other, they were wrenched apart. Hannah slipped into an ancient world, discovering how her ancestor had received the ruby clasp - her talisman. Somehow she survived the ensuing tragedy and Max's love was strong enough to bring her home. Since then, Hannah has had no awareness of her ancient counterpart and wonders whether the slender thread that united them had been broken, lost beyond time, leaving only a memory.

On a spur of the moment trip to Rome, familiar dreams recur. Unable to recognise where her ancestor is, but realising that she is not on Masada, Hannah struggles to understand the reason behind her visions. Then, a chance meeting with two friends sees Hannah and Max invited to join an excavation team, one whose goal is to determine what lies beneath the ruins of Pompeii. Although excited to be a part of such an investigation, Hannah experiences a growing sense of unease, an unnamed fear circling at the edges of her consciousness.

Her worlds begin to converge and Hannah realises to her horror, that her fear, this reconnection of minds, must be related to Vesuvius and that the woman she is bound to was actually in Pompeii before the eruption. Hoping she can somehow warn her ancestor without being drawn back into her other life, Hannah tries to convey her knowledge through her dreams.

As before however, fate intervenes. After entering a house, which bears a Hebrew inscription, Hannah falls back through time. Although familiar with this fusion of souls, she still has to rely on her instincts to adjust to life in ancient Pompeii. A world where her ancestor is a physician to gladiators engaged in mortal combat, where riotous mobs run amok and where a ghost from the past returns to haunt her. All the while knowing she needs to save her family from the devastation that will befall this town.

Will Hannah escape the cataclysmic eruption? Can she persuade her loved ones to flee before burning debris engulfs the town? Will she ever find her way back to Max the love of her life waiting, not so patiently, millennia away? Or will echoes be all that remain?

Embers of Destiny

Hannah's Heirloom ~ Book Three

AD80 ~ It is a year since Hannah and Maxentius escaped from the cataclysmic eruption of Mt Vesuvius and, after a pleasant interlude in Rome, they must now embark on a new journey. This time to the troubled frontier of Northern Britannia, recently subjugated, yet maybe not quite pacified.

This harsh borderland is a far cry from the luxuries and relative security of Rome, and danger lurks where least expected. A garrison of soldiers, some rather disgruntled with their isolated posting and it's new commander; local tribes people, although outwardly accepting of their erstwhile enemy, may still harbour a burning resentment that their lands have been occupied.

Meanwhile, in the modern world and now married to Max, Hannah Vallier is working in the archives department of a museum on Hadrian's Wall; cataloguing artefacts from some of the original wooden forts, recently discovered following a series of aerial surveys. While most of the finds are mundane, Hannah is shocked when she comes across an all too familiar item. It is her, or rather her ancestor's pomegranate; the one carved by Maxentius in the aftermath of the massacre at Masada, carried from there to Pompeii and then on to Rome.

Confused as to how it could be here in Northumberland, Hannah searches a new database for answers, finding a fragmented inscription indicating that Maxentius and Hannah had indeed been posted to Northern Britannia; that Maxentius had been commander of a garrison, the fort for which, coincidentally, had been almost exactly where she was now sitting. Realising what this might mean, Hannah needs to talk to Max, who is away on business.

Before they get the chance, disaster strikes! Believing the love of her life to have been killed and unable to deal with her grief, Hannah retreats into the past, re-connecting with her ancient family. Unfortunately, scant historical evidence for this period means that Hannah is unaware of what might be looming, instead she must trust that any information she holds will be enough to save them once again.

Adjusting to a world on the frontier of Empire, Hannah meets the local wise woman and, as they share their love and knowledge of healing, a tentative friendship blossoms. The burgeoning cordiality between the garrison and the locals is jeopardised however, as a multitude of challenges conspire to undermine the fragile peace. Hannah realises that the threat might come from a most unexpected quarter, for there is one within the fort whose enmity will have dire consequences.

At the same time, Hannah's heart whispers that maybe, just maybe Max is still alive and that he is calling her home.

Will Maxentius be able to preserve the hard won trust of the locals, or will everything descend into madness? Is there any hope of discovering who is inciting such hostility before it's too late? Can Hannah learn to trust her heart, or will she remain forever caught out of time, her destiny floating away like embers on a breeze.

Etched in Starlight

Hannah's Heirloom ~ Prequel

Maxentius

Only eighteen years of age, army recruit Lucius Maxentius Valerius, arrives in Armenia, a world away from the comforts of Rome. Rather than a career in politics, as his family would have preferred, he has chosen a life in the military. Being a soldier in the Roman Army is not for the faint hearted; there is no such thing as an easy campaign and, here in the wilderness of Armenia, they face the Parthians, a formidable enemy, one whom the Romans underestimated once before — to their downfall. This does not deter Maxentius; he has long wanted this life.

It becomes apparent, that Maxentius is a born solider. His uncanny ability to anticipate the actions of the enemy, desire to understand and empathise with the local populace and reasoned perspective on any given strategy, gains the young man the respect of comrades and his superiors and he is promoted with unusual rapidity. A soldier with such instincts is a desirable commodity and, after four years in Armenia, Maxentius is dispatched to Masada, an isolated outpost in the middle of Judaean Desert, taking command of the local garrison. Although a rather mundane assignment, it would be a welcome respite after several years of warfare.

Hannah

Hundreds of miles away in Jerusalem, a city descending into chaos, a young girl is training to be a healer under the watchful eye of her uncle. Not your conventional Hebrew maid, Hannah bat Avigail, forgoes traditional feminine pastimes, spending her days treating all manner of wounds and ailments. Relishing the challenge, Hannah dreams of becoming a physician.

The city is rife with dissent and clashes between advocates and opponents of Roman rule are commonplace. Every day

Hannah and her uncle deal with injuries more typical of a battlefield than a civilised society. Worse, her brother and his friends are caught up in the violence and she fears for their lives.

Deprivation and disease add to the increasing instability, inflaming the agitators and encouraging radical groups to join forces hoping to oust the Romans once and for all. In a desperate bid for weapons, a band of rebels venture into the desert, to a fortress guarded by a Roman garrison.

Hannah's brother refuses to leave his sister alone in an increasingly lawless city and so she travels with him, accepting that, if nothing else, her skills as a healer will probably be required.

Masada

In the aftermath of the attack on Herod's citadel, Hannah finds and, against her brother's wishes, treats three badly injured soldiers. Unexpectedly, one of them touches something deep inside her; something that, despite him being an enemy and a captive, she cannot ignore.

Maxentius regains consciousness to the knowledge that this impregnable citadel has fallen and that he is likely one of only three of his garrison to survive the ambush. Uncertain of his future and in a haze of agony, he realises he is in the care of a young woman. A young woman, whose startling green eyes and impish smile, will turn his world upside down

In the days that follow and against impossible odds, they come to realise that they are more than healer and captive, their fate already etched in starlight.